AN HEIRESS FOR THE MARQUESS

MARQUESS

LORDS OF VOLUPTAS - BOOK TWO

KATHY LEIGH

Published by Blushing Books
An Imprint of
ABCD Graphics and Design, Inc.
A Virginia Corporation
977 Seminole Trail #233
Charlottesville, VA 22901

Kathy Leigh
An Heiress for the Marquess

eBook ISBN: 978-1-64563-966-4
Print ISBN: 978-1-64563-967-1
v1

INTRODUCTION

Voluptas: a Latin word meaning pleasure, delight, satisfaction, enjoyment, gratification

CHAPTER 1

LONDON 1806

$\mathcal{L}$ord Theodore Vincent Simon Raeburne twirled the champagne glass in his elegantly gloved fingers and sighed. His eyes wandered restlessly over the ballroom of Montgomery House, passingly admiring how the glow from hundreds of candles in the crystal chandeliers deepened the vivid reds and yellows of the roses, dahlias and tulips arranged in massive vases around the perimeter. The duchess had done a marvelous job of transforming the usually rather stately ballroom into a vibrant grotto. From his perch in the gallery, he watched the sway and swirl of silks and satins as the elite members of London society gathered to celebrate his cousin, the Duke of Broadwell's, fortieth birthday. Low laughter and mingled voices mixed with the merry sounds of the violins as the musicians set the pace for the dancers. Lord Theodore, however, was not feeling particularly cheerful. He ran an irritated hand through his carefully arranged hair and sighed again.

A languid voice interrupted his disconsolate contemplation

of the dancers. "Are you trying to decide which mama it would be easiest to dupe so that you can lure her daughter onto the terrace or into the garden for a little private dance?"

The marquess let go of his gloomy thoughts and turned to greet his friends with a grin. He raised his champagne glass in a mock salute as he replied to the Earl of Sherbonne's flippant comment. "I am sure you have already selected the most likely candidates for an illicit little *rendezvous*."

Viscount Anthony Donnington and Baron Adam Loxley chuckled but the earl just shrugged. "I believe in making hay while the sun shines. When someone is kind enough to offer me a selection of pretty girls, I consider it ill-mannered of me not to enjoy such delectable morsels of femininity and send them home with dreams of earldoms dancing in their heads."

Lord Theo scoffed lightly and then the humor in his voice faded as he nodded towards the crush of guests in the ballroom. "Actually, I was just observing the latest debutantes and thinking that not one of them piques my interest. Year by year, there's a constant stream of young ladies, all vaguely attractive, all supremely fashionable, all equally as stiff as wooden dolls."

Sherbonne shrugged. "It isn't as if we're planning to marry any of them."

The marquess looked at his friend for a moment before replying as nonchalantly as his rioting thoughts allowed him to. "Perhaps not, but I have recently begun to bore of the insipidity of casual acquaintances. Perhaps a grand passion, true love, a lasting relationship, would be more enriching, more satisfying, than simply flirting endlessly." His eyes wandered across the milling dancers. "All these debutantes so eager to attract our attention, and yet I have no desire to spend any time with even one of them. The only woman who does not bore me is Amelia."

Sherbonne frowned and his usual laconic drawl was replaced with concern. "Are you jealous of the duke? You're not in love with his wife, are you?"

Theo huffed a wry laugh. "No, I am not in love with Amelia, but I am a little jealous of their love for one another. I have begun to despair of ever finding a woman I could love the way my cousin loves his wife." He kept his eyes on the dancers in the ballroom. He did not want Sherbonne or his other friends to see the wistfulness in his eyes as the image of a gangly schoolgirl, mud streaking her face, her blue eyes vivid with compassion as she comforted a lamb flashed into his mind. He had too much sense than to hanker after a girl who was probably even now repeating French phrases in the schoolroom.

Sherbonne clapped his shoulder. "Well, that's no reason not to enjoy yourself now." The earl leaned against the balustrade, his tall, lean body occupying the space as if he was master of the room. "What you need is an evening at Briar House. You haven't been there in a while. A few hours of intense physical pleasure will shake you out of the doldrums."

Theo gave a brief shake of his head and his short laugh conveyed his frustration. "Somehow, the thought of a night of unbridled passion without love to give it meaning is not as appealing as it once was." He tried to banish the memory of dancing blue eyes and a lopsided dimple that had haunted his dreams for the last few months.

Adam Loxley, elegantly dressed in a claret coat that fit smoothly across his broad shoulders, slapped Theo on the back. "What? Lord Theodore Raeburne, connoisseur of pleasure and lover of beauty, so jaded at twenty-eight years old that he does not find any lady worth his attention!"

Theo gave a wry chuckle as he placed his empty champagne glass on a side table. "When you put it like that, Lox, it does sound arrogant of me. The truth is, though, I am weary of the endless sameness of the debutantes and the fleeting pleasure of a night of sex."

Viscount Anthony Donnington, who had been eagerly keeping a watch on the arrivals, turned to Theo. His green eyes blazed with fiery passion. "You are right. The nearer I am to turning thirty, the more convinced I am that pleasure without love does no one any good."

Loxley and Sherbonne groaned in unison, and the earl muttered, "As if Donny's infatuation isn't enough, now Theo is bailing on us, too."

Donnington scowled, but Loxley forestalled his retort, ever the peacemaker. He gestured at the dancers below them. "Theo might have a point. I am tired of listening to mindless chatter about whether Lady Augusta's chartreuse ribbon perfectly matches the cerise of her gown or whether the height of a feather in a bonnet is an inch too short to be fashionable. It is enough to send any proper man running." He gave an exaggerated shudder. "It's enough to make one consider foreswearing the company of women forever."

The Earl of Sherbonne placed his hand over his heart in a dramatic gesture and staggered back. "What! You will forsake the pleasure to be found in the silky curves and warm bodies of women, the delight of a tight cunt clutching your cock, or a warm mouth sucking you hard?"

The other men, all members of the club known as the Lord of Voluptas, guffawed at Sherbonne's antics and the absurd suggestion that Loxley would turn celibate and abandon the pursuit of pleasure.

Baron Loxley shook his head with a laugh. "I am not quite ready to enroll in a monastery and seek the tragedy of celibacy, but I cannot imagine spending a lifetime with one of those prissy, prattling dolls who have no original ideas and who are horrified by the mere thought of physical pleasure. I agree with Theo. So few ladies have the confidence and intelligence to be a suitable partner through all the years of marriage."

Donnington sipped his champagne and frowned. "I suppose girls and women cannot be blamed. They are brought up to believe that intellectual ideas are the purview of men. Any lady who has an original idea is called a blue stocking and shunned by the fashionable set." He paused to watch a new surge of guests enter the ballroom and, seeing that Miss Blakeney was not among them, continued. "It helps to remember that they have not had the advantage of our education at Eton and Oxford. It is only the very rare lady who has risen above what her governesses instilled in her as proper conversation for ladies, and so we have to endure their trivial babble while we admire their pretty... faces," he ended with a smirk.

The four friends surveyed the swirling mass of guests in the ballroom silently for a few moments. From their perch in the gallery, they had a clear view of the parade of young debutantes preening and strutting as they tried to entice an eligible bachelor into forming an attachment that would lead to marriage.

After a few moments, Loxley snorted. "Such prancing and simpering are enough to warn every self-respecting bachelor to stay far away!"

Sherbonne shook his head with a melancholy air. "What a gloomy lot you are tonight. They might not all aspire to Lady Amelia's vividness or Miss Blakeney's perfection, but I have spotted some dainty little morsels who, I am sure, can be encouraged to enjoy a few wicked moments with me out on the terrace. I am not on the lookout for a wife, just a pleasurable encounter."

Adam lifted three glasses of champagne from the tray of a passing footman and handed one to Donnington, one to Theo and swallowed a mouthful of the third. Sherbonne had ensured his own glass was never empty.

Viscount Anthony made a strangled sound as a lady with shining, blonde hair entered the ballroom and then he swore softly under his breath. "It's not her. Do you think her aunt has decided not to bring her?"

The baron grinned as he explained to Theo, "Donny has been

dragging Sherry and me around the ballroom all evening in search of his paragon."

Sherbonne laid his hand on Donnington's shoulder. "Don't worry, old chap. Even the strait-laced Miss Blakeney will make an appearance at the duke's birthday ball. She will be here soon and then you can spend the evening pining for her from afar and afterwards you can go home to your lonely bed and pump your cock while thinking of all the things you didn't say to her."

Amidst the laughter, Theo added, "Perhaps tonight you will actually ask her to dance!"

Sherbonne took a small step back. "It's quite easy. Should I remind you how it's done? You approach the lady you have selected, the incomparable Miss Clarissa Blakeney, bow prettily, just the way they taught us at Eton, and say, *Miss Blakeney, if you are not already engaged, may I have the pleasure of the next dance?* And then she says..." the earl cleared his throat and raised his voice to a falsetto, imitating a debutante, "*oh, Viscount, it would be my delight and pleasure. I have spent all my waking hours hoping that you would dance with me tonight.*"

Donnington laughed with his friends but protested, "I have danced with Miss Blakeney on a few occasions."

The group of friends was guffawing by the end of the earl's little pantomime, oblivious to the glares of the guests near enough to be offended by their raucous laughter. They were silenced by the discreet clearing of a throat near them. "Lord Theodore, is there anything I can get for you or your friends?" The duke's butler, Carter, had appeared on the gallery and stood quietly next to them.

Theo grinned at him. "I think we have everything we need, Carter. Thank you."

The butler bowed and moved away, his duty done.

Theo chuckled with his friends. "Good old Carter, always ready to remind us how to behave, as if we were still unruly boys at school and not grown gentlemen with titles and property of our own." He turned back to his perusal of his cousin's guests. "I suppose the proper thing to do is to go down there and brave all the mamas who are determined that we would make the best husbands for their empty-headed daughters, simply because of our illustrious names and pretty fortunes that we haven't lost in riotous living." He scanned the seats near a row of potted palms where the girls who had not been asked to dance were seated. "It does seem that quite a few young ladies are without partners, and as gentlemen, we should do the right thing and ensure that the evening is not without some pleasure for them."

His friends murmured their agreement and all turned to the staircase. But just as they were about to make their way to the lower level, Donnington sighed. "Oh, she is here. She has come."

Theo glanced towards the main door of the ballroom. Miss Clarissa Blakeney, dainty in a soft pink dress, was entering with her aunt. He shrugged, knowing that his friend would not be very good company for the rest of the evening. The viscount would spend his time trailing behind Clarissa, hoping that she would smile at him. Theo chuckled.

And then he froze.

His eyes were riveted on the young woman who had entered just behind Miss Blakeney. Gleaming chestnut curls were held in place with glittering diamond pins that sparkled in the candle-light as the pretty girl almost bounced beside her mother. Her white dress swirled around her like a cloud. Even from this distance, she exuded energy and excitement, quite unlike the carefully cultivated restraint and air of ennui adopted by the usual debutantes.

The marquess swore under his breath. He had not expected to see Charlotte Drake at his cousin's ball. He descended the stairs slowly, his mind racing. When had Charlotte Drake grown old enough to attend balls or to enter London society as a debu-tante? The last time the marquess had seen her, she had been barefoot and fishing in a river that marked the border between his property of Oakdene and her father's estate, Summerhill, in Worcestershire. Somehow, the glittering diamonds and fashionable silk ballgowns looked incongruous on her. He was caught by the memory of how the deep blue of the autumn sky was reflected in her eyes, how her unruly chestnut curls had tumbled riotously down her back and how her skirt, muddy from riding and torn by the brambles, did nothing to dim her wild beauty. She had been a nymph, a dryad, who belonged in that autumn landscape, the embodiment of some ancient goddess come to life. That image of her had fueled many of his fantasies when he lay in bed alone at night and stroked his cock.

Lord Theodore paused on the steps leading into the ballroom and studied Charlotte. Her elegant dress and sophisticated arrangement of her hair revealed that she was older than he had thought. She was not a sixteen-year-old schoolgirl, but a debutante entering into the whirl of London society and the competitiveness of the marriage mart. His cock thrummed with approval at the sight of her, but he took a few deep breaths and drew on the control he had mastered to keep himself from acting foolishly. It would not do to rush down the stairs and claim her for his own, keeping all other contenders for her attention at bay. He was transfixed by her loveliness.

As Lord Theodore made his way into the main part of the ballroom, he realized Miss Charlotte Drake had already captured the attention of at least half the young men in attendance. Within minutes of her arrival, her name was being whispered up and down the long ballroom. Each whisper was accompanied by remarks on the fineness of her dress, the quality of her pearls, the magnificence of the diamonds in her hair. He heard the word *heiress* passed from group to group, like the sibilance of the wind before a storm.

CHAPTER 2

*M*iss Charlotte Drake was having a dreadful evening. She tugged at the folds of the exquisite white silk dress she was wearing, a frown crinkling her usually smooth forehead. She longed to run her fingers through her hair, removing the pins that confined it in an elaborately fashionable arrangement on the top of her head. She was sure that at least three of the diamond pins were piercing her skull. It had taken two hours to make her presentable for this ball, her first appearance as a debutante in the London season, and she felt like a doll, dressed up and ready to be played with. She had never really liked playing with dolls or being dressed up in pretty dresses. She preferred the easiness of riding habits and simple garments that allowed her to move freely outdoors.

"Come along, Charlotte. If you stand near the light from these candles, you will be seen to good advantage. That dress is made of the finest silk and the cut shows your figure well. You will draw the attention of all the right people, especially if you do not slouch." Mrs. Drake smiled complacently as she surveyed the crowded ballroom. She tugged the ribbon on her daughter's dress straight. "And do smile, dear. You want the gentlemen to believe that you are pleased to be here."

Charlotte pulled away from her mother and turned to a thin, slightly built man who was leaning against the wall beside them. He had entered the ballroom with them, and his air of studied nonchalance hid his irritation with Mrs. Drake's fussing or Charlotte's frustration.

Charlotte's voice was soft but urgent. "Hugh, you will dance with me, won't you? You promised. I would be absolutely mortified if I had no partners at my very first ball in London."

Hugh Parsiville arched a thin eyebrow. "If you absolutely insist, then I will lead you out. However, I think your mama has rigged you out in a decent enough outfit. Any of the gentlemen on the prowl here tonight will be eager to make your acquaintance. There are always fortune hunters at events such as these, gentlemen who have gambled away their family fortune at the card tables, and the jewels at your throat will definitely attract their attention."

Charlotte gasped. "Surely, you exaggerate. I cannot believe that anyone could be so reckless. I could not be convinced to associate with any gentleman who displayed such irresponsibility."

Hugh laughed, but his eyes remained cool and dismissive. "You are a naïve little chicken. That's one of the things I admire most about you. I assure you that many society gentlemen are very reckless with their money. It is one of the exhilarating pastimes gentlemen of leisure indulge in. I have seen whole family fortunes lost in a single night's play of cards. One of the easiest ways to rectify the situation is to marry an heiress. I have no doubt that within twenty minutes you will be surrounded by men eager to be better acquainted with your inheritance. They will woo you with promises of eternal love that will end the moment the marriage is settled and they have paid their debts."

Charlotte bit her lip and surveyed the room, suspicion

clouding her eyes. "How am I supposed to know which of these gentlemen want to dance with me because they like me and which are only interested in my fortune?"

Hugh shrugged. "It's a safe bet that most of those who ask you to dance have heard that your father is very rich, that you are his only heir and that his estates are not entailed." He leaned closer. "Of course, as this is a private ball, it would not do for you to refuse to dance with anyone who asks you, but I will ensure that you do not fall for their wiles." He surveyed the ballroom and his eyes narrowed. His voice was harder when he continued. "You do have a tendency to become sentimental over anyone who shows you the least bit of attention, and you need someone who knows the ins and outs of London society to take care of you. I will ensure you do not make a fool of yourself."

Charlotte's cheeks flushed an indignant pink. Hugh's reminder of her foibles, her past indiscretions, drained her confidence. She lowered her head, but Hugh took no notice of her distress and continued his lecture on the intricacies of navigating London society. "It would be best to treat every gentleman as someone who is interested only in your fortune. Even those who have been lucky at cards and whose fortune is still intact will be tempted by the promise of all that Summerhill offers. No matter how many pretty compliments you receive about how pretty your eyes are or how charming your smile is, remember that it is your inheritance they really see."

Charlotte shuffled her feet and took a deep breath. Her mother's voice, explaining to a new acquaintance which *modiste* had designed her dress and how the pearls Charlotte wore were only a small part of the collection of jewelry she had inherited from her grandmother, floated over the silence. Charlotte shook her head and sighed. She would find no support from her mother. Before they had arrived in London, Mrs. Drake had spent hours and hours describing the kind of match she expected Charlotte to make. Her mother would push her to dance with every gentleman who had a title, no matter how old or impoverished. Her ambition was to see Charlotte married to a member of the aristocracy, and so the Drake family would be elevated from prosperous landowners to the grandness of the nobility.

Charlotte bit her lip and turned wide, anxious eyes to Hugh. "I am so glad you are here with me, Hugh. You have been a good friend to me and I know I can trust you. With Papa detained at Summerhill because of his illness, I am adrift in London society. Your help is a great comfort."

Hugh smirked. "I am always glad to be of service to you, as long as you do not trot me out onto the dance floor. You know I can't stand prancing up and down and making polite conversation when I could be playing cards and discussing the upcoming races at Newmarket."

Charlotte's face fell and she took a step backwards. "Oh, Hugh, I am sorry. I don't mean to be a nuisance. I am sure I will manage comfortably on my own. Please go and find your friends."

Hugh began to turn, eager to escape to the cardroom for a game of faro, but he was blocked by the sudden appearance of Lord Theodore, who looked right past him and focused on Charlotte.

Charlotte dropped the folds of her skirt that she had been clutching when the deep, rich baritone that haunted her dreams washed over her. Her heart fluttered and her throat felt tight and dry. Coherent thought fled as the marquess said, "I beg your pardon, Miss Drake, but I noticed you have not yet graced the dance floor. I wondered, if you are not engaged, could I have the honor of the next dance? The sets are just forming."

Charlotte gaped, unable to process her thoughts or articulate an answer. She felt the heat of blood rush to her face. She tried to remind herself that she was now a debutante and should be confident and poised. She was no longer the tongue-tied schoolgirl who sat stupefied at the dinner table whenever the marquess dined at Summerhill. Taking a deep breath, she raised her eyes to the face that filled her dreams. A glint of amusement brightened Lord Theo's dark brown eyes and the little dignity she had managed to hold on to scattered. Lord Theo was studying her with such keen appraisal that she could not breathe. He was standing so close to her that his six-foot-two-inch frame appeared even more imposing than usual. His broad shoulders blocked her view of the rest of the ballroom.

Only once had she been at ease, comfortable, confident in the presence of the marquess. Only once had she been able to ignore how daunting he was. That day ranked as the most precious of her memories. Even as she stood now, speechless in a London ballroom, gawking at the only man she really wanted to impress, memories of that glorious afternoon flashed through her mind.

Charlotte cantered Lady May in a steady rhythm across the newly harvested fields and easily jumped a low hedge her mother had told her was too high for a lady to attempt. She threw back her head and laughed, relieved to have escaped her mother's constant carping and the groom who was expected to accompany her on her rides. She turned her face up to the vivid blue sky, adorned with heaps of brilliant white clouds, and her heart soared with hope and the joy of having just turned eighteen and on the verge of all the pleasures life held for her.

On the other side of the hedge was a path, seldom-used but one she loved. From here she had a clear view of the high chimneys and domed turrets of Oakdene. The main country residence of Lord Theo, Marquess of Raeburne, was magnificently situated against the lower slopes of a gently rising hill. Soft yellow stone walls were warm and welcoming under the mellow autumn sun. To the south, spreading chestnut trees and grand old oaks continued to watch over the house as they had done for centuries. Charlotte had never been inside the house, but her favorite daydreams were woven around the beauty of the estate and the handsome owner of all that splendor.

She slowed Lady May to a gentle walk and let her mind roam free.

Drawing on her memories, she pictured the earl galloping across the fields on his favorite black stallion, his strong hands guiding his horse and his firm thighs gripping the saddle. In her imagination, he saw her and reined in his horse, matching his pace to hers so they could walk their horses side-by-side. In her daydream, she engaged in a lively, witty conversation with the marquess, such as had never occurred in real life. Their delightful dream discussion ranged from Mrs. Radcliffe's latest novel to the best mares for breeding that spring. Not once did Charlotte stumble over her words or find her tongue tied in knots. In her dreams, she was articulate, poised and responded to the repartee of the marquess with scintillating sallies of her own.

She was just, in her mind, explaining to Lord Theo why she sympathized with Wordsworth when he proclaimed, "... that best portion of a good man's life, His little, nameless, unremembered, acts Of kindness and of love," when her thoughts were rudely interrupted by the sudden piteous wails of a lamb. Startled, she reined in her horse and looked around. It took her only a few minutes to locate the half-grown creature that had fallen into a deep ditch. The lamb was scrambling desperately, trying to clamber out, but every frantic wriggle caught its wooly fleece more securely in the brambles. It was trapped.

Charlotte dismounted quickly, tied Lady May's reins to a nearby tree and scrambled into the ditch. Heedless of the mud, she set about trying to free the half-grown lamb. The four-foot ditch and the slipperiness of the mud defeated her attempts at rescue. Her attempts were futile. The more she tried to help the lamb, the more entangled it became in the brambles. She stamped her foot impatiently and pushed her loosened curls back from her forehead with a muddy hand, leaving a streak of dirt on her face. She placed her hands on her hips, despair and desperation filling her heart, and looked around for some way to cut back the brambles. With a sigh of despair, she realized she could not help the lamb on her own.

She scrambled out of the ditch, but the sound of horse's hooves clipping briskly along the path brought her to a standstill. Mortification swamped her when she recognized Lord Theo on his large, black stal-

lion. Horrified, she tried to brush the mud off her dress and straighten her hair. The marquess had already brought his horse, Diablo, to a halt and she could feel the weight of his gaze as he took in every smudge, every trace of mud and the way her skirt had been ripped by the brambles.

He raised an eyebrow, but his voice was polite and conveyed no surprise at finding his neighbor's daughter in such a bedraggled condition and quite clearly unaccompanied by a chaperone. "Good afternoon, Miss Drake. Can I offer my assistance?"

Charlotte blushed, but the lamb gave a particularly plaintive bleat and looked at her with such despair that her desire to help the little creature overcame her usual shyness. She turned to the marquess, her hands outstretched. Lord Theo was already dismounting from his hunter and removing his coat as she entreated, "Oh, Your Lordship, would you? I haven't been able to loosen the brambles. Actually, the lamb wriggles and squirms so much that I think I might have made the situation worse rather than helping him. I was just about to go home to find someone to come and help."

The marquess rolled up the sleeves of his pristine linen shirt, and in spite of her concern for the lamb, Charlotte found herself riveted by the corded muscles of his forearms. He rummaged in his saddle bag and pulled out a hoof knife then quickly climbed into the ditch. The muscles of his back were clearly visible beneath the fine material of his shirt, and Charlotte turned an even brighter pink when she saw how his breeches bulged with the swelling of his manhood.

The marquess began to pet the lamb, speaking in low murmurs while he ran his hands over the soft, wooly fleece. Charlotte was mesmerized by his strong, capable movements and the gentleness of his voice. She wondered what it would be like to feel those hands caressing her arms, stroking her back and running through her hair. A deep shudder of desire swept through her. It was only when the marquess looked at her quizzically and asked if she was all right that she broke out of her daydream with a blush and scrambled after him into the ditch.

For the next half an hour, Charlotte and the marquess worked side-by-side, setting the lamb free from the sharp brambles. The marquess was as little concerned about the mud as she was, and even when a branch swung back and swiped his face, leaving a long scratch on his cheek, he just laughed and brushed away the drops of blood. Moment by moment, Charlotte's admiration for Lord Theodore increased.

It was impossible to avoid her hands from touching his frequently as they untangled the lamb, and at times she even found herself brushing against his strong thighs. Every time they touched, Charlotte felt a jolt of electricity surge through her. Her skin tingled and ripples of heat coursed through every part of her body, until they gathered in a warm pool in her most intimate parts. She tried to focus on the lamb, but it was impossible to ignore the sensations the marquess aroused in her.

The marquess, apparently oblivious to the energy that flowed between them, instructed her to hold the lamb while he cut away the branches. Charlotte tried to distract herself by singing softly under her breath, and before long Lord Theo began talking about music, then poetry and books.

Soon Charlotte forgot her shyness and how intimidated she usually felt near the marquess. She passionately defended her love of Sir Walter Scott's The Lay of the Last Minstrel when Lord Theo criticized it as a fanciful romance and declared that it would be best if the Scots remembered that they owed allegiance to England. She was surprised when he, instead of dismissing her ideas as naïve and childish, listened to her argument respectfully. He even conceded that perhaps Scotland had a right to sovereign rule. Charlotte was not used to having someone listen to her views. Her mother constantly reminded her that young ladies were not expected to have their own opinions.

All too soon, the last bramble was cut away. Lord Theo lifted the freed lamb into his arms, checked it over carefully to ensure that no serious harm had been done, and then settled it on his horse. With a heart filled with both euphoria and a strange sense of loss, Charlotte watched the marquess ride off to return the lamb to the shepherd. She

was left to make her own way home, accompanied only by her memo-
ries of a delightful afternoon.

Charlotte blinked twice and adjusted her vision to focus on the marquess who, now fashionably elegant, stood in front of her at the duke's ball. Nothing in the cynical quirk of his mouth or the glint in his eye reminded her of her pleasant companion from that glorious afternoon. She remembered that she had seen Lord Theodore only once after the incident with the lamb.

She had been fishing in the river that ran between Summerhill and Oakdene when the marquess rode past on Diablo. He had not stopped, only given her a terse nod as his eyes swept over her disheveled condition. She had rucked her skirt up around her waist and removed her shoes and stockings to make it easier to wade in the shallow water. Her dress was wet and clung to her. Under his silent gaze, she hastily tried to pull it down to cover her bare limbs, but before she could do more than sputter a greeting, he had passed without a backward glance.

CHAPTER 3

*L*ord Theo was bemused but enchanted. Charlotte Drake was blushing an adorable rosy pink, but her eyes were distant and dreamy. The demure young lady in a fashionable white silk evening gown bore little resemblance to the wild hoyden he remembered from the countryside. In her fashionable white silk evening gown and elegantly styled hair, she was definitely a young debutante old enough to be wooed, not the out-of-reach, awkward, gawkish schoolgirl he had thought her to be. The combination of her demure shyness and her delightful enthusiasm did strange things to him.

Her dark hair and vivid blue eyes gave her an otherworldly appearance against the pallor of her skin. The soft folds of her white silk dress swirled around her like the morning mist rising off the rivers at Oakdene. She could be a fairy come to play in this grotto Lady Amelia had created for the duke's ball.

It thrilled him to know that she could break through the barrier of her shyness to challenge his ideas and offer her opinions and yet she still yielded to his calm authority and was still intimidated by his powerful dominance. He would find great pleasure in exploring the nuances of her character and body.

Blood rushed to his groin and his cock pulsed with a glorious ache, eagerly anticipating how wonderful it would be to find relief in her sweetness. But the marquess knew how to control his lascivious desires, so for now he exerted his iron will and his cock, after giving two hard throbs, subsided.

He held back a chuckle as Charlotte shifted her weight from one foot to the other and then raised wide blue eyes to him. She opened her mouth, but before she could politely accept his invitation to dance, a smooth drawl answered, "Why, thank you, Lord Raeburne, but Miss Drake is engaged for the next set. She was just about to step out with me."

Theo's eyes hardened as he watched Hugh Parsiville place a possessive hand on Charlotte's arm. It took all his breeding as a gentleman not to pull him away from Charlotte and punch his nose. His lips straightened into a hard line and a hard knot of disappointment clenched his stomach when Charlotte looked at Parsiville with a smile and covered his hand with hers. "Oh, Hugh, I thought you did not want to dance!" Charlotte finally found her voice.

Theo bowed stiffly and took a step backwards.

Parsiville stood up a little straighter and looked at Theo but spoke to Charlotte. "Don't be such a little goose, Charlotte. You seem to have forgotten most of what I said to you. You really should pay more attention."

Theo bristled at Hugh's tone, but Charlotte did not appear to mind Parsiville's harangue. With an effort, he held back, deeply aware that he did not have the right to protect Charlotte, although his every instinct urged him to draw her into his arms and keep her safe now and for always.

He kept his voice steady and politely civil. "Well, in that case, let me not delay you. The musicians have begun the tune and you will need to join one of the sets." He stepped aside to give Charlotte and Hugh access to the floor. As Charlotte trotted after Hugh without looking back at him, he felt a strange mixture of annoyance and regret. He had lost the one woman who had the power to fascinate him before he had even begun to woo her.

≈

CHARLOTTE STUMBLED AFTER HUGH, raging at her slowness in accepting Lord Theo's invitation. She took her place across from Hugh at the bottom of the second set of dancers in the lower part of the ballroom, with a scowl. Hugh's behavior puzzled her, but he had given her no choice.

As she waited for the dance to begin, she gazed around the ballroom. She had a clear view of the first set of dancers, and her mouth tightened when she saw the marquess lead another young lady to join the line. She blinked back the tears that stung her eyes. It had not taken him long to find a willing partner, a sophisticated young lady who preened as Lord Theo bowed to mark the beginning of the dance.

Hugh's irritated mutter reminded her that she needed to focus on her dance partner instead of sending furtive glances at Lord Theo. Reluctantly, she placed her hand in Hugh's to let him lead her in the first movement of the cotillion. He said nothing, simply scowled into the distance. She tried to think of something to say that would mollify her friend. He might not have the broad shoulders, handsome face and imposing manner of Lord Theo, but she could never forget how much she owed Hugh, how he had supported her when she least deserved it.

As she paced out the steps of the dance, so carefully taught to her by the fussy dance master her mother had hired, she ventured, "Hugh, please don't be angry with me. I know you didn't really want to dance. I am sorry."

Hugh merely huffed and so, as she circled him, she added, "I do not think I could have come to any harm with Lord Raeburne. After all, he has often dined at Summerhill and I am acquainted with him." She ignored Hugh's frown as she added, "Papa admires and respects him."

Hugh scowled. "You need to make up your mind. You ask me to support and guide you as you make your way through London society, and the first time I do so, you object."

Charlotte murmured an apology, "I do appreciate your advice, but I am a little confused."

Hugh gripped her hand almost painfully while he slowly dragged his feet through the steps of the dance. "Your father likes the way Raeburne manages his estates, but he would not be happy if he knew about your silly schoolgirl infatuation. You open yourself to scorn and ridicule by this foolish obsession with a man who has no interest in you."

Charlotte held her head high and her eyes flashed with indignation, which did not quite hide her lingering fear. She said nothing as Hugh continued his tirade. "You hold your reputation very lightly, but it would not be very comfortable for you or your mother if you became known as the kind of girl who chases after men." His eyes traveled down Charlotte's body and then he concluded, "In your situation, it would be better to not have even the whiff of indecency near you."

Charlotte tilted her chin and tried to keep her expression impassive. When she had circled around Hugh and was facing him again, she managed to answer with some composure, "Admiring a gentleman for his attributes is not being obsessed with him."

Hugh snorted. "Last autumn, you prattled endlessly about how valiant and noble he was, as if he had all alone defeated Napoleon, when he had done nothing more than demean himself, laboring like one of the workers on his farm, to take a stupid lamb out of a muddy ditch."

Charlotte flushed heatedly. "Hugh, perhaps we should change the subject," she protested, but as she twirled, she admitted to herself that Hugh might be right. She really was fixated on the marquess, while he had shown little interest in her.

Charlotte's eyes wandered to where Lord Theo was dancing in the other set. She was drawn to the marquess as surely as iron filings to a magnet. She watched him in silence for a few moments, admiring the elegant grace of his movements. He was as much at home in a ballroom as when he galloped his horse across the fields of Oakdene.

Hugh's eyes followed the direction of Charlotte's furtive glances and his mouth straightened into a grim line. He was not going to let his quarry go, not when he could almost feel the weight of the fortune that marrying Charlotte would bring him. He drove his point home inexorably. "Lord Raeburne can have his choice of any lady in London. His taste runs to all that is refined and fashionable and his usual company consists of the most accomplished, most elegant of high society ladies. Don't mistake his politeness for interest in you. He will never attach himself to a scrap of a girl who prefers riding through the mud to playing the harp or herding sheep to painting water colors, and who spends her time with the sons of farmers."

Hugh's words stung deeply and Charlotte barely restrained herself from slapping him, proving just how unsuited she was for this sophisticated world of fashion. She took a deep breath and concentrated on the sedate and complex dance steps, so at odds with her riotous emotions. She was livid that Hugh had hinted at her secret, but his words also reminded her of how he had covered up her scandal, ensuring that no one would ever know of her disgrace.

She made one last feeble stand in her defense, goaded by memories of how kind and amiable Lord Theo had been to her on that one splendid afternoon. "I do not believe that Lord Theo would have asked me to dance if he considered me unsuitable."

Hugh sniffed. "Do not confuse polite social manners for real interest. That was nothing more than the consideration due to the daughter of his neighbor and the owner of the property he has made no bones about wanting to purchase."

Charlotte stumbled, forgetting for a moment the carefully learned steps the dance master had drilled into her. "He wants to buy Summerhill?"

Hugh gave a terse nod. "Adding your father's estate to his would vastly increase the value of Oakdene. Of course, every gentleman in this room tonight would like to get his hands on Summerhill. It is, after all, one of the most prosperous estates in England."

Charlotte had resumed dancing, but her feet felt heavy and her movements were wooden. Hugh leaned closer to Charlotte. His voice was soft, almost menacing. "Just remember, none of the gentlemen who find your fortune so attractive would continue to show any interest if they heard even a whiff of your secret. I am the only one who knows you well enough to over-look your indiscretion."

Charlotte blinked back the tightness in her eyes that warned her of gathering tears. She dug her fingernails into her palms, hard enough to leave deep indentations. The pain incongruously soothed the agony that reminders of her dark secret usually brought. Hugh was the one she needed to trust, not a fanciful dream that could never come to pass. She plastered a bright smile onto her face. "Perhaps, Hugh, the best way to protect my honor and my father's dignity would be to form an attachment with an eligible gentleman as quickly as possible. Once I am married, all should be well."

Hugh scoffed slightly. "No need to rush headlong into marriage with the first person who shows you any attention."

Charlotte flushed. Hugh had, once or twice, intimated that he would be prepared to marry her, but he had never openly declared his intentions. She was also sure that in spite of his kindness to her, he did not love her. She knew, without a doubt, that she did not love him. As she twirled, she caught sight of the marquess. Her breath caught in her throat and her heart stopped beating. Never, with Hugh, did she feel the intoxicating fire of desire that Lord Theo roused in her. With a soft sigh, she pulled her eyes away from the marquess. Marriage had very little to do with love. Her girlish dreams had no place in the real world.

She danced in silence for a few moments and then ventured to look at Hugh. His expression showed both smugness and annoyance. His words had been harsh, had cut deeply, but that had been her fault. She knew he did not like to dance and she had spent most of the time ogling another man. He deserved better from her. If she was a little more amenable, a little more accommodating of his wishes, then he would not be irritated by her.

She cleared her throat and spoke softly, not quite looking at Hugh. "Papa's recent ill health prevented him from coming to London, but I am sure that he would welcome you at Summerhill, especially if you wanted to speak to him about our... attachment, our situation," she stumbled to an awkward halt.

Hugh shrugged. "All in good time. I am enjoying the season in London and don't want to rush off into the countryside every few days. It would do you well to get a little town polish before you marry."

Charlotte couldn't help retorting, "I prefer the country to the city and my father says that it is a sign of real nobility when a gentleman shows an active interest in his lands and the people who work on them." Her voice dropped as she ended. "I am not sure I would be happy in the city for very long."

Hugh's eyes darkened with anger. "I am very well aware of your father's views but I have no interest in grubbing around in the dirt the way the Marquess of Raeburne does. I prefer to live in the city."

The musicians ended the dance tune with a flourish and the dancers bowed sedately and began to drift off the dance floor, but Charlotte stood where she was, misery etched in every line of her face. Hugh grabbed hold of her arm and pulled her to the line of chairs where her mother was seated with the other chaperones.

Charlotte tried to soothe her friend. "I am sorry, Hugh, I don't mean to be disagreeable and contrary. It is just that everything is so unsettled. I just think, maybe, if you talked to Papa, and my future was settled, I would be less agitated."

Hugh's grip on her arm tightened until it hurt. "There will be time enough to discuss the future later. Now, if you will excuse me, I see some gentlemen who have promised me a little wager on a game of faro tonight." He bowed and moved off rapidly, not giving Charlotte a chance to answer him.

She sighed and hovered forlornly at the edge of the dance floor. Hugh loped off, dodging around groups of guests as he threaded his way to the card room.

In a matter of minutes, though, she was approached by a gentleman in a bright blue coat who asked her to dance. She smiled politely and followed him onto the floor, but her thoughts were in turmoil. She hated London. She longed for the peaceful tranquility, the simplicity of life at Summerhill, where she was free to dream, where she could forget about annoyed friends and her fragile reputation that would shatter like the shell of an egg at the slightest murmur of the darkness that was locked tightly in her heart.

CHAPTER 4

The sun gleamed on the hardwood floor of the breakfast parlor of Raeburne House. Lord Theo Raeburne poured himself another cup of coffee as he read through the letters his secretary had left for him. Nothing was too urgent. His businesses and estates were prospering.

He picked up the last letter in the pile, and a frown creased his forehead. His plans for expanding the work on his estates would have to wait. For over a year, he and Mr. Drake had been discussing how the latest ideas of crop rotation and selective breeding would benefit the farmers, producing greater yields increase the prosperity of the region. Theo's ideas would not be complete if Oakedene and Summerhill were not both included in the plans. But now his neighbor was ill, very ill.

Theo swallowed the last of the coffee in his cup with a heavy heart. He admired and respected Mr. Drake and had spent many pleasant hours playing chess with him, but his steward was doubtful that Mr. Drake would see another autumn. His reverie was disturbed when Dawson, his butler, stepped forward to replenish his empty coffee cup. Theo nodded his thanks and resumed his perusal of the letter. Perhaps he could visit Mr. Drake.

He shook off his gloom and turned his mind to more practical matters. If Mr. Drake was not well enough to continue the negotiations, he would have to begin all over again with his successor. That would set back his plans, and the marquess had already laid out considerable sums of money to purchase the newest machines and begin draining the fields that lay between the two estates.

With a wry shrug, his mind drifted inevitably to Charlotte Drake. His mouth twisted. Although he had not danced with Charlotte at his cousin's birthday ball, he had been very aware of her every moment of the time. He had lain awake for many hours after he arrived home, recalling every tilt of her head, every smile of her lips, every sway of her hips. And then, like a schoolboy with no other outlet for his unruly passions, he had grabbed his dick and pumped, milking it of every drop of pent-up passion.

Now, thoughts of her again flooded his mind, even though she appeared to be out of his reach. He glanced at the letter lying beside his plate. Charlotte Drake was her father's sole heir. When she married, her husband would be legally responsible for what happened to Summerhill. A bitter taste flooded his mouth. He stabbed at piece of ham, remembering how her face had lit up with relief when Hugh Parsiville had joined her at the supper table.

With a snarl that startled the Golden Spaniel that was sprawled under the table, hoping to receive tidbits of ham, Theo tossed his fork onto his plate. Absently patting the spaniel's head, he pondered for a moment the travesty of Parsiville becoming the proprietor of Summerhill. But more than that, the horror of Charlotte's yielding all her sweet trust, all her delightful innocence, to the feeble selfishness of Hugh Parsiville sickened him.

A grim determination hardened the contours of his face. Charlotte was not yet lost to Hugh Parsiville. He would make his own intentions clear to her. He would woo her and win her.

He picked up the letter from his steward once more, deciding that perhaps it would be best if he paid Mr. Drake a visit before long.

A peevish voice interrupted his musing, "Well, brother, I thought after a night cavorting at the duke's ball, you might be in a more pleasant mood."

The marquess tossed aside the letter and looked up to greet his sister. "Good morning, Winifred. I thought I would see you at our cousin's ball. It was quite a splendid and lavish event."

Winifred flounced into a chair, beckoning a footman to pour her some tea. "Oh, I am not so fond of our cousin's company since he married that little upstart of a wife."

Theodore watched his sister as she buttered a breakfast roll. When she bit into it, he observed, "You mean you were not very happy when you realized that I would no longer inherit all of the duke's property."

Winifred scowled. "Well, you are his heir until his wife presents him with a son of his own. I can't see why he should have bothered to marry and rob you of an inheritance. It appears that your current wealth is not sufficient to cover current expenses in this household."

Theodore took a deep breath and counted to five before responding, keeping his voice as calm as he could. "Winifred, you receive a very generous allowance each quarter, more than many ladies in your position. It is not unreasonable to ask you to live within that allowance. Even if I thought it prudent to increase your allowance, which I don't, most of my available funds are allocated to the extensions and development of the estates. I am building for the future of the Raeburne name."

Winifred tossed her half-eaten bread roll onto her plate. "It's absurd and I don't care about future generations of Raeburnes. It is the current generation that should matter. Is it too much to spare a few pounds for a new bonnet? The milliner refused my order. She said I was stretched beyond my limit."

"Of course, I do not want the current family to suffer at the expense of the future, but you have already had eight new bonnets this season. I would have thought that enough for any lady." He folded his napkin as Winifred sipped her tea. "You must know that all your debts come to me, and that while I have settled the accounts you have run up, I have also placed restrictions on your expenditures and the amount of debt you will be allowed to incur. It is not in your best interest to be so heedless. One day you will marry and need to manage household accounts. It would be most unpleasant if your extravagance caused problems between you and the man you eventually marry."

"I will marry someone rich enough and generous enough to buy me all the bonnets I want. I will certainly not marry someone as stingy and as unkind as you are!"

Theo's usual placidity was riled. "When am I to meet this elusive gentleman? I assure you I will give him permission to marry you as soon as he asks," he bit back.

Winifred ignored this comment and returned to the issue of the bonnet. "Am I to take it that you refuse to pay the milliner and so I must cancel my new bonnet?"

Theo raised his eyebrow. "Yes, sister, I am not paying for your latest extravagance. If the bonnet is that important, you can wait for next quarter's allowance and purchase it then."

"But it will be out of fashion by then and I will want a different one!"

Theo rose from the table. "Then you will have to live without it. Please excuse me, but I have pressing matters that need my attention."

∽

LORD THEO GRUNTED with satisfaction as he landed a punch right in the center of the Earl of Sherbonne's jaw. Lord Laurence laughed as he staggered back and threw up his hands." Enough! I concede. You're in top form today."

"I am not sure that the art of pugilism is best used to vent oneself of frustration," the cultured tones of Gentleman Jim observed from the side of the ring where the marquess and earl had been sparring.

Theo gave a wry chuckle. "It is a great way to release tension!"

Lord Laurence rubbed his jaw and tossed a towel to his friend. "You might find a target less easily able to bruise." A wicked gleam brightened his eyes. "Although I can use my injuries to garner much sympathy from solicitous ladies."

Theo, who was using the towel to get rid of the sweat that coated his hard muscles, groaned. "Incorrigible!"

The earl shrugged, but as the friends moved towards the lockers where they had stored their clothes, he commented, "I would willingly sacrifice my comfort for your well-being, and yet, even though we have been sparring here for more than an hour and you landed a few heavy blows, the air of tension you had when we began has not entirely disappeared."

It was Theo's turn to shrug. "I'm all right." He grinned at his friend, but the laughter didn't reach his eyes. "Thank you for being available to bear the brunt of my frustrations."

They had washed their torsos and were now pulling their shirts over their heads. Loxley and Donnington, who had also been practicing their pugilistic skills, joined them.

Loxley paused in buttoning his shirt. "What has you so worked up this morning, Theo? Are you still harping on about the lack of suitable marriage prospects at the duke's ball last night?"

Theo punched Loxley's arm. "I have more important things to think of than Sebastian's ball."

The four gentlemen, looking very much like men about town, in well-tailored coats and elegantly tied cravats, thanked Gentleman Jim and sauntered out onto Pritchard Street. As they clambered into Sherbonne's waiting carriage, Donnington looked thoughtfully at Theo. "You behaved rather oddly last night. You lurked on the edges of the dance floor doing a very good impression of a gargoyle for most of the time."

Theo joined in the general laughter, but his face quickly resumed the disgruntled expression he had worn most of the morning. He tried to deflect the conversation from a discussion of his concerns. "Where to now, gentlemen?"

Donnington sat up, his eyes brightening. "Miss Blakeney mentioned that she would be shopping this morning. I might have suggested that I could treat her to an ice at Gunter's."

Loxley laughed while Sherbonne groaned.

Theo smiled. "It seems that progress has been made in your pursuit of the paragon."

Donnington looked smug. "Miss Blakeney is usually very fastidious about dancing only once with any partner at a ball, and yet," he paused dramatically, "she accepted my offer twice."

Amidst the back thumping, cheering and clapping, the carriage pulled out. Sherbonne drawled, "So now I suppose we need to congratulate you on entering into nuptial bliss. At the rate you are pursuing Miss Blakeney, she might just agree within the next decade or so."

Donnington ignored the jibe and looked smug, "My expertise in the art of wooing and seduction gives me particular insight into Theo's situation."

Loxley sat forward. "Do tell. What have you deduced?"

Donnington shrugged. "Theo is besotted with a young lady, one, I would venture to guess, who does return his admiration."

The marquess attempted to smile, but he only managed a snarl. "Theo is sitting right here."

The others ignored him. "That is an interesting theory and I believe you might just have hit the nail on the head."

Sherbonne groaned. "Et tu Brute! Then fall Caesar. It seems as if this love thing is contagious. I thought we had all declared we would remain bachelors until we had supped of all the great banquet of life, and yet first, Donnington has become sentimental and starry-eyed over his paragon and now, Theo has been wounded with Cupid's arrow. Are none of us safe?"

When Adam stopped laughing, he asked Theo, "Who is this enigmatic beauty whose loveliness has pierced your heart?"

Theo shook his head. Sherbonne lost the look of cynical levity that was his customary public face. "You really have fallen in love? Is that why you have been acting so strangely lately? Why did you not tell us?"

Theo said nothing but looked pointedly at Donnington.

Loxley laughed. "Well, if you do begin acting in the same love-sick way that Donnington does, then you deserve to be mocked." His laughter subsided into sincere concern. "There was a new debutante last night, a dark-haired beauty adorned in diamond pins and a very beautiful pearl necklace. You approached her once but never danced with her."

Sherbonne slapped his thigh with his glove. "Ah! She attracted a large amount of attention from everyone. She is pretty in a sweet, country way and I heard rumors of a very large, very attractive dowry."

Donnington frowned. "Theo, you aren't in some financial difficulties that require you to marry a fortune? I thought you were solid. Besides, I thought you too noble-minded to cheapen the sanctity of love and marriage through fortune-hunting."

The carriage had drawn up in Berkeley Square and the four friends strolled towards Gunter's Tea Shop. Theo slapped Donnington's shoulder. "All my current enterprises are prospering. I have no sudden need to bolster my inheritance with a marriage of convenience. I have too much pride to surrender my principles to such ignobility."

Sherbonne entered the popular pastry shop and surveyed the crowd. He observed dryly, "You might have nice principles to guide you, but there was a large wake of vultures circling her last night." Having satisfied himself that there was no young lady he wished to flirt with, he followed Donnington to the side of the room where Miss Blakeney was sipping a cup of tea with her aunt. Sherbonne placed his arm around Theo's shoulder. "Who is your little heiress? I know I have never seen her before. Such a pretty young thing would not have escaped my notice."

Theo growled but when Sherbonne grinned at him, he answered, "Charlotte Drake is the only child and the sole heir of my nearest neighbor in Worcestershire. I know you have heard me speak of Mr. Drake. I occasionally dine with the family when I am in the country."

Donnington had spotted Clarissa Blakeney, in a swirl of pale pink muslin, and was engaged in nodding and smiling at her, while Loxley secured the attention of a waiter and placed an order for tea and cakes. Sherbonne, after having greeted his mother who was seated at a nearby table, turned to Theo. "So, you were just being neighborly last night when you asked Miss Drake to dance."

Theo, glad to escape the teasing of his friends, nodded. "Yes, but she did not need my help. She was already engaged to dance with Hugh Parsiville." He managed not to spit out the name.

Sherbonne raised a skeptical eyebrow, but before he could respond, Donnington, startled enough to drag his attention away from Clarissa Blakeney, declared, "Parsiville! He owes me about five hundred pounds from a game of faro at Brooks' a while back. In fact, he owes money all over town. He is not the kind of gentleman I would trust near any lady of my acquaintance."

Adam nodded. "He goes through life complaining about how

life never treats him fairly, but he neglects his estates and drains the little profit they procure. Do you remember the only time he was asked to play cricket for the school team? He was out for a duck because he didn't bother to run, and then he criticized the umpire as unfair and biased."

Such reminders of just how much of a blackguard Hugh Parsiville was did nothing to appease Theo's mood. Sherbonne added his bit, "His estates are in disrepair and rumor has it that before long, unless he can secure a large fortune, he will be languishing in the Marshalsea. No wonder he is so attached to your little heiress."

Theo raised an eyebrow. "She is not mine." He added sotto voce, "At least not yet." Just then, Charlotte Drake entered Gunter's, trailing behind her mother. Her sudden appearance drew all of Theo's attention.

Loxley gave a low chuckle. "I have never seen you so obsessed with a young lady. I believe Donny is right. You are in danger of falling in love."

Sherbonne bit into an éclair and swallowed rapidly before saying, "It seems that Theo has been keeping secrets from us. I believe his infatuation with the heiress goes back to last October. It would explain the mystery of why he has been so odd recently."

A look of annoyance flashed through Theo's eyes, but he responded calmly, "I have found Miss Drake to be a charming young lady with very interesting ideas."

Sherbonne lost his habitual bantering tone. "You are serious about her."

Theo did not answer, but even as he attempted to stiffen his shoulders and set his jaw more rigidly, his eyes flashed with a tenderness and vulnerability that was all the answer Sherbonne needed.

The earl placed his arm around Theo's shoulders. "If she is the lady who will bring you happiness all through your life, then you know that we will support you, especially against the wiles of Hugh Parsiville."

Theo looked at his friend with an affectionate smile. Many saw only the sardonic facade the earl presented to the world and did not know the intelligent, noble and caring gentleman he truly was. "Thanks, Laurie. But I cannot make her love me against her wishes, and if she has chosen Parsiville, then no matter what my feelings are, I must respect her choice."

Loxley, who had just noticed Parsiville enter the shop, shook his head. "Don't give up the battle just yet, Theo. Until Miss Drake announces her betrothal, there is still time to help her understand that there are better options."

CHAPTER 5

*C*harlotte descended from the carriage onto the crowded pavement of New Bond Street. She tugged her pelisse tightly around herself as she tried to avoid being jostled by the surging masses of shoppers. Two ladies, accompanied by three footmen laden with parcels and packages, swept past Charlotte and she hastily returned their greeting just as Mama plucked at her arm, maneuvering her towards the milliner's.

Before they could enter the fashionable establishment, a portly gentleman, clad in a vivid green coat and wearing tight yellow pantaloons blocked their way. He twirled a walking stick, embellished with brightly colored ribbons as he bowed low. "Mrs. Drake, Miss Drake," he drawled. "How charming to see you." Lord Beauchamp had sat near them at supper at the duke's ball, and Charlotte had marveled at the paleness of his skin. She was certain he would never dare venture out into the sunshine.

Mrs. Drake returned his greeting, but the widowed earl was leering at Charlotte. She had to take his proffered hand and tried not to let him see her shudder as his limp fingers rested just a moment too long in her hand.

"You were quite the belle of the ball at the Duke of Broadwell's little shindig the other evening. I was terribly disappointed that your dance card was so full that I did not have my chance to cut a caper with you. That could be remedied if you would do me the honor of attending a little soiree that my mother is hosting on Friday evening." His voice dripped with unctuous oiliness and Charlotte felt as if she had dipped her hand into a particularly slimy pond. It was only her mother's eyebrow raised in warning that prevented her from wiping her fingers on her dress.

Mrs. Drake gave a triumphant smirk and quickly accepted, "We will gladly attend, thank you, Lord Beauchamp." She pinched Charlotte's arm. "Thank the gentleman, Charlotte."

Charlotte sputtered out a polite response but could not bring herself to be happy about the prospect. She did not think it would be an honor to dance with such a man. As Lord Beauchamp strutted away, Mama looked at her with a mixture of approval and irritation. "You are a very fortunate young lady, Charlotte. I worked hard to secure us an invitation to the duke's ball. I knew it would be the perfect place for you to make your first public appearance and draw the attention of the most eligible, titled gentlemen. If you follow my advice, before the end of the season, I have no doubt that I can secure you a marriage with one of them. However, you could show a little more enthusiasm and gratitude. Even the most eligible of gentlemen need some hint of interest from you. It would not be improper for you to be a little more forthcoming when a gentleman pays you such marked attention."

Charlotte huffed as she followed her mother into the milliner's shop. "I would rather never marry than have to suffer the company of a man such as Lord Beauchamp. I could be very happy living alone in the peace and beauty of Summerhill." But even as the words left her mouth, a vision of Lord Theo's handsome face and strong body rose in her mind. Living at Summerhill with the marquess was still her favorite daydream. She bit her lip. No matter how much her heart beat faster when she thought of him, it was clear that Lord Theo did not dream about her. After Hugh had so deftly intercepted Lord Theo's invitation to dance at the duke's ball, the marquess had not even looked her way for the rest of the evening. Her dance card had been full, but the only gentleman who would have made her evening worthwhile had not even attempted to speak to her again. He had very happily partnered the sophisticated, fashionable ladies who had thronged him and his friends.

Charlotte's musings were interrupted by the sound of raised voices as she stepped into the milliner's shop. She paused just inside the door and stared at a tall, good-looking young woman, a few years older than she, whose face was blazing with anger.

"That is absurd," she spat out. "I must have this bonnet for Lady Henrietta's Venetian breakfast tomorrow. I did not think that my brother was in such dire straits that I cannot take a simple bonnet on credit."

A grim lady, in a deep grey silk dress, squared her shoulders and faced the virago. "I am sorry, Lady Winifred, but until your bill is settled, I cannot let you have any new items. Now, if you will excuse me, Mrs. Drake and her daughter are here to try on the hats I have made for them."

The tall lady tilted her chin and stared at Charlotte as she swept out of the shop without another word, leaving Mrs. Drake and her daughter to the attention of the milliner.

AN HOUR AND A HALF LATER, Mrs. Drake dispatched a footman, laden with parcels from the milliner's, and turned to Charlotte. "I do hope Madame Rouget will be able to finish the rest of the hats before next week. The peach-colored creation will do very well for Lady Bradford's luncheon party." Charlotte scowled but said nothing. She had thought the milliner's design was too fussy and likely to be uncomfortable, but it was no use arguing with her mother.

Her head was throbbing from the hustle and bustle of Bond Street and the endless trying on of hats. She longed to return to the tranquility of the garden at Drake House, but her mother was determined to be seen in the most fashionable places in London. She meekly trailed behind her as they entered Gunter's Tea Shop. The celebrated establishment was crowded and noisy, causing Charlotte's head to ache even more.

Mrs. Drake made her way through the crowd, nodding and smiling at people they barely knew. Finally, she stopped beside a table and smiled ingratiatingly at the very Lady Bradford and her daughter, whose luncheon party they had been invited to attend. Mrs. Drake beamed. "Ah, Lady Bradford, Lady Augusta, how delightful to run into you here. I have just this morning sent my reply to your kind invitation and, indeed, we have spent an exhausting morning trying on the most delightful array of hats. Charlotte finally decided on a charming peach bonnet that is perfect for such an occasion."

Lady Bradford did not look very pleased to see Mrs. Drake or Charlotte, but with a stiff nod, she invited them to join her for refreshments. Gratefully, Charlotte sank into a seat and smiled tightly at Lady Augusta whose critical eye swept over her from head to foot before she offered a curt greeting. Charlotte couldn't help remembering that the marquess had danced the supper dance with Lady Augusta.

She pressed her fingers to her forehead, in an attempt to ease the ache, and tried to concentrate on the menu. She was deciding whether to try the strawberry ice cream or indulge in a cream puff when Hugh Parsiville appeared at her side. Relieved to see a familiar face, she smiled at him. "Oh, Hugh, it is good to see you. How are you?"

He bowed a greeting at the other ladies as he answered Charlotte, "I am well enough. I am expecting today to be pretty good. I have just come from Tattersall's where I was given some sure tips for this afternoon's races at Newmarket."

Charlotte shifted uneasily but scolded herself with a reminder that all gentlemen indulged in gambling and it was a harmless pastime. "I wish you luck."

Hugh shrugged and surveyed the room. He frowned when he spotted the marquess and his friends lounging towards the back of the shop but said nothing. However, when a grim-faced gentleman stalked towards Hugh, Parsiville made another slight bow and sauntered away. Charlotte watched him go, a frown puckering her forehead. While Lady Bradford and Lady Augusta were instructing a somewhat bewildered waiter in the correct method for steeping a pot of tea, Charlotte took the moment to whisper to her mother, "We should have asked Hugh to join us here."

Mrs. Drake's lips flattened into the disapproving line Charlotte hated. "Oh tush, child. I really do not know why Hugh so fascinates you. He is only a distant cousin of your father's and has no title. Remember that our purpose in London is to mingle with the elite of society so that you can make an excellent match. Your father's money and connections will open doors to your success. Why, we are seated with a countess and her daughter and you have already attracted the attention of barons and earls. One of these days, I will be calling you *my lady*!"

Charlotte felt the blood rush to her face. Mrs. Drake had not spoken as quietly as Charlotte, and her last words carried over the hubbub of chatter in the tea room. Charlotte wriggled under the hard scrutiny of Lady Augusta and flushed a deep red when some of the gentlemen she had danced with at the duke's ball turned to her with curious looks.

The hubbub of chatter had fallen off and Charlotte cringed at the hiss of laughter that rippled around the room. Her mortification increased when she caught sight of the tall, imposing figure of the Marquess of Raeburne. He was leaning against a table, and when she looked at him, she couldn't help noticing the flash of irritation in his eyes.

Charlotte gripped her hands tightly in her lap and stared at the table. The bitter truth of Hugh's warning words settled like a stone within her heart. Men would seek her fortune but would not love or even admire her. She heard Lady Bedford murmur something about how some people were determined to buy their way into the aristocracy. She dared not raise her eyes to look at any of the people around her. They probably saw her as a hard, calculating woman who was using her riches to lure one of them into a marriage of convenience.

She was startled when a large hand rested on her shoulder. She glanced up to see Lord Theo standing beside her, his eyes soft with compassion and concern. With a contented sigh, she leaned into the sure, steady comfort of his touch. He tightened his grip on her and she could feel the sweep of his thumb brushing her lightly beneath her light, linen pelisse.

She gave him a tentative smile, but just as she began to think she could escape the humiliation of the last few moments, a gentleman who had paid her much leering attention at the ball stopped at their table. He slapped the marquess on his back. Early as it was in the day, he reeked of brandy. "I say, Raeburne, old chap," he slurred, "I think you should give some of the rest of us a chance before you hog this newest picking. Better leave the heiress to those of us who need a boost to keep us going." He nodded towards Charlotte. "I've heard her dowry's at least eighty thousand and her father's estate will all be hers when the old man pops off, which could be any day now if rumor has it right."

All the customers who filled the elegant tea shop were now silent, riveted on the little drama playing out in front of them.

Charlotte heard someone nearby comment, "Better than the latest offering at the Drury Lane."

Charlotte could hardly breathe. Tears stung the back of her eyes. She felt dizzy. The air was heavy. The room was too hot. She wanted to go home. She made a feeble attempt to push her chair back, ready to flee.

Just before her humiliation spilled down her face in tears, the marquess, whose hand had not left her shoulder, gave her another reassuring squeeze. His thumb smoothed a soothing circle over the back of her neck. Just for a moment, she pretended that Lord Raeburne was more than a solicitous neighbor, more than a kind friend who had come to her defense. The firm pressure of his hand anchored her and kept her from bolting from the room in a fit of dramatic and overwrought passion. She held her breath, comforted by his touch but unsettled by the unexpected intimacy of his caress. She turned her face to him and, once again, she found it difficult to breathe. The heat of his touch unfurled tendrils of warmth through her body and she softened against him, wishing she could find shelter in his arms.

The marquess was not looking at her, however. He beckoned the proprietor of the establishment, who was hovering a few feet from the table, wringing his hands in his spotless white apron. "I believe that Sir Trenwith is ready to leave. You can add his refreshments to my bill. Please ensure that his carriage is called." Lord Theo's voice was calm and quiet but conveyed a depth of authority that insisted on being obeyed.

Mr. Gunter bowed hurriedly. "Yes, indeed, your lordship. I am sorry that this contretemps has spoiled your enjoyment of your refreshments. His carriage is already at the door. Sir Trenwith, if you would like to come with me?"

Mr. Gunter hustled Sir Trenwith from the room. Slowly, the previous level of chatter returned and Charlotte found it possible to breathe again, although the comforting weight of

Lord Theo's hand on her shoulder still sent shivers down her spine.

The marquess only removed his hand when, with a bow to Lady Bradford and her daughter, he dropped into an empty chair.

CHAPTER 6

*L*ord Theo was finding it difficult to control the swell of his cock as it bulged in his breeches, pulsing lewdly and pressing against the buttons of his fly. The sweet gratefulness of Charlotte's response to his assistance in getting rid of Sir Trenwith fired all his dominant instincts.

Charlotte looked so sweet, so vulnerable, so much as if she needed him to care for her as she sat demurely at the table in the middle of Gunter's, nibbling on a cream puff. Her pale blue dress enhanced the brilliant blue of her eyes and heightened the delicious pink flush of her cheeks. Wisps of hair had tugged loose from her pins and were framing her face. Her slightly disheveled appearance reminded him vividly of how unkempt, how free, she had been that afternoon when they had rescued the lamb. Here, in the fashionable swirl of London society, her eyes did not sparkle with the intense passion that had fascinated him and there was no hint of the unbridled laughter that had echoed in the crisp autumn air. He was determined to stoke her dampened passions back to life.

She bit into the cream puff, and a smudge of cream remained on her lip. His cock jerked, and without thinking, he brushed his thumb over the soft pink swell and cleared away the cream. He sucked his finger lightly to clean it. Charlotte turned a brighter pink and Lady Augusta gave a soft snort. He would need to be careful not to allow his inappropriate responses to damage Charlotte's reputation.

As if to remind him that she was not his, the soft sneer of Hugh Parsiville's voice drifted across the shop, "It is unfortunate that even gentlemen forget to show their breeding when they find themselves in the presence of an heiress."

Charlotte stiffened, but this time Lord Theo did not respond. He was grateful when his cousin the duke and Lady Amelia stopped beside their table. The duke bowed a greeting and cast a raised eyebrow in Theo's direction but said nothing. It was the gentle delicacy of Amelia that rescued Charlotte this time.

"It is very good to see you, Miss Drake. May I sit here for a moment? I must offer you my apologies for being a poor hostess at my dear duke's ball."

Charlotte looked up with startled eyes, but her polite protest died on her lips when Lady Amelia winked at her and continued blithely. "I neglected you most horribly, but I would be very grateful if you would allow me to make up my deficiencies."

Charlotte shook her head. The duchess was a delightful lady, extremely beautiful and quite a bit younger than the duke, only a year or two older than Charlotte herself. She had none of the detached boredom or supercilious arrogance Charlotte had so quickly come to detest in the ladies she had encountered in London. But Charlotte was tongue-tied. She had experienced a bewildering array of emotions that morning, and Lady Amelia's sudden and unexpected warmth and friendliness brought tears to her eyes.

His grace, the Duke of Broadwell, leaned over his wife and ran his finger down her cheek. The gesture was so tender, so intimate, that Charlotte felt both the heat of voyeuristic embarrassment and a deep yearning for someone to love her in just such a way.

The duke's voice was low but carried the unmistakable authority of someone used to being obeyed. "My dear, do get to the point. It seems that you have not yet overcome your propensity to ramble and we will need to *discuss* it when we return home."

Charlotte shivered at his tone, but Amelia just laughed. She did, however, focus her thoughts. "Miss Drake, I would really like to become better acquainted with you. I am arranging a little party to attend the opera next Thursday evening and I would be delighted if you would join us."

Charlotte almost giggled at the triumphant look the duchess gave her husband, but the low clearing of Lady Augusta's throat near her reminded her that she had made too much of a spectacle of herself already. She turned to her mother, very aware that a look of pure delight suffused Lord Theo's face. "Mama, do we have any other engagements on Thursday evening?"

Her mother's usual self-assurance had deepened to a self-satisfied smugness. "You have received so any invitations that I cannot immediately recall all of our engagements, but I will send her grace a reply as soon as I have consulted my daybook."

Charlotte's impulsive outcry that no other engagements could possibly matter more than spending an evening with Lord Theo was cut off before she had spoken a word by the drawling voice of Hugh Parsiville drifting over her head, "The opera! How boring. I can never understand the fascination ladies have for the wailing and ranting in a language one cannot understand. The only reason to waste an evening at the opera house is the chance to speak to other gentlemen who have also been dragged there under protest."

Charlotte was a bright pink, but Lord Raeburne stared at Parsiville, raising an eyebrow, an action he had learned from his cousin. "In my experience, gentlemen with refined taste and intelligence find the opera more agreeable than the cardroom or Tattersall's."

Annoyance, and something more, something much like a flash of rage, crossed Parsiville's face and Charlotte shrank back into her seat. But Hugh was used to dealing with snubs and he ignored the marquess, holding out a hand to Charlotte. "I believe you said something about going to Hatchard's. I am walking that way if you would like to come."

CHARLOTTE WALKED BESIDE HUGH, taking quick steps to keep up with his unusually rapid pace. He had said nothing since they left Gunter's, and uneasy guilt gnawed at her insides. Once again, Hugh had adroitly maneuvered her away from the company of the marquess, and yet she was finding it hard to be grateful for his intervention. She seethed as she thought how Hugh had not intervened when Sir Trenwith had embarrassed her, only when the marquess had shown any interest in her.

They entered the large bookshop, but she was feeling too miserable to enjoy the rows and rows of dark wooden shelves laden with books. Hugh glanced around as if he was looking for someone. A group of gentlemen talking in low tones behind some shelves containing books on classical history caught his attention. He took an eager step in their direction and then hesitated, glaring at Charlotte. "I suppose you can't get into much trouble in a book shop. I need to speak to some gentlemen."

Charlotte nodded. "I shall be perfectly happy browsing."

Hugh paid scant attention to her comment. He moved away from her, not even glancing back as he joined the gentlemen he had come to see. Charlotte sighed but quickly let the wonder of the books absorb her interest. She wandered along the shelves, breathing in the peaceful ambience of leather covers and newly printed pages. Soon, she found a collection of Charlotte Smith's

Elegiac Sonnets and began idly skimming through the pages, reading a line here and there. She was contemplating the poet's description of spring flowers when the mention of Lord Theodore's name intruded into her thoughts. Spurred by curiosity, she marked her place on the page with her finger and looked up to see three ladies, all of whom had danced with the marquess at the duke's ball, conversing near the end of the row.

"Do you not agree that Lord Raeburne was looking particularly splendid last night? His coat must have been made by Weston," began one young lady.

"I believe the marquess is finally contemplating marriage. I was deeply gratified when he approached me twice for a dance last night, even though he usually makes a point of never dancing more than once with any lady at a ball." The second lady, whose head was wrapped in a bright yellow turban embellished with sweeping feathers, managed to look both smug and coy. "I do believe I would make a fine marchioness."

The bright blue and green feathers on the first lady's turban trembled. "There is no need to be vulgar, Lady Harriet."

The yellow-turbaned lady retorted, "I noticed that he did not dance with you at all last night."

"My dance card was full," the blue and green lady hastened to explain.

Charlotte found herself edging closer to the group of ladies. A tightness clutched at her stomach at the thought of the marquess being married to someone who was not her. She was so intent on hearing the conversation that she did not see anyone else, not until she bumped into the solid presence of the marquess, which had just entered the alcove. With a muffled shriek, she sent the book in her hands tumbling to the floor.

Charlotte bent down to retrieve it, her face burning with embarrassment. She dared not look at Lord Theo, but she was very aware of the soft sneers of the ladies. She stood up, smoothing the pages of the book, and irritation swamped her humiliation. The ladies had swooped around the marquess, like a mischief of magpies fighting over a shiny ring.

"Your Lordship," simpered the first, "I was just telling Lady Harriet and Miss Agatha how delightful it has been to have you dine with us so often recently. Mama is very fond of your company and she looks forward to seeing you at her little musical evening on Thursday."

Charlotte gasped. The ladies fell silent, staring at her as if she were a particularly repulsive insect that had disturbed their luncheon. She was aware of the weight of Lord Theo's gaze on her but kept her eyes averted, studying the spine of the book as if she needed to memorize every inch of the deep, red leather.

"It is such a pity that one is expected to endure the crassness of country manners here in the middle of the metropolis," the third lady, who had not previously spoken, observed blandly. "There is something quite vulgar about trying to attract the attention of a gentleman through dropping one's possessions and making inarticulate sounds. I suppose when one has a large fortune, one does not need to learn the niceties of society manners."

The yellow-turbaned lady attempted to look coy as she simpered, "Poor Lord Raeburne! I am sure it must be tedious to have unsuitable young ladies attempt to attract your attention, but I know that you are not fooled into thinking that silk gowns and diamond pins and the hints of a large dowry make a lady worth pursuing."

"You are very right, Miss Cartwright. I am somewhat fastidious regarding the ladies whose company I keep," Lord Theo replied. Charlotte shivered at the hard edge in his voice. She wanted to flee, but her only way of escape was to push past the little group. She remained where she was, trapped in the alcove. "And now, ladies, if you would excuse me, I came here to look for a new translation of the poems of Catullus."

Miss Cartwright had not noticed the coldness of Lord Theo's

tone. Her voice resonated with triumph. "Oh, but of course, Lord Raeburne. I do admire a gentleman who reads intellectual works. I must find Mama. We came in to purchase the next volume of Maria Edgeworth's *Moral Tales for Young People*. Such an edifying work for ladies to read."

In spite of her discomfort, Charlotte giggled at this announcement. Her own mama had bought the set of books, but Charlotte had been much more interested in reading Mrs. Radcliffe's latest novel.

Lord Theo was stepping away from the ladies, but Miss Cartwright had one last sally to offer. "I look forward to hearing your opinion of my performance on the harp at Mama's musicale on Thursday."

Lord Theo stopped and looked at her. "Oh, that is a delight I will have to forego, Miss Cartwright. I received your mother's invitation after I had already committed myself to joining Lady Amelia at the opera on Thursday."

Relief flooded Charlotte, even as Miss Cartwright sputtered and disappeared into the main part of the shop, trailed by her companions. She took a deep breath and looked up, straight into the eyes of the marquess. "Oh, I thought you had gone."

A smile glimmered in his eyes, but he answered her seriously, "No, I am still here. As I mentioned, I am looking for a book of poetry, and this is where the poetry books are kept."

Charlotte bit her lip and ran her finger along the edge of the book she still held. "Yes, of course. I am sorry." She tried to step forward but Lord Theo had moved closer, his impressive body trapping her against the shelves. He loomed over her, so close that she could feel the heat of his body seep into her, warming her like summer sunshine breaking through the clouds of the thunderstorm that raged within her. She took a deep breath, but her thoughts were jumbled and she could not think of the right words.

She looked up when he ran the tip of his finger down the

contour of her cheek. Her breath was coming in short, sharp bursts and made her breasts rise. She flushed a darker red when she realized that the marquess was watching how they swelled as she breathed deeply. Slowly, he raised his eyes and focused on her face, a glimmer of a smile in his dark eyes that did nothing to ease her discomfort.

"Well, Miss Drake, are you enjoying the delights that London has to offer?"

THEO SMILED WITH SATISFACTION. Charlotte Drake looked lovely. Her soft green dress clung to her in all the right places. Her light blush sent the blood pulsing through his body and his cock was hard as a rock, as it had been since he had seen her in Gunter's earlier that morning.

At his question, a look of indignation flashed in her eyes. "London is crowded and there is nothing to do here but try on dresses and bonnets and then wear uncomfortable fashions where other ladies can admire your clothes."

He chuckled. "You do not like clothes?"

Charlotte's eyes skimmed over his blue silk waistcoat, embroidered with a deeper blue paisley pattern, his cravat elegantly tied in a cascade style, and his tightly fitted blue velvet jacket. Her eyes dropped, focusing on the mother-of-pearl buttons that fastened his waistcoat. "Papa often says *vestis virum facit*, and I know that one can tell much about a person from what they wear."

Theo chuckled. "I prefer to think that it's not the clothes that make a man, or woman. I have seen dandies dressed in the height of fashion who have little substance to their characters."

This time when Charlotte raised her big blue eyes to his face, relief and confidence flooded them. "That is such a helpful point of view. I do like pretty dresses, but I like them to be comfortable as well. And I find it tedious to stand still while a modiste prods and pokes and pins dresses for endless hours."

Theo brushed his finger over her cheek. "And yet the end result is so charming, quite a change from the clothes I have seen you wear in the countryside." He reached for the book she was still clutching and eased it out of her tight fingers. "I see, however, that you have found that there is more to London than modistes and milliners."

Charlotte nodded. "I have never seen such a splendid shop before, but I do not think I could ever truly be happy in London." Her voice was wistful. "The buildings are so tall and so crowded on top of one another, and the roads are all cobbled with stones, and hard. There is so little grass and so few flowers. I did not imagine that so many people could be in one place at one time. I find it difficult to breathe when there are so few trees and the sky seems so far away. I miss the sounds of the birds. It is not easy to hear them over the rumble of cartwheels and all the footsteps clattering on the pavements."

Theo was delighted by her sweet spontaneity. "You are a rare woodland creature, a veritable nymph. I am sure that even if you lived in London for years, society could not tame your delightful wildness."

A shutter seemed to quench all the fire in Charlotte. The marquess frowned, unsure of why his compliment should make her uncomfortable. Slowly, he ran his hands over her arms, following the curve of her waist and soothing her with gentle strokes. He drew her closer to him, tucking her head against his chest. He nodded when he felt her body soften against his.

His every instinct compelled him to protect and comfort her, as if she were the little lamb they had rescued. He breathed deeply, filling his senses with the soft fragrance of violets. He reached for her hand and cradled her fingers against his palm, pressing his thumb against her hand, enjoying the way her body trembled in response. Gently, he brought her hand to his mouth and slowly kissed each fingertip through her soft gloves.

"I prefer the country too," he murmured against her hand. "But London has its pleasures, and soon, with someone who knows the ins and outs of it to guide you through the maze, you will be as comfortable here as you are at home in Summerhill." His hands moved slowly, surely, over her body, persuading her that he would lead and guide her into whatever pleasures awaited her. His cock jerked against his tight breeches, bulging lewdly as it anticipated the pleasures of her sweet body.

Charlotte was not convinced. She shook her head, pulling away from his embrace, and nibbled her lip in a way that he found quite distracting. Her mouth was made for pleasure and he had a sudden urge to push her to her knees in front of him, right here in the middle of Hatchard's on a busy morning with customers milling among the books, and teach her to take him in that sweet, hot mouth.

But Charlotte's next words showed that she was still mulling over what he had said earlier. "I do not have the skills to be a social butterfly, flitting from one overcrowded ball to another, primping and preening to impress the right people. I don't even know who the right people are. I only know that I am not one of them."

She stumbled as she tried to move out of his embrace, but he placed his hand on her waist to steady her. Leaving his left hand on her waist, he cupped her chin in his right one and tilted her face up so she had to look at him. The vulnerable trust in her eyes did something strange to his heart. The tip of her tongue peeped out of her mouth, a delectable invitation for him to explore her more completely. He brushed his thumb along the bow of her lips, savoring the softness. He wanted to taste her, to run his tongue over every inch of her delicious body and learn to know her. She whimpered softly as he pressed harder against her mouth. He wanted to hear those moans become loud screams of ecstasy as she called his name at the moment of climax.

But she would never surrender to him fully until she was sure of her own worth. He needed to encourage her to be confident in herself. His voice was husky with desire but contained just enough dominance to compel her attention. "Little lamb, you do not need to primp and preen, as you put it. You are delightful as you are." His mouth quirked up in the beginning of a smile. "No matter how crushed a ballroom is or how many people ride through Hyde Park, trying to attract the attention of the Beau Monde, you have a beauty that shines brightly."

Charlotte scoffed, but she nuzzled his hand as she protested, "That shine comes from the diamonds and pearls of my dowry."

The marquess suppressed an irritated growl. "You are more, far more, than your inheritance. It is not attractive when you try to be cynical or when you demean yourself." To emphasize his point, he leaned closer and just touched her lips with his. Her blue eyes opened wider, startled by his kiss, but as he touched them again, she pressed against him, urging more.

Theo let her go when he heard footsteps approaching. The slow affected drawl of Hugh Parsiville was jarring. "There you are, Charlotte. Have you done all you need to? I have completed my business and I promised your mother I would return you in good time for lunch. Come along."

Charlotte stumbled back, turning to Parsiville with relief. She dropped a brief curtsey to Theo and hastened after Parsiville, leaving the marquess to bring his raging hard on under control.

CHAPTER 7

$\mathcal{E}$arly the next morning, Lord Theo was ushered into the blue drawing room at Drake House. He took a deep breath as Charlotte Drake rose from the table where she had been working on a piece of embroidery. When he glanced at her sewing, she scowled and pushed it under a book that was lying open beside her. The marquess bit back a grin. Charlotte Drake was not a "Curly-locks" who would sit quietly sewing a straight seam for hours, like the girl in the nursery rhyme. She was the kind of person who needed to move, to feel the freedom of the wind in her hair and the sunshine on her face.

Charlotte was prettier each time he saw her. Her dark hair was fashionably but simply arranged in a knot on the top of her head and tendrils framed her face, drawing attention to her soft skin and bright eyes. Theo admired the pale blue dress she was wearing that did not hide the tempting curves of her figure. He had to concentrate very hard to keep control of his unwieldy cock, which had leapt in delight at the delectable sight of Miss Charlotte Drake and was now throbbing against the seam of his tight breeches. He hoped neither Charlotte nor her mother would notice the unseemly bulge. Trying to ignore his aching groin, he greeted the mother and daughter with all the civility he could draw on and then focused on Charlotte.

"Miss Drake, I trust that I am not disturbing you, especially so early in the day, but I wanted to bring you these while they are still fresh with dew." He held out a bunch of bluebells.

Charlotte took them with an exclamation of joy and buried her face in their sweet-smelling mass. It was such a charming vision that he did not mind the exorbitant price he had paid for flowers in London that grew wildly and abundantly in the woods of his estate.

Charlotte's voice was almost muffled by the flowers. "Oh, thank you, Lord Theo. These are such a delightful reminder of the countryside. They bring home a little closer." She glanced around the room at the elegant displays of hothouse and culti-vated flowers in formal vases. "Somehow, these other flowers do not contain any suggestion of meadows and forests or even of gardens, whereas your bluebells transport me directly to the woods around Summerhill."

Mrs. Drake had been paging through a copy of *The Ladies Journal* on a settee near the fire. She sniffed and muttered some-thing about roses and tulips being more appropriate offerings from a wealthy suitor. Theo ignored her. He understood his little lamb. She would have smiled politely at an offering of formal flowers and sent them to a servant to have them arranged. Charlotte was a wood nymph, a delightful wild spirit for whom the beauty of woods and streams was essential to her happiness. Lord Theo knew that the way to woo her, to win her away from a clod like Hugh Parsiville, was to touch her soul.

He smiled and held out the other parcel he had brought with him. "You left Hatchard's so quickly yesterday that you forgot your book."

With a cry of delight, mingled with the reminder of just why she had left the book behind, Charlotte took the neatly wrapped parcel from the marquess and untied it. She opened the book and paused when she saw he had written an inscription on the flyleaf. It was a simple message, simply *To Charlotte*, followed by the date. But Charlotte blushed deeply and ran her fingers over the dark blue ink.

The marquess, who was now seated beside her at the work table, covered her hand with his, and then flicked through the pages until he found Sonnet VIII. He smiled at Charlotte. "This has always been one of my favorites. It reminds me of Oakdene."

Charlotte tilted her head to look up at him. Her eyes were soft with memories of the woods and fields of her home. Suddenly, she dropped her eyes, and her face flushed a pretty pink. She ran her finger over the words on the page and began to read. Her voice echoed the elusive fragrance of violets that almost always clung to her.

"AGAIN THE WOOD, and long withdrawing vale,
  In many a tint of tender green are drest,
  Where the young leaves unfolding, scarce conceal,
  Beneath their early shade, the half form'd nest
  Of finch or woodlark; and the primrose pale,
  And lavish cowslip, wildly scatter'd round,
  Give their sweet spirits to the sighing gale.
  Ah, season of delight!"

SHE SIGHED as she paused in her reading. "How I would love to be able to capture the beauty of home in words like these."

Lord Theo held her hand in his. A deep sense of satisfaction settled in his heart. "I am glad you are able to appreciate the pleasures of nature." She raised her eyes to his once again, and he continued, "I enjoy the way nature marks the turning of the seasons, how different flowers bloom in each month of the year."

He gave a low chuckle. "Even when I was just a boy at school, my friends often teased me by calling me Farmer T."

The entrance of the housekeeper with a tray of refreshments broke the spell. Charlotte pulled her hand away from his and quickly rose. She picked up the bluebells. "I need to place these in a vase." She moved across the drawing room, coming to a standstill some distance from him, where a low cherry wood table stood in front of a mirror. "I will place these here, and then their loveliness will be increased."

Theo sat back in his chair, watching her with a tender smile on his face. As he watched her bend over the bluebells, he could picture her in the woods, her hair tumbling free, her body naked to his eyes, curvaceous and bounteous, suggestive of the abundance of nature. She was an earth goddess, and he was ready to worship her. Her breasts might, for the moment, be contained within the stays that bound them, but the luscious shape of them pushed up into generous mounds, tempting his mouth to suckle them. Her skin was soft and creamy, and he longed to run his tongue over every part of her, becoming intimate with every crevice and every curve. Getting to know her would be like feasting on milk and honey.

Charlotte kissed the petal of a bluebell and Theo was riveted to her mouth, so delicate and pink, and so ready for the kisses that he would bestow on her, that he would draw from her sweet lips. Even now, he could remember the merest taste he had had in the bookshop.

His cock had been hard as granite since he had seen her enter Sebastian's ballroom a few nights ago. Even though he had squeezed and stroked his dick in his bath and in his bed, dreaming of Charlotte until his seed had spewed out onto his stomach and thighs in long, creamy ropes of promise, he was still hard. He did not think the ache and stiffness would ease until he could sink into the warm, welcoming depths of her body and he could release his pleasure into her pussy.

But he was in her mother's drawing room and manners dictated that he should maintain a semblance of a civilized demeanor. With a quick shake of his head, he reminded himself of the real purpose of his visit. "Miss Drake, Charlotte, although we are not in the countryside, London does have some places where nature can be enjoyed. I would like to take you for a ride in the park if you are not otherwise engaged."

Mrs. Darke, who had been sitting discretely a few feet away, allowing the marquess to converse with her daughter, now intervened. "My dear Lord Raeburne, that is a lovely suggestion, but it is not yet the fashionable hour of five o' clock when the elite of London are usually seen in the park."

Theo raised an eyebrow. "I thought it would be best to go now. The fashionable hour finds Hyde Park somewhat over-crowded and crushed. I thought it would be more pleasant to go when it is possible to enjoy some peace." He rose, picking up his gloves and hat. "I have my curricle and a pair of chestnuts in the street. Unfortunately, if Charlotte is not able to join me, I must take my leave, as it is not good for the horses to stand around for too long."

Mrs. Drake quickly set aside her feeble objections. She beamed, even as Charlotte shook her head. "Charlotte would be delighted to drive out with you, Lord Raeburne. It will take her only a moment to fetch her bonnet." She was ringing the bell even as she spoke. "The straw bonnet with the blue ribbon, dear," she advised Charlotte, pushing her from the room.

Theo made his way down the stairs, followed by Mrs. Drake. Charlotte entered the foyer a moment later, fastening the ribbons of her bonnet. He led her out to his curricle, energized by the frisson of electricity that pulsated between them as she placed her hand on his arm. Her quick startled glance at him indicated that she felt it too. Theo was no stranger to the plea-sures of sexual intercourse, but never had he experienced the deep pulse of passion that existed when he was near Charlotte.

Yet she was innocent, unfamiliar with the kind of pleasure he was used to. He needed to take it slowly so that she was not frightened away by the intensity of what was brewing between them.

"That is a very fetching bonnet," he remarked as he helped her into the curricle, admiring how the bonnet framed her face and the ribbon heightened the blue of her eyes.

"Thank you. It is one of the new ones Mama selected. She seems to think it is necessary to have a bonnet for every dress, but I don't really care much for them. I think one or two are all that is necessary to protect me against the sun."

Theo took the reins from his groom and settled into his seat. "You don't? I thought all ladies considered a dozen new bonnets each season as absolutely essential to life."

Charlotte turned a pretty shade of pink. Her teeth played with her lip. Theo watched her, fascinated and bemused as he took the reins from his groom and set his chestnuts to a brisk pace. He was accomplished in the art of flirtation and was used to ladies accepting his compliments with smiles and thanks. Yet Charlotte responded quite differently. She became more distant, less open, to his advances. She was an intriguing puzzle he needed to unravel.

CHARLOTTE STARED straight ahead of her. She touched the ribbon of her bonnet and blinked hard, thinking over Lord Theo's remark about ladies and their bonnets. Her answer had proven her to be gauche, unsophisticated. She was not a fashionable society lady, able to converse about the latest styles and which color of ribbons was the most elegant. The marquess had raised his eyebrow when she blurted out her lack of interest in bonnets. She must be an object of amusement to him.

From the corner of her eye, she glanced at the handsome

profile of the marquess, trying not to let him see that she was staring at him. Her heart thudded in her chest, as she was thrilled to be sitting beside him, but she was confused. He had not danced with her at the duke's ball and yet he had defended her honor in Gunter's when Sir Trenwith had caused such a scene. And now he had called on her, brought her the very flowers she had been longing for, and he was driving her out. She shook her head. In spite of the kiss he had given her in Hatchard's, she did not think he could be serious about wooing her. She shook her head. She could not understand why the marquess was paying her such attention when he could have the company of every sophisticated and accomplished lady in London.

As the marquess maneuvered his curricle expertly and effi-ciently through the busy London streets, she tried to understand why he was spending time with her. She turned to him with a determined tilt of her head. "Thank you, Your Lordship, for this outing and for your assistance yesterday. I know you must be very busy with all your affairs. I am sure that you have many better things to do than spend time with me." She swallowed hard and when he said nothing, she wound down, "Please accept my apologies, Your Lordship. Mama is not aware that you are courting Miss Cartwright. She would not have insisted that I ride out with you had she known."

Lord Theo swore softly under his breath, but a butcher's cart lumbered into the road just in front of his curricle and he had to concentrate on keeping his high-stepping chestnuts from bolt-ing. As soon as the horses were calm, he turned to Charlotte, his eyebrow raised. "Miss Cartwright?"

Charlotte nodded, her eyes bright with the strain of holding back tears. "I am not sure of the conventions of London society, but I believe Miss Cartwright would not approve of your keeping me company." She straightened her shoulders. "Although I am sure she will find anecdotes of my foibles amusing when you share them with her and your other friends."

As Theo turned his horses through the gates of Hyde Park, he looked at Charlotte, the intensity of his dark eyes silencing her. None of the humor that usually softened his air of unquestionable authority and implacable command was evident in the hard glint. Charlotte shivered. In spite of the tremor of fear that coursed through her, her heart softened even more at that hard, dark look. The strength of his broad shoulders and noble bearing made her feel safe.

The marquess shook his head. "Miss Cartwright?" he repeated. "I have no arrangement with Miss Cartwright or any other young lady." For a moment, a glint of his usual humor flashed in his eyes. "I hear rumors every week or so that I am about to be betrothed to a hopeful debutante."

Charlotte subsided, sinking back against the comfortable swabs in Lord Theo's curricle. Blood rushed to her face and her blush deepened when an emotion she could not identify filled his eyes. His momentary amusement faded and his voice echoed the hardness in his eyes. "That is not, however, of real consequence. Your suggestion that I asked you to ride out with me only so I could find a reason to mock you is disturbing."

Charlotte cringed, trying to find words to answer the marquess. She opened her mouth, but no sounds emerged.

The marquess filled the silence. "Miss Drake, your suggestion that my friends and I amuse ourselves by mocking young ladies does not speak very highly of your estimation of my character or that of my friends, gentlemen I esteem highly and whom I trust completely."

Charlotte was numb with dismay. She sat stiffly next to the marquess, consternation robbing her of any explanation. He drove along Rotten Row for a few minutes. He took the reins and his crop in one hand and, with the other, covered Charlotte's trembling fingers. When he next spoke, his voice was softer. "My real concern, however, my little lamb, is that you believe you have foibles, as you put it, that would bring down ridicule on you. What foibles, what quirks, did you expect me to find matter for amusement?"

Charlotte's voice rasped with unshed tears. "I-I am not fashionable or sophisticated, like the young ladies with whom you spend so much time. I have neglected the kind of accomplishments that debutantes are expected to have." She stumbled to a halt, unable to continue the list of her weaknesses.

The marquess turned his horses down a side lane, away from the popular thoroughfare used by most members of the fashionable set in London. "If you were sophisticated, you would not be seated beside me right now." He caressed her hand, running his thumb in circles over her palm and along her fingers. "I would like to help you see yourself the way I do, as a charming, sweet, sensitive woman."

The tears that had been stinging the back of Charlotte's eyes tumbled over her cheeks at Lord Theo's unexpected words. She gulped softly and brushed her cheek with the back of her hand. "Your Lordship, please accept my deepest apologies. I meant no insult or offence to either you or your friends. I do need to try to think through what I say before letting the words rush out of my mouth."

The glimmer of humor returned to Theo's eyes as he nodded. "You are forgiven, my little lamb. It seems to me that you need someone strong to help you control your impulses and to assist you to gain confidence." He lifted Charlotte's hand to his mouth and placed a kiss on the tip of one finger as the horses pulled the curricle down a very beautiful tree-lined avenue. "It will, however, require you to trust me, to accept my guidance, my advice, my discipline."

Charlotte tried to pull her hand out of Lord Theo's firm grasp, but he simply tightened his hold, trapping her. She bit her lip and gazed at her hand in his, absorbing the comfort and steadiness he exuded. "Discipline?" Her voice was a soft murmur. "I have spent much of my time trying to escape from Mama's discipline. She has often described me as wild and uncontrollable." Even as she spoke, a guilty image of her dark secret rose in her mind. Lord Theo was treating her with such kindness now, but if he realized just how wicked she was, he would give her the cut direct. She glanced at him, biting her lip so hard that she drew a drop of blood. The metallic tang filled her mouth and grounded her.

Lord Theo was watching her closely, and his strong jaw and thick, dark hair distracted her for a moment. But then she noticed the hard scrutiny of his dark eyes and she squirmed. She had to look away to try to regain some equilibrium.

Lord Theo's voice was low, gentle and yet edged with authority that compelled her to pay attention. "Discipline is not something to be feared. It does not take away your individuality or force you to conform to some impossible image set by society. Learning to control your impulses and emotions gives you the strength and power to fulfill your potential. It gives you the freedom to be yourself."

They rode on for a few minutes in silence while Charlotte pondered what the marquess had said. A chattering squirrel leaped from one branch to another of a nearby tree, and Charlotte watched it, her eyes bright with delight. When it disappeared and the only sound came from the jays and sparrows that were focused on their own business, Charlotte turned to face Lord Theo. "I am not sure that I really understand what you mean. It does not make sense that you would want to waste your time with me, even at such an unfashionable hour as this when few people come to the park." She glanced hesitantly around the deserted path and then forgot her troubles for a moment in the beauty of a row of cherry trees, arrayed in deep pink blossoms as if they were ready for a ball. She sighed at the loveliness.

Lord Theo smiled and tilted her face towards him. "There are some lovely things to see in London. It is not all smoke and cobbled roads." As he spoke, Lord Theo ran his finger softly over her mouth, tracing the shape of her mouth. Charlotte drew in her breath with a soft gasp. Through the soft leather of his gloves, he ignited sparks of desire in her.

Charlotte felt her body tremble and her skin tingle, as if she could feel him everywhere. Her breasts felt swollen and heavy and pushed up higher, pressing against the confinement of her corset. Her nipples bunched into hard little points that ached against the firm linen of her petticoat. She moved her thighs restlessly against the cushions of the curricle seat in an attempt to quell the surge of heat that pulsed in her groin. Her body thrilled to Lord Theo's attention, and she surrendered to his advances, abandoning all attempts to behave like a proper society lady.

Lord Theo's eyes were focused on her face with an intensity that seemed to pierce right through to the very center of her being. She found it difficult to breathe. His hand moved away from her lips and cupped her face. "Do you really want to imitate the staid and somber ladies of the *ton* who have no under-standing of pleasure? You should not sell yourself short. You have considerable charms, not the least of which is your willing-ness to explore pleasure."

Charlotte tried to squirm and pull her face away, but the marquess held her firmly, even as he kept control of the horses that moved slowly up the avenue. She closed her eyes and, when she opened them, tried not to look into the deep brown velvet of Lord Theodore's disconcerting gaze. Her voice was husky with suppressed desire, but also with the agony of her situation. Ignoring the painful memory of her secret, she answered, "I am aware that my charm lies mostly in the inheritance I will receive from my father." Her body stiffened. "From all that I have heard, My Lord, you are not knocking on poverty's door and it is not imperative that you marry an heiress."

Charlotte bit off her words when Lord Theo's shoulders stiffened and his mouth straightened into a hard line. Could it be that his position was not as secure as her father thought it to be? Was the marquess entertaining her because he wanted her fortune? Strangely, her plight had loosened her tongue, and instead of being tongue-tied in Lord Theo's presence as she so often was, she babbled, "My mother has cautioned me that a lady should only ride out with a man at the fashionable hour and only keep to the main paths. I believe she made an exception because of your friendship with my father, but I do not want my reputation to be tainted. I still have hopes of entering into a respectable marriage."

Theo had slowed his horses to a walk during Charlotte's rambling explanation. Now he stopped them altogether. They were under the shade of a large, sweet chestnut tree, hidden from the view of any idle passer-by who might wander along the quiet path. He dropped the reins and slid his left arm around her slender shoulders, drawing her closer to him. His right hand cupped her face, keeping her focused on him. He perused her intensely for a few moments, gently soothing her with slow sweeps of his hand down her back. He waited until she softened against him, her shoulders losing their rigidity and her eyes losing their anxious expression under the soft caress of his fingers.

Eventually, he spoke, his voice a low, intimate rumble that conveyed far more than his words did. "My little lamb, I have never set much store by society's approval, and respectability is so often a cage that society erects to keep us from experiencing all that is good in life."

"It's different for a man," she protested.

He nodded. "Unfortunately, it is true that society holds men and women to different standards, and it takes courage to be yourself and follow your heart. The young woman I got to know in Worcestershire showed that kind of courage when she muddied her dress to rescue a lamb. Your openness, your unaffected manners, your sweet spontaneity, all of these qualities set you apart from the usual society ladies, and that I find so charming and delightful." To corroborate his words, he drew her hand to his mouth and kissed her knuckles, one by one.

Then he looked at her again with a sardonic lift of his eyebrow. "As for driving out now rather than at five o' clock when the park is crowded with members of society who want to be seen, I know that you are longing for the countryside, for a place where you can escape the hustle and bustle of the crowds, and so I thought you would prefer to see it now and not when there are so many people crowding the paths that it is impossible to move and one can hardly see the flowers and trees because of the carriages and horses that jostle along the paths." Theo indicated the view with a sweep of his arm. "My friends and I often ride in the park at this hour so that we can exercise our horses properly and enjoy the solitude."

As he spoke, he tugged Charlotte's gloves off, leaving her hands and arms bare. She shivered as a light breeze blew against her skin. She watched the marquess, fascinated by how dainty and delicate her hands looked in his firm, strong ones. She sighed and surrendered to the inevitable. She could not resist him. She did not want to resist him.

Slowly, he raised her hands to his face, inviting her to explore the handsome contours, just as he had explored hers. He moved her fingers along his jaw. She pressed her fingers against his skin, relishing the feel of the smooth skin and the firmness of his features.

"Society has ideas that are restrictive and often cause more harm than good. My philosophy, and that of my friends, is that pleasure is the highest good and we seek to do good in all we do, even if it is at times at odds with the judgment of society." The marquess let his hands roam over her body, adding their persuasion to his argument.

Charlotte was not completely convinced. The marquess was very persuasive, but the memory of her secret prevented her from surrendering to the desires of her body. Her body pressed closer to him even as her mind insisted that she should demur.

Lord Theo pulled her hand towards his mouth. Tenderly, he kissed the fingertip of each finger on both hands. By the time he had finished that task, her breath was uneven, ragged. All thoughts of society's conventions fled and all she could focus on was the pleasure of his touch. He was gazing at her hands as if they were the most fascinating objects he had ever seen. He turned them over and kissed her palms. Then his tongue slid from his mouth and swept over her upturned palms. She shivered. He looked at her, his eyes heavy with desire. She wanted to press herself closer to his large body, to nestle into the comfort and safety his presence offered. But she sat still, trying to reconcile the effect he had on her with his words, her mother's teachings and her own carefully guarded secret.

The marquess kept her hands in his, slowly rubbing her fingers as he studied her face for a few moments. Desire and uncertainty chased one another in her eyes. He was pleased when she left her hand in his, when she stroked his finger with her thumb. There was a tenderness in his eyes and voice that hinted at the growing affection he felt for his enchanting nymph. "My little one, you find pleasure when I touch you. My caresses calm and comfort you and my kisses evoke desire and delight. Pleasure is not something to be denied. Do not fight what your heart knows is right." Theo smiled softly and kissed her temple, her cheek, her forehead. "Surrendering to pleasure does not make you wicked."

Charlotte dropped her head and a soft but anguished cry escaped her lips. She could not let Lord Theo know how close he had come to the truth of her dark secret.

"Look at me, little lamb," Lord Theo instructed.

After a moment, Charlotte raised her eyes. The marquess was

watching her as if nothing else in the world could ever interest him. She trembled. His dark eyes focused so intently on her, she was sure he could read her every thought, could see her every dream, could understand her every desire. She wanted to draw her arms around herself, to protect herself, but Lord Theo was holding her hands firmly and she could not move them. A slow ripple of fear, mingled with desire, coursed through her. She felt the slickness between her thighs increase and hoped that she would not leave a mark on the elegant light grey cushions of Lord Theo's curricle.

Theo cupped Charlotte's neck. His tight hold kept her focused on him, conveyed his need to possess her in every way. It was strangely comforting. He untied the ribbons of her bonnet and removed it, admiring how the rays of sunlight highlighted touches of bronze and copper within her dark chestnut curls. He leaned forward and gently pressed a kiss to her forehead. Then drawing her closer to his chest, he continued, "There are many of us who have found that pleasure is the highest good, that understanding how to control one's yearnings, understanding the parameters of pleasure is a better philosophy than denying and suppressing it. If you can learn to trust me, then you will discover the truth of this too."

Charlotte sat very still. The voice of the marquess was like an enchanter's spell, weaving a magic web over her. It was so tempting to surrender to his promises, but a niggling thought, an echo of Hugh's warning, held her back. She could not accept that the marquess was wooing her because he wanted to know her, because he liked her. She voiced her hesitancy, "I'm not sure I really understand. I am not the kind of lady gentlemen form attachments with."

The marquess tilted her face and looked deeply into her eyes. "My little lamb, you should not be so ready to dismiss yourself. I am concerned about how you insist on undervaluing yourself. You need to learn to appreciate how precious you are. I think every time you belittle or undermine yourself, I will need to remind you just how valuable you are." A sardonic smile flashed across his face. "That might include some punishment for disparaging something that I consider valuable."

Charlotte's eyes widened at this and her mouth dropped open, but no sound came out. A shudder rippled through her at Lord Theo's words. He took both her hands in one of his and put his other arm around her shoulders, drawing her closer to his side. She snuggled into the warmth of his riding coat, enjoying the fragrance of green woods, bergamot and cedar that surrounded him. He smelled of home.

Suddenly, Charlotte realized that the marquess was removing the pins from her hair and running his fingers through the loosened strands. His lips brushed over her hair. She knew she should pull away, but the sensations were so wonderful that she wanted more. A low moan fell from her lips.

Theo leaned closer to her, blocking out all other thoughts, all objections. His lips found hers. Gently, softly, his mouth touched hers. It was almost just a whisper, just a light breath teasing her at first. Slowly, he traced the shape of her lips with his. Then he molded his mouth over hers and took possession. Sparks shot through her. His mouth was strangely soft and supple against hers.

She pressed against him, returning his kiss, inviting him to explore further. The marquess tasted her, drawing her into his mouth. She softened against him, opening herself to his touch. His tongue ran along her lips, outlining their shape, and then he licked the seam and she stifled a moan. He slid his tongue into her mouth, plunging into her, capturing her, taking her, claiming her. His tongue danced with hers, tantalized her, possessed her.

She rubbed against him, trying to find relief for the aching heaviness in her breasts. Theo continued exploring her mouth, holding her head close to him, his hand tugging her hair so that a faint tingle rippled from her head down through her body to her private parts. His lips never left hers, his tongue exploring every part of her mouth. Charlotte was finding it difficult to breathe. Her head was dizzy and her eyes could not focus, but she did not want this intimacy to end. She wanted to stay wrapped up in Lord Theo's arms forever. For the moment, Charlotte allowed the words and the caress of the marquess to settle into her heart. Just for the moment, she felt wanted, desired, contented. Pleasure washed over her. She smiled, pretending that her life could be like this, that she had no secret to mar her happiness.

But as she opened her mouth to his hot kisses, the sound of cantering hooves clashed along the path. Charlotte pulled away with a start. She looked around her frantically, patting her hair and grabbing for her gloves.

Lord Theo watched her, a satisfied smile on his face. When he saw the panic in her eyes, he reached over and smoothed her hair, tucking some of the wayward strands behind her ear. Then he began twisting her ruffled locks back into position, fixing the pins gently into place. Finally, he placed her bonnet on her head and tied the ribbon neatly, pressing a kiss on her nose as he finished. All the while that he was fixing her bonnet, she was fumbling with her gloves, struggling to get her fingers into the right places. Lord Theo gently took them from her and eased the gloves over her fingers, carefully buttoning them neatly at her wrists. He did not bother to look at the riders who were quickly approaching the curricle.

Two horses came into view and then drew to a halt alongside the curricle. The Earl of Sherbonne and Baron Loxley shouted cheerful greetings as they recognized Lord Theo and Charlotte.

Charlotte blushed deep red and tried to pull her hands away from Lord Theo's grasp, but he held her firmly, greeting his friends as if being found in a sheltered spot in the park with a girl in his arms was not unusual, was not something to be ashamed of. Perhaps, for them, it was not.

As the curricle, now accompanied by the earl and the baron, set off through the park, Charlotte tried to calm her riotous thoughts and savor the memory of Lord Theo's attention. She settled back into the seat, intent on enjoying the ride with the marquess. She let her imagination roam into a world where Hugh Parsiville and her dark secret did not exist. She dreamed that the marquess could fall in love with her as she had fallen in love with him. She built a little castle in the air, which looked remarkably like Oakdene, where she and the marquess lived happily ever after.

CHAPTER 8

*C*harlotte stumbled as she hurried to keep up with the Duchess of Broadwell as she made her way through the brightly lit foyer of The Royal Opera House, Covent Garden. Charlotte stared around her in dismay, dizzy and bewildered, at the surging mass of people, all moving in different directions. The bright lights and the constant noise were disconcerting. She was terrified that if she lost sight of the duchess, she would be abandoned in the turmoil of London society forever.

Suddenly, a hand settled on the small of her back, a large, warm, comforting hand whose touch she was beginning to recognize. She glanced up. The Marquess of Oakdene was beside her, guiding her through the chaos, protecting her from the crowds. She took a deep breath. She was safe. Her face broke into a relieved smile.

He grinned back at her as they began to climb the stairs to the upper floor where the duke's box was situated. Before long, they reached the relatively quiet space where a deep red velvet curtain sheltered them from the turmoil in the corridors. A footman closed the door and the noise subsided to a distant murmur. Charlotte took a deep breath and looked around her.

Lord Theo stepped back to let the ladies find their seats, and Charlotte felt bereft, as if she had lost her comfort. Her eyes followed the marquess as he began talking to his cousin about the race at Newmarket where one of the duke's horses had won that afternoon.

Lady Amelia turned to Charlotte with a slight shiver. "I hate the entrance to the opera. No one ever seems to know where they are going, and so many people just loiter in the foyer, waiting to be seen and gossiping about who has arrived with whom." The duke broke off his conversation with Theo and slid his arms around his wife, drawing her into a tight embrace. He murmured soft words to her and kissed her tenderly.

Charlotte was not used to such open displays of affection. She shuffled uneasily, not sure where to look. Heat rushed to her face. Hastily, she moved away from the demonstrative couple. She leaned against the front of the box and surveyed the crowds filling the stalls below, glad to escape the discomfort of such unusual intimacy. The other guests of the duke ignored their host and simply began to seat themselves.

Charlotte hardly noticed the opulence of the theatre or the brilliance of the audience. She was deeply conscious of the marquess a few feet away from her, and the easy camaraderie of the rest of Lady Amelia's party reminded her that she was out of place. Lady Amelia had been very kind, and the other guests were friendly, but Charlotte was an outsider. She did not know the people or places they talked about, and she had never been to an opera, so she had nothing to contribute to the easy banter that passed among the others.

Lady Sherbonne brushed past her as the formidable dowager selected a seat right in the middle of the front row. Charlotte smiled politely and glanced at the other guests. Her face flushed a deep red. "Please accept my apologies," she said to anyone near enough to hear her. "I did not mean to block your access to the chairs." She took a step backwards and bumped into Lady Amelia.

With a laugh, the duchess, her face bright and her eyes happy with the memory of her kiss, caught Charlotte's arm. "It is I who should be apologizing to you, my dear Charlotte. I love the opera, but I once had an unpleasant encounter in the foyer and I tend to rush to get to our box. I find the crush unpleasant and the duke is very concerned if anything upsets me even slightly. He was comforting me, and I have neglected you. But, come, you must sit here next to me so that we can talk comfortably."

The duke raised an eyebrow at this, but Charlotte, intimidated by the stern look on his face, tried to move to the back of the box. Amelia grinned up at her husband. "My duke, I know better than to talk while the singers are on stage, although I can remember when you used a performance of *The Magic Flute* to have a very interesting discussion with me."

The duke ran his hands over his wife's body, resting them on her lower abdomen. His voice was low and controlled, but Charlotte was close enough to hear what he said to his wife. "My little treasure, impertinence is never acceptable, and your current condition will not keep you from a spanking."

Amelia's face lit up with a mixture of desire and anticipation, but Charlotte gasped. The duke and his wife both glanced at her and then Lord Sebastian raised his eyebrow in his inimical way and addressed Lord Theo, who was leaning against the back of a chair near them. "If you have serious intentions regarding this little one, then you need to begin training her. If she is going to spend time with us, she will need to know and accept our ways," the duke commented drily.

Theo looked at his cousin and raised his eyebrow in imitation of the duke's favorite gesture. He gave a mock bow. "Yes, Your Grace." But his eyes were serious when he turned to Charlotte. He knew his cousin was right. In spite of his conversation with her in the park, Charlotte was clearly uncomfortable with the open and easy affection between Sebastian and Amelia. It would take much more to set Charlotte free from years and years of society's conditioning. It would be awkward if she flinched every time someone mentioned spanking.

The marquess ushered Charlotte into her seat, his hand lingering on her shoulder. He leaned forward so that his mouth brushed her ear and his words were a warm whisper. "My little lamb, are you comfortable?"

Charlotte nodded, but her hands were twisted in the folds of her dress and her bottom lip was caught between her teeth. Theo frowned. "Charlotte, there are certain things that we need to establish." She glanced at him, a puzzled look on her face. He held her gaze. "You are no longer the timid schoolgirl who could be excused for not speaking at the dinner table. It makes me very happy when you give spoken answers to my questions. That way, there can be no misunderstanding or miscommunication."

Charlotte blinked a few times, consternation deepening the creases around her mouth. There were some things she could never share with the marquess. She fumbled with her reticule, trying to remember what specific question he had asked her.

He repeated his words quietly. "Are you comfortable, little lamb?"

Charlotte swallowed. She dropped her eyes and gazed at her gloved hands. Lord Theo's penetrating gaze was disconcerting. Never had anyone looked at her as if they could see right into the depths of her heart. If she did not look at him, perhaps he would not suspect that she had a secret. "Thank you, my lord, I am very comfortable."

Lord Theo's intense eyes did not waver. He ran his fingers down her throat and traced the soft skin where it disappeared into the lace of her décolletage. She shivered as his voice wrapped around her in a sultry cord. "I prefer an honest answer to a socially acceptable one, little one. I can see that your skin is flushed and there is a tightness around your eyes that suggests you are not very comfortable. What is it that distresses you?"

Charlotte bit her lip and glanced at the duchess, who was arranging for refreshments to be served to her guests. The duke was behind her, his hand on her shoulder. They were standing very close together, much closer than society deemed respectable even for a husband and wife in public. Charlotte looked down at her lap. Her answer to the marquess was the soft brush of a breeze in spring. He had to lean very close to hear her. "I admire and like Lady Amelia very much, I really do. And part of me wishes for the freedom she has to love her husband so openly. But my mother believes that ladies should find no pleasure in physical caresses. She says that love is a vulgar country matter and only the peasants and those who have no finer feelings indulge in such vulgarity."

Theo just managed to stop himself from scoffing at this. He knew Mrs. Drake well, knew she considered any emotion to be beneath her. And Charlotte's very earthy nature was in constant struggle against her mother's strictures. "It is a great tragedy that love has been dismissed as crass and that marriages are so often nothing more than a convenient way for a gentleman to add to his family fortune or a lady to raise her family's status."

Charlotte raised her head quickly, looking at the marquess with large eyes that hid none of her trepidation. "Surely, every mother wants her daughter to be well married!"

"Indeed, arranging for a good marriage is the business of all of the mothers in society, but the understanding of what makes a good marriage is not shared by everyone." He tilted his chin to indicate Lady Amelia and her guests. "We have very different views from most of society and I believe that because we value the goodness of pleasure, we are much happier than people who are trapped in a loveless world."

Theo stroked her arm and brushed his fingers over the swell of Charlotte's breast, just visible above her lace fichu.

Charlotte shivered at Lord Theo's caress but obediently did as he suggested. For the first time, she really looked at the faces of the people around her. They were relaxed, content. They showed none of the anxiety and strain usually seen in members of the *haut ton* that came from following the rigid expectations of society and the need to impress those who mattered.

Charlotte could feel the blood rush to her face when Lord Watford nuzzled his wife's neck at the back of the box. Her eyes drifted to the front of the box where Lady Amelia was seated beside her husband. The duke had pulled his chair so close to his wife's that their thighs were touching and his hand was molded around the top of her thigh. His thumb moved in insistent circles while he spoke to Lady Sherbonne, who paid scant attention to the way the duke was caressing his wife.

When Lord Theo noticed the direction of Charlotte's eyes, saw how her breasts tightened, how her skin flushed with desire, he placed his hand on her leg, imitating the way the duke was touching Lady Amelia. Gently, slowly, the marquess moved his hand up towards Charlotte's hip. She looked at him, her lips parted and her eyes glistening with anticipation.

The marquess nodded. "We believe that pleasure is the highest good and we pursue pleasure in many forms."

Charlotte frowned at him. "But the duke said he would spank Lady Amelia. I do not see how that is either good or pleasurable."

Theo chuckled. "A great deal of pleasure is derived from a good spanking, especially when there is a mutual desire to please one another. Amelia deliberately goaded Sebastian earlier because she wants to feel his discipline." He smiled as Charlotte squirmed and seemed about to protest. "Let me ask you a question. Did you notice how Amelia responded to the duke's suggestion?"

Charlotte nibbled her lip, confusion flittering through her eyes. "I am not sure what you mean."

Theo explained, "Did she appear distressed, or angry, or upset when Sebastian said he would spank her?"

Slowly, Charlotte shook her head.

Theo quirked his eyebrow. "You have already forgotten that I have asked you to use words when you answer me. I think you want to know just what it would feel like to be spanked because you deliberately disobey me."

Charlotte gasped, but her buttocks clenched tightly. She studied Lord Theo's strong, firm hands and had a deep urge to know the feel of them against her bare bottom. Theo squeezed her thigh and she gave a startled mewl at his reminder that he was waiting for her answer.

Charlotte wrinkled her forehead, trying to remember the look on her new friend's face. She had been so shocked by the duke's mention of spanking his wife that she had not really noticed his wife's reaction. But as she thought back, she remembered the gleam in Amelia's eye and the half-formed smile on her lips. She glanced at the marquess and then down at her lap, embarrassed by the conversation. "The duchess was almost eager for the duke to do what he said," she whispered.

Theo smiled. "She was. In fact, I would say she was very eager."

Charlotte shook her head. "I am still confused. It is all very strange. All my life, I have heard that to feel pleasure in response to the touch of a man is wrong and yet," she glanced around at the people who were now settling down to enjoy the opera, "amongst these people, it is quite natural."

Theo rubbed her thigh and his fingers sought the crease at the top of her leg. She squirmed but her hips titled upwards, encouraging his touch and urging him to continue his exploration.

She closed her eyes and swallowed hard. "It is very pleasurable, my lord, but I am sure it is very wicked of me to allow you to do that."

As the orchestra began the overture and the audience subsided into silence, Theo leaned closer to Charlotte, his voice a murmur in her ear. "You are not wicked, my little lamb, and neither are the people in this box. You are a sweet, passionate woman, open to pleasure, and it will give me great pleasure to help you find the freedom of your passion."

THEO ATTEMPTED to focus on the music, but the thrill of anticipation surged through his body. It would be a delight to train this young woman, to introduce her to the pleasures her body could experience. She was such a spontaneous, sensitive and compassionate woman and she would soon come to accept the beauty of love in all its forms.

He studied her face. He was learning to read every nuance, every thought, every feeling that showed itself so readily in her eyes. As the music played, he envisaged taking her in his bed, thrusting his hard, heavy cock into her sweet, warm, tight pussy. Her eyes would open wide with passion and then glaze over with pleasure, and her face would flush the prettiest shade of pink as she climaxed beneath him. His dick throbbed at the thought of how her body would tighten around him, milking him of every drop of pleasure.

He had seen how open she was to pleasure, how sensitive she was to love. The barriers to enjoyment that society had placed around her would soon crumble as he taught her to love him. Even now, her breasts rose prettily, delightfully, with her every breath and he wanted to nuzzle in the crevice between them, run his tongue over the soft skin and indulge in the taste of her. Soon, he promised himself, very soon, he would learn to know her body more fully, even as he was learning to know her heart and soul. As Charlotte leaned forward, absorbed by the beauty of the music, he knew that he would marry her. With a start, he realized that he was half in love with her already and it remained only to convince her to love him too. Hugh Parsiville could never give her what she needed. The sooner he made his intentions known, the better it would be for them all. In the morning, he would leave for Oakdene to talk to her father.

CHAPTER 9

*C*harlotte glanced around her nervously, wondering how many people could see the way Lord Theo was touching her. Lady Amelia looked at her, a knowing smile on her lips.

Charlotte smiled back. The young duchess was so different from the Miss Cartwrights and Lady Augustas who conducted themselves with the sophisticated boredom expected from members of the *haut ton*. Lady Amelia was fashionable and elegant, yet she said the oddest things and shared her thoughts with confidence and enthusiasm. It was a puzzle, but one that Charlotte was happy to unravel.

The duchess turned to Charlotte with a delighted laugh under cover of the music. "I am so glad that you are here. I believe we are destined to be the best of friends." She ran her hand down the duke's arm and then turned back to Charlotte. "Much as I love my duke, and he loves me too, he is a bit older than I am and I do long for friends my own age."

Charlotte was warmed by the kindness, but she shook her head. "Duchess, much as I appreciate your offer of friendship, I am not sure how long I will be in London."

The duchess pouted. "Oh, dear, there is much wrong with your reply. You do not sound as if you would like to be my friend." The duchess wriggled in her chair and her eyes dropped down. For a moment, in spite of the elegant dress and diamonds she wore, she looked like a schoolgirl who had been deprived of an outing.

Charlotte found her heart softening at the vulnerable look that crossed Lady Amelia's face. She reached out and took Amelia's hand in hers. "I'm sorry, Your Grace. I did not mean to be rude or to suggest that I do not like you." She took a deep breath. "It is just that I am quite overwhelmed by all of this and I am not certain of my own future."

Amelia nodded, her eyes filled with sympathy. "Do you know that I had never come to London before I married the duke? I felt horribly out of place and it took me quite a while to become accustomed to the hustle and bustle of society."

Charlotte stared. Perhaps she and the duchess had more in common than she had realized.

Amelia squeezed Charlotte's hand. "I would like to tell you something of my story. We will have tea sometime soon, but in the meantime, you must realize that you do belong, that you are one of us now. Theo is very attracted to you. I have never seen him behave with any other lady the way he is with you."

Charlotte stiffened. Lord Theo's hand was still caressing her thigh, and she could feel his grip tighten when he heard Amelia's words.

Charlotte again shook her head. She spoke so softly that only Amelia could hear her whisper, "It does not seem possible that someone so sophisticated, so elegant, so handsome could be interested in me."

Amelia giggled but could not reply as the first act of the opera began. Charlotte sat stiffly for the first few minutes of the performance, but as the dramatic story of *Fidelio* unfolded on the stage, the soaring music and intense emotions drew her in. She leaned forward and rested her arms on the edge of the box, her eyes fixed on the singers as they enacted the story of love and loyalty.

The heavy weight of Lord Theo's hand sent ripples of hot desire pulsating through her body, igniting a fire in her core. It was difficult to concentrate on the music. He stroked his fingers along the seam between her legs, pushing slightly so that her legs fell open beneath the pressure. Her pussy clenched and her hips rose slightly, involuntarily, offering an invitation for him to go farther. With a soft chuckle, he ignored her body's silent pleas and kept his hand tantalizingly just out of reach of her most intimate place, which was aching for attention. His fingers lightly caressed the tender softness of her inner thigh through the soft silk of her dress. She shivered.

The scene on stage changed, and during the lull, Charlotte was aware that Amelia was looking at her. In spite of the comforting caress of Lord Theo's hand on her thigh, Charlotte squirmed. She felt embarrassed that her new friend could see just how wanton she was, and yet strangely, unexpectedly, the powerful passion and pleasure the marquess was igniting in her was increased by knowing that Amelia was watching.

A smile lit up Lady Amelia's face. She turned to the duke, who was leaning back in his chair, one leg crossed over the other as if he was relaxing in his favorite armchair in his library at home. "Oh, my darling duke, this is going to be so much fun! I am so glad that Theo and the other younger men are beginning to be serious about finding brides of their own so I can have some friends of my own age."

Charlotte shook her head and blurted, "Oh, Lady Amelia, I would not presume too much."

Lady Amelia said nothing, but looked pointedly at Lord Theo's hand, which was still on Charlotte's thigh.

The fingers of the marquess tightened around her thigh, almost digging into her sensitive flesh, sending shivers of pain through her that somehow evolved into pleasure. She bit her lip to hold back the little cry that wanted to escape and tried to focus on the duchess.

She was saved from having to respond by a sudden guffaw from the Dowager Countess Sherbonne. "I still don't believe my son plans to find a wife before I pass from this world! Yet before my own dear Lord Sherbonne died, Laurence promised his father that he would carry on the family name, yet he has shown no interest in marrying and providing me with the grandchildren I so desire." She bit a piece of cake that the footmen had been handing around and quaffed some of the wine in her glass. "Of course, considering the way he behaves, I probably have any number of illegitimate grandchildren peppering the countryside!"

Charlotte blushed at this unexpected and rather impolite conclusion to the dowager's speech, as a general wave of laughter greeted this outcry. The Earl of Sherbonne leaned forward from his seat near the back of the box. "Mother, you are not anywhere close to dying and I am not going to marry before I reach the grand old age of thirty-five! There are too many willing pretty girls for me to enjoy before I even think of shackling myself to one of them." In imitation of his mother, he too took a deep drink from his wine glass and then added, "And you do not have any illegitimate grandchildren. If you did, I would bring every single one of them to Sherbonne Manor and encourage them to exasperate you every day of your life."

Charlotte twisted her hands in her dress as Lord Theo nodded at his friend, a broad smile brightening his face. "Spoken like a true bachelor, Laurie. The world is full of delightful young ladies to be enjoyed."

A tight fist gripped Charlotte's heart. Lord Theo's words confirmed that he saw her as nothing more than someone to flirt with. He did not share her deep feelings, her growing love.

With a suppressed cry, she tried to push Lord Theo's hand

off her thigh. He turned to her with a puzzled look. Blood rushed to her face. She stiffened her shoulders and tried to appear ladylike and dignified, but her eyes were filled with sadness and her chin trembled. Lord Theo frowned but removed his hand. And Charlotte immediately missed the warmth and intimacy of his touch.

LORD THEO ENJOYED opera and usually paid close attention to the music, but this evening his attention was divided. He was fascinated by Charlotte, by her intense involvement in the story, by the tears that glistened in her eyes and the heaving of her breasts when a particularly emotional scene played out. Her reaction gave him assurance that when he wooed and won her, she would offer herself fully to all he longed to show her about love.

He slid his arm around Charlotte's back and cupped the curve of her shoulder. Even though layers of clothes prevented him from touching much of her skin, he relished the warmth of her body. He was gratified when she nestled into the curve of his arm. His eyes wandered over her face and he thought disparagingly of how society taught wonderful women like her that passion was wicked and then encouraged men to seek physical release outside of their marriages, so breaking the vows they made to their wives before God. When he married, he would find his pleasure with his wife, and the more time he spent with Charlotte, the more he was convinced that she was just the woman he could enjoy being with for the rest of his life. But she was still torn between the expectations of society and her own desires. She yielded to his touch, but she was clearly perturbed by much of what he was showing her.

As the first act drew to an end and the audience stirred, eager to be seen by the crowds, Theo took two glasses of wine from a footman and offered one to Charlotte. "Well, my little lamb, is the opera to your liking?"

Her eyes were still dazed and a little unfocused as she turned to him. She nodded, a slight smile curving her lips. "Yes, my lord. It is more wonderful than I had imagined it could be."

Theo smiled. "I did tell you that London has pleasures that could rival some of the joys of the countryside."

She looked at him thoughtfully. "The opera might be enjoyable, and there are other marvels that cannot be found in Summerhill, but on the whole, I believe that I would prefer to spend my life in the country with only occasional excursions into the city."

Theo sipped his wine and observed her. "That is a very interesting view, my little lamb, even though it is not one shared by much of society."

Charlotte stiffened and tilted her chin upwards. She smoothed her hands over her dress, lingering on the place where his hand had rested for most of the first act. Her eyes wandered over the audience, most of whom were drifting from box to box, sharing the latest *on dits* and showing off their brilliant finery. She took a sip of wine and breathed deeply.

Theo watched her while he drank his wine. Finally, he touched her cheek, causing her to turn to him with a start. Theo smiled softly. "My little lamb, I do not care very much what society thinks. I prefer to follow my own ideas, as long as they do no harm to those around me." He stroked her cheek. "And I admire that you, too, know your own mind, that you have opinions that are at odds with the way society thinks. It bodes well for the future."

Charlotte's forehead creased as she tried to puzzle out Lord Theo's meaning. "It is difficult to reconcile one's own views with the expectations of society. Mama wants me to be respectable and accepted by the *haut ton*, by those who matter in the world."

Theo growled. "Those who matter," he repeated. "You use that phrase far too often. Who are the ones who matter?" He glanced at the people in the duke's box. "These people could all be considered those who matter in society, and yet we do not simply accept conventional opinions. We do not flaunt our differences, but we hold fast to them, as long as we do not offend anyone. We believe it is better to be honest with ourselves rather than accept the hypocrisy of a society that preaches restraint and considers love vulgar, yet accepts that most gentlemen, unsatisfied by their wives, seek release with mistresses and prostitutes."

Charlotte mulled over these words as the orchestra began resuming their seats for the next act. She surveyed the audience with a *moue* of a frown between her eyes. Finally, she turned to the marquess with a shake of her head. "It is all so complicated. Are you saying that many of the people here only present a façade of respectability, that their lives are in fact fraught with wickedness?"

With a smile, Theo ran his finger over the lines that creased Charlotte's pretty face, easing away the worry. "There are some who value respectability above all else, but many are not honest with themselves or others. I abhor the hypocrisy found in the aristocracy. I value honesty, sincerity, openness, which is why I like being with you."

As the music swelled and the opera continued, Theo squeezed her leg and then ran his fingers lightly up to the crease where her thigh joined her hip. His fingers were so very close to the most intimate part of her. She felt ripples of excitement course through her body as he stroked her.

He leaned towards her, so close that his mouth almost brushed her ear. She shivered. "The pleasure of physical touch is very natural and greatly to be desired. It is not wicked when the focus of pleasure is goodness." He tugged at the tendrils of chestnut hair that framed her face. She turned big, trusting blue eyes to him as he continued, "So often, denying pleasure leads to spitefulness, small-mindedness, pettiness. Learning how to enjoy pleasure, to control desire, brings about a sensitivity to those around one. You, my little lamb, are not wicked. Your yearning for intimacy, your desire to be touched are indications of the depths of your compassion and kindness. When you respond to what your body was naturally created to enjoy, you experience the power of pleasure and goodness."

Charlotte leaned against the marquess, yielding to his words and touch. On stage, Leonore's plaintive aria told of her passion. Charlotte shivered, as the words filled the auditorium and at the slow, steady caress of Lord Theo's hand on her body.

The sensations built up in her body, reaching a crescendo just as Leonore reached the end of her song. Lord Theo took hold of Charlotte's hand and placed it on his thigh, encouraging her to imitate his movements. She took a deep breath and then exhaled as the heat of his flesh warmed her fingers.

The muscles of Lord Theo's leg were hard and firm. She was eager to explore how his body differed from hers, how his hardness contrasted with her familiar softness. She pressed her hand firmly onto his leg and carefully, surely, steadily moved it along his muscles. His solidity, his firmness, his strength gave her confidence, made her feel safe and secure enough to let her fingers travel towards the bulge of his manhood.

She heard the marquess draw a breath that sounded almost like a hiss. Her hand found the top of his leg. She dug her fingers into the place where his thighs joined his torso and felt a little rush of power when his legs parted to allow her better access. Heat poured off him. She pulled back and her hand continued its path along the top of his leg. She hesitated when her fingers encountered the solid ridge bulging against his thigh. She knew she was touching his manhood. She paused but quickly resumed her exploration. Her fingers examined the shape, the thickness of him. She molded her hand around him, trying to fit her fingers round the fullness of his shaft. She squeezed, trying to hold it, grasp it, lift it.

Lord Theo groaned and his cock jerked in her hand. She bit back a startled gasp and dropped the heavy shape of him. She glanced at his face, anxious that she might have hurt him. His face was tense. His eyes were glazed, the lids half closed. He was watching her, his eyes moving from her hands on his groin to her eyes and back again slowly.

Lord Theo smiled at her and nodded his approval, giving his permission for her to continue. She touched him again, squeezing lightly. His manhood seemed to swell thicker and grow longer under her eager fingers. She stroked the bulge that pressed against the seam of his breeches. She could see it now, outlined beneath her hand. Even through the soft silk of his breeches, she could feel the heat pulsating from him. An unexpected urge to see his manhood uncovered rushed through her mind. The thought was so overwhelming, so compelling, so wicked, that Charlotte groaned.

A sudden shift in the music brought her back to the realization that they were in the theater. She looked at Lord Theo's face and then with dazed eyes slowly gazed around her.

She pulled back slightly, but the marquess gave a brief shake of his head and placed his hand over hers on his groin. He began to move their joined hands up and down his length, firmly, rapidly. He showed her how to squeeze him and how to stroke him with firm, even movements, using the soft silk of his breeches to add to the stimulation. He pulled her hand up and down his rigid length for a few moments. Suddenly, he stopped, a look of tense concentration on his face. Charlotte drew in a sharp breath as she felt a surge of wetness under her fingers on Lord Theo's breeches.

The marquess grinned at her. He leaned closer and whispered, "You are a naughty little lamb. You made me come, right in the middle of the opera house."

CHAPTER 10

*C*harlotte pulled her cloak more tightly around herself and tried not to look at the marquess who was seated opposite her in the carriage. She paid scant attention to the light chatter that passed between the Duke, Lady Amelia and Lord Theo as they made their way back to Montgomery House after the opera. She was suddenly appalled by her earlier actions. Now, in the quiet of the carriage, the echo of Hugh's voice filled her mind, warning her of the need to protect her reputation and the reminder that her only attraction to any gentleman of Lord Theo's caliber was her large inheritance.

She clasped her hands in her lap and turned to look out the window of the carriage as she mulled over all that had happened at the opera house. The streets were dark, lit only by the light that spilled out from the windows of houses and from the boys who ran alongside carriages with lanterns.

As the duke's carriage turned a corner, Charlotte gave a sharp cry. Immediately, the marquess leaned forward, taking her hand in his. "What is it, little one?"

"That girl, that poor girl," she uttered incomprehensibly.

Her words did not confuse the duke. Immediately, he rapped

on the roof of the carriage and his coachman brought it to a neat standstill. Lord Sebastian had opened the door even before the footman had time to descend from his perch. Theo followed him out.

Amelia peered through the open door while Charlotte continued to watch through the window. The group who had caused Charlotte's outcry had not noticed the carriage had stopped or that two gentlemen were rapidly descending. Four or five men, dressed in elegant evening clothes that marked them as members of the *haut ton*, surrounded a girl of about sixteen. She was cringing, pulling her arms around herself tightly. Her eyes were wide with fear. One of the men was gripping her shoulder while another was groping her breasts. Her dress was torn. All of the men were laughing.

"Come, come, my darling, you're never going to make a living on the streets if you pretend to be so innocent," the man who was groping her smirked.

"Push her up against the wall so we can all have our turns with her, and then we can get on to the club. I feel a lucky streak in dice coming on," urged one of the others as he took a swig from a hip flask and passed it to one of his friends. They were all clearly inebriated and did not need more brandy to fuel their lust.

"I think the lady is not going to be used for your vile little games. Let her go." The duke's voice rang with such authority that all the men stopped and looked at him. The girl crumpled to the ground and covered her face.

The first man glanced at her and then back at the duke. "She's no lady, and why should you care what we do with her? Who are you to interfere with our pleasure? She's a hussy, a harlot, and good for nothing but to spread her legs and let us fill her holes until we've had enough of her."

A flash of rage crossed the duke's face, but his voice remained calm and cold. "I am the Duke of Broadwell and I am extending my protection to this girl. I suggest you leave and go on to whichever club is foolish enough to allow you to be members." The men, hardly old enough to have graduated from college, shuffled at the biting tone, the unmistakable authority of the duke. Slowly, they began to shuffle away.

Eventually, only Sebastian, Theo and the girl were left. The girl lowered her hands and looked up at her rescuers. "Thank you, sirs," she whispered. She moved slightly, attempting to rise to her feet and at the same time cover herself with the torn edges of her dress.

Lord Theo reached out and helped her up. "Is there anywhere we can take you? Where is your home?"

The girl pulled her torn dress over her bosom and looked at the ground. "I'm all right, thank you, sir."

Just then, Amelia, who had now left the carriage, slipped between the two gentlemen and the girl. She slid her arm around the girl's shoulders and implored, "My darling Duke, I do believe she has nowhere to go and if we leave her on the street, she will be assaulted again. We need to help her."

Theo looked at his cousin. "Amelia is right. The girl needs us to help her. She needs a place of safety where she can be protected."

Sebastian nodded slowly. "We will take her to Montgomery House for now."

CHARLOTTE SAT in the duke's drawing room, bewildered by the sincere concern he and his guests showed towards the young girl they had rescued. All of Lady Amelia's opera guests were gathered together, but the earlier festive air had turned more serious as they discussed how best to help a girl most people would shun and dismiss for her wickedness. The girl, whose name was Mary, had been bustled off by the housekeeper as soon as they had arrived at Montgomery House. The matronly woman who ran the duke's London home had shown no surprise or shock, simply taken the girl under her wing with promises of a hot bath and a nourishing meal.

Charlotte couldn't help remembering how, not that long ago, her mother had dismissed a parlor maid who had been found kissing one of the footmen in the kitchen garden. Mrs. Drake had insisted that Charlotte be present when the maid, Tessie, was discharged. Charlotte had shuddered when her mother called Tessie a depraved and wicked trollop and lamented that she had harbored such degeneracy in her house. The intensity of her mother's scorn and repulsion had frightened Charlotte. The words had festered in her soul. They had touched too near the truth of her own secret.

Charlotte gave a slight shake of her head and tried to concentrate on the conversation around her. "Our homes for boys have been very successful, but there is nowhere for young women like Mary to find the help they need," Lord Theo was saying.

Lady Sherbonne nodded. "I was upstairs when Mrs. Duffy was assisting the child. Mary worked as a kitchen maid, but her pretty face was too tempting for one of the footmen. He promised her the world but put a child in her belly instead. She's pregnant. Of course, when her condition was discovered, she was dismissed as immoral and given no reference."

Lady Watford sighed. "Poor child, and yet her story is not an unusual one. So many girls end up on the streets for similar reasons. They are cast out as wicked and have no options."

The duke paused in his pacing of the room. "What can we do? It would not be sensible to place her in the homes with boys."

Lord Danforth, a remote, austere gentlemen who intimidated Charlotte just by his presence, gave a light snort. "We have focused our assistance on young boys because they can easily be placed in the trades we prepare them for, but it is very different with girls who have spent time on the streets. No one will employ a girl whose character is questionable."

Charlotte sat frozen with horror at the truth of Lord Danforth's words. There was no hope for girls, for women, who were tainted with scandal. What would they think of her if they heard any rumor of her secret?

Amelia stood up, her hands clasped in front of her. "That is just the kind of attitude that we need to challenge. Surely, the girl is not to blame for her situation. How dreadful it will be for her if she is sent back out on the streets after we have given her hope."

The duke placed his arm around his wife's shoulders. "Hush, dearest. Danforth wasn't suggesting that we will turn Mary out, only pointing out the difficulties of women who are victims of society's own narrow-minded morality." Amelia leaned against her husband and smiled apologetically at Lord Danforth.

Lord Theo, who had been staring into the fire for most of the conversation turned slowly to face his friends. "That property I bought some time back in Cheapside could be turned into a safe place for women and girls, a place where they could learn some crafts and skills that would give them the opportunity to earn an income without having to seek a position with intolerant people."

Amelia nodded enthusiastically. "Yes, I am sure that would work. I am sure we could find people to teach them ways to earn their own living so that they could support themselves and their children."

Just then, footmen carried in a light supper of Welsh rarebit, devils on horseback, petit fours and other delicacies, and the duke nodded at his guests. "That's settled then. We will begin refurbishing Theo's property and looking for a matron and other teachers who can train the girls. I have no doubt that we will soon outgrow the space available. And now, let's enjoy ourselves."

The party broke into smaller groups and the chatter turned to lighter matters. Charlotte nibbled a macaroon as she thought about all that had happened. She was surprised and pleased when the young duchess sat down next to her.

"Thank you for drawing our attention to Mary's plight this evening. Because of you, she and many others like her will have a better life." The duchess took a bite of a petit four. "I would like you to be involved in setting up and running the home."

Charlotte smiled. "I am not sure if that would be possible. I do not believe my mother will approve."

Amelia shrugged impatiently. "That might be so for the moment, but before long you will be married and free to make your own decisions." Lord Theo's deep laughter drifted across the room and both ladies turned to look at him.

Charlotte turned bright red. "I have heard that wives are not free to follow their own ideas. They need the permission of their husbands before they engage in such projects."

Amelia frowned. "I cannot imagine that Theo would prevent your involvement. After all, it is his donation that is going to make it possible."

It was impossible for Charlotte to turn a brighter red. Her heart beat hard against her ribs, as if she had just run across a meadow at Summerhill. She sputtered, "Lady Amelia, I am not sure what Lord Theo's intentions are. I cannot presume that he means anything beyond politeness because of his friendship with my father."

Amelia took Charlotte's hand in hers. "I have seen the way Theo looks at you. No other woman has ever brought that look to his face. Mark my words, it will not be long before he proposes. He likes you very well indeed." She grinned. "And he definitely enjoyed the way you touched him at the opera."

With a startled cry, Charlotte withdrew her hand from Amelia's and covered her face. Mary's predicament had brought home to her just how reckless she had been. "Oh, it is not gracious of you to remind me of my indiscretion and folly," she uttered, her voice tight and strangled.

The low, velvety voice of the marquess wrapped around her, soothing and igniting her at the same time. "Little lamb, do not be ashamed of the beauty of your passion. Accept your desires as something good, something to be cherished and nurtured, not quenched and denied."

Charlotte lowered her hands and peeked over her fingers at Lord Theo, who was now sitting on the settee beside her. Amelia had disappeared.

Theo slowly, gently, pried her fingers away from her face and enclosed her hands in one of his. He smiled at her, his eyes showing a tenderness that stole Charlotte's breath.

THEO CROSSED the room quickly when he had heard Charlotte's anguished sob. Now he sat beside her, stroking her hair and speaking softly to her. He had been so occupied with finding a solution for Mary that he not offered Charlotte the comfort and reassurance she needed. The scene in the opera house would have left her feeling raw and vulnerable.

Charlotte took a deep breath and tried to look away from him, but he caught hold of her chin in his fingers and tilted her face so that she had to look into his eyes. She squirmed under his close scrutiny, her eyes wide with confusion, with fear, but also with a hint of desire. He drew encouragement from the trust he discerned as she settled into his touch and looked steadily at him.

The marquess leaned over her, trapping her against the back of the settee. He moved his hand up her arm and down over her shoulders, down, until he cupped her sweet breast in his hand. It was a perfect size, just filling his hand with its soft promise of passion. He fondled her breast for a few moments and then traced his path back to where her smooth skin emerged above the lace trim of her dress. With one pad of his finger, he drew a slow line from one side to the other. Finally, he cradled her head in one large hand and drew her closer to him. His lips touched hers in a soft caress.

She opened her mouth to welcome his touch. He licked her lips slowly, savoring her taste. She whimpered as her breasts swelled and her nipples puckered. She pressed closer to him, moving her lips against his. His tongue slid into the welcoming warmth of her mouth. He sucked her tongue and drew it into his mouth, softly at first and then harder.

Charlotte's hands grasped Theo's arms, digging her nails into his muscles as she yielded to his kiss. His touch became more intense as he claimed her, devoured her, possessed her.

After a long while, he drew back, running his fingers down her face. "Mine," he whispered. "You are mine."

A clatter of coffee cups startled Charlotte and she pulled away from the marquess with a low, anguished cry. "Oh, how can I be such a wretched, wicked fool?"

Theo's face hardened, but he held Charlotte still as she tried to wriggle loose. He drew her into the shelter of his arms, tucking her safely against his shoulder. She was so petite, so dainty, and she fit so perfectly against his body, as if she was made to be there.

"Charlotte, you are not a fool and it does not honor me when you continue to demean yourself. I think it is time for you to face the consequences of your tendency to belittle someone I admire."

Charlotte uttered a little cry at this, but the marquess was implacable. He glanced across the room to where his cousin was sitting in a comfortable armchair, his wife kneeling complacently at his feet, resting her head against his knee while he watched Theo and Charlotte. The marquess raised an enquiring eyebrow. Lord Sebastian nodded and then spoke, his voice clear above the hubbub of chatter. "You can go to my study, unless you would prefer to mete out her punishment here, in front of the rest of the guests."

Theo grinned but Charlotte's horrified expression was enough incentive for him to choose the duke's first suggestion. He rose, taking Charlotte's hand to help her to her feet. "Thank you, Seb, but I think for now, this little one would be more comfortable in private, although I believe one day, she will enjoy being displayed in public."

Charlotte gasped, but Lord Theo did not give her time to respond. Taking her arm gently, he led her out of the drawing room and into the duke's library.

CHARLOTTE STOOD APPREHENSIVELY in front of the large leather couch, her hands twisting in front of her. Theo placed his hands on her shoulders and gently turned her around to face him. She was so close that she could smell his bergamot and sandalwood scent, mingled with something that was uniquely his own. The heat of his body sent tendrils of warmth through her. She tried to remember the posture the marquess had taught her and dropped her hands to her side while lowering her head just enough to show that she surrendered to him.

He touched the top of her head and then rested his hand possessively on her shoulder. His voice was grave. "My little lamb, do you understand why I am going to punish you?"

Charlotte nodded and then quickly cleared her throat to say, "Yes, my lord. I said some things about myself that were not very complimentary."

Lord Theo nodded grimly. "Yes, that is a good way to explain it. It is not an attractive tendency."

Charlotte dropped her head and avoided Lord Theo's gaze.

She stood in silence for a few moments, contemplating his words and anticipating what was about to happen.

"Go to the end of the couch and bend over the armrest, then place your hands as far along the cushions as you can reach," the marquess instructed calmly.

Charlotte looked at him for a moment, and then, compelled by the certainty in his eyes, walked slowly to the place he had indicated. She stared at the couch for a moment and then leaned forward. The couch had been built for men and the armrest was quite high, rounded and firm, yet the warm leather was supple and inviting. She wriggled as she tried to make herself comfortable.

Lord Theo moved round to stand behind her and admire the pretty picture she made. Her arms were reaching forward, grabbing the seat cushion. Her head rested on her arms. Her bottom was nicely positioned over the edge of the armrest. Theo placed his hands on her waist and maneuvered her until her thighs were straining just a little so that her feet were only just able to touch the floor. Her arse rose perfectly, round and ready for his attention. "Soon, I will use ropes to tie you in the position I want, but for now, I want you to keep as still as you can."

Charlotte tensed at his words and he ran his hand over the pretty globes. "My little lamb, you need to relax. Try not to clench these lovely mounds. It will be much more pleasant for you if your muscles are loose. Keep still and hold your position while I deal with you. You may, however, cry, sob, even scream. The servants will not mind and nobody in the drawing room will be able to hear."

Charlotte squirmed under the slow caress of his hand, but she did not speak. He smiled. "Do you understand what I have said?"

"Yes, my lord." Her voice was muffled against her arm.

"Your dress and petticoats are in my way," he remarked casually, as if he was talking about nothing more significant than the weather. Theo felt Charlotte stiffen beneath his hands, but he stroked her bum through her dress in slow, steady movements, and soon he felt her surrender to his touches. Her body softened and she lost the tense tightness of embarrassment.

He continued to talk as he tugged her dress towards her waist. "You will receive twenty strikes and you will count each one and thank me for each one before I give you the next."

He felt her take a deep breath before she answered, "Yes, my lord."

He had pulled her dress and petticoat up together, and now her buttocks were exposed to his gaze. He stood for a moment, simply admiring the pretty sight. Stockings were fastened just above her knees and then her silky white thighs with the shapely muscles of a girl who rode horses often and well led up to a heart-shaped arse. She was made for pleasure, his pleasure. Two pristine globes trembled as he ran a single finger over their surface. His touch was slow, soft, sure. He caught a glimpse of her pussy, pink and shiny, between her legs.

His cock was throbbing, ready to explode at the vision before him. He really had refrained from sexual intercourse since last Christmas. Somehow, since the afternoon he had spent with this sweet girl at Summerhill, rescuing a lost lamb, his desire for other women had vanished. His focus had been on her, even though he had thought she was still a schoolgirl out of his reach. But now she was his and his cock was ready to conquer the new worlds of pleasure she offered.

He raised his hand and brought it down sharply on her right buttock. The flesh quivered and turned even whiter and then a soft shade of pink.

"Ow, ow, ow," Charlotte cried out. "That was sore." She tried to move her hand to rub her stinging buttock, but Theo caught hold of it and placed it back where it belonged.

The marquess ran his hand over the soreness. "Yes, my dear, that is sore, but I need to hear you count," he reminded her impassively as if he were simply discussing whether he would take his tea with or without milk.

Charlotte stifled her cries and sobbed out, "One. Thank you, my lord."

"It's a pleasure, my little lamb. I will do whatever I believe is necessary to help you stop belittling yourself." He raised his hand and brought it down on her left buttock. She cried out again, but this time she remembered to count. The spanking continued, with the marquess placing his strikes evenly over her buttocks and thighs and Charlotte sobbing out the numbers.

CHARLOTTE WAS FINDING this experience very strange. She was stretched out over a couch in the Duke of Broadwell's library, her buttocks bare, her pussy exposed to Lord Theo's gaze and she was being spanked. Yet the strangeness excited her. She found herself melting under Lord Theo's touch, and her heart filled with trust for him and a warmth that could only be described as love.

At first, each time the marquess brought his hand down on her bottom, the sting had been unbearably painful. His hand was large, and he was a strong man and did not hold back. But as the spanking continued, she found herself floating into a languid state. Her body felt limp, her mind peaceful. Warmth spread through her. Her eyes drifted closed.

Suddenly, Lord Theo was pulling her off the end of the couch and wrapping his arms around her. She rested her head against his chest, breathing in the heady scent of his presence. He was talking to her, but the words were a distant murmur. Then she was being lifted and eased onto his lap. She snuggled into him, even as she winced at the burn on her bottom.

"It's all better, my little lamb, it's all over," the marquess murmured as he hugged her.

She nestled into his chest, drawing warmth and comfort from him. His voice was soft, soothing, and it washed over her like warm summer rain. Her bottom was sore against the hardness of his thighs as she settled into his lap, but she had never felt quite as content as she did now. Slowly, she realized that the marquess was kissing the top of her head and loosening the pins that kept her hair in place. Soon, her hair was falling freely over her shoulders and down her back. He ran his fingers through the mass of curls, tugging so that her skull tingled. She tilted her face to him and he kissed her, slowly exploring her mouth.

CHAPTER 11

*H*ugh Parsiville paced the length of the drawing room at Drake House. Charlotte sat at the table, trying to keep her stitches even, but the sampler was beyond repair. She was really much better at helping on the estate than at the accomplishments ladies were expected to pursue.

With an exasperated glance at Hugh, Charlotte wished that her mother had not left her alone with Hugh while she went to discuss the week's menus with the housekeeper. Mrs. Drake would not forget propriety so far as to leave Charlotte unchaperoned with other gentleman callers, but she considered Hugh harmless because he was a distant cousin of Mr. Drake.

Charlotte tossed her sewing down and followed Hugh's pacing with her eyes, irritation evident in every feature. "Do sit down, Hugh. You are making me quite dizzy with your incessant pacing."

He came to an abrupt stop in front of the table. "So, did you have a good time at the opera? Are you finding your new friends to your liking?"

Charlotte blushed and flinched at Hugh's sneering tone. She could not let Hugh know just how much she had enjoyed the things she had done with the marquess. She prevaricated. "The duchess is very pleasant and not at all what I expected. It is very easy to converse with her."

Hugh began pacing again. "I am sure she is delightful. Is the Marquess of Oakdene to your liking, too?" Before Charlotte could say anything, Hugh continued. "You're becoming quite the subject of gossip and conjecture. They've opened the books on you at White's."

Charlotte stared at him, confusion filling her eyes. "I do not understand what you mean."

"They're laying bets on how soon the marquess will shackle himself to you. Of course, he made his move so quickly that all the other contenders had no chance to put in their offers."

Charlotte blushed. "I do not believe that Lord Raeburne is serious about forming an attachment with me. I have heard that he has been courting Miss Cartwright."

Hugh once again stopped in front of her. His gaze wandered over her. "Perhaps you are too naïve to have understood his intentions; nevertheless, he seems to be remarkably interested in what you could bring into a marriage." His voice dropped as if he was talking more to himself than to Charlotte. "I might still have some cards up my sleeve. All might not be lost."

He resumed his pacing. "Perhaps you should give the marquess some reason to want to be attached to you, beyond your inheritance. It might not be such a bad idea for you to encourage the marquess. Of course, he is very keen to acquire Summerhill, but you could sweeten the pot for him through flattery and flirtation. If he takes over the management of Summerhill, it is likely to become even more profitable."

Charlotte was staring at Hugh openly now, bewilderment clear in her eyes. "Is it really necessary to be both cryptic and crass, Hugh? You are not making much sense."

Hugh looked at her thoughtfully. She tried not to cringe at the sardonic twist of his mouth. She was not going to tell him that she had seen nothing of the marquess since that glorious night almost a week ago when Lord Theo had kissed her, spanked her, and aroused sensations in her body that were beyond her wildest fantasies. She had been a fool. She had taken Lord Theo's passionate declarations as promises of a future together while he was only indulging in passing pleasure with her. No matter how foolish she had been, she could not eradicate the memory of his touches. Each night since then, her dreams had been filled with visions of his eyes gleaming with passion, his firm hands exploring her body, his deep voice washing over her.

But she had seen nothing of him, heard nothing from him, since that night. He had not called on her, nor had he been present at any of the parties or dinners or balls she had attended. He had not sent a note or flowers. The bluebells he had brought her after the duke's ball had faded and she had reluctantly allowed the housekeeper to throw them out. His interest had waned as quickly as it had arisen and she was left with the ashes of a dream.

Hugh finally sat down. He scowled at the cup of tea Charlotte poured for him. "Am I supposed to drink this swill? Isn't there anything decent for a man to drink?"

Charlotte shifted uneasily. "It is only eleven in the morning. Mama does not allow the servants to serve strong drinks until after five."

Hugh snorted. "That is all very well for foolish females, but men have different needs." He reached into his pocket and pulled out a hip flask. He tipped some brandy into his tea.

Charlotte watched his performance, her shoulders stiff and her lips in a disapproving line. Hugh did not hold his drink well. When he had taken a mouthful of the reinforced tea, she ventured a return to his earlier point. "You said that the marquess is interested in Summerhill?"

Hugh grunted. "He's been talking about little else for years.

Everyone knows that he has some odd notions about experimental farming and he wants more land to extend his projects. He is enough of a businessman to know the best way to procure land is to marry it."

Charlotte twisted her fingers together in her lap. Her heart was a heavy stone and her stomach twisted into a tight knot. She should have listened to Hugh right at the beginning. Her only value was in her father's fortune. Theo would never be interested in her. He was no different from the dozens of suitors who vied for her attention at balls and clamored to be seated next to her at dinners and then spoke of nothing but the profitability of Summerhill. Lord Raeburne wanted Summerhill and she was simply the means for him to get it. All his fancy words and passionate seduction were just a ploy to entice a naive girl.

She studied her fingers as they twisted into intricate patterns in her lap. Those fingers had played with Lord Theo's manhood at the theater. She was a silly girl to think that someone like him could have any affection for her. He did not want her, only what she could bring into a marriage.

She looked at Hugh, who suddenly seemed a bit blurry. She blinked hard to stop the tears from falling. It was difficult to speak about something that Hugh had avoided, but despair drove her. Her only escape from the machinations of impoverished gentlemen lay in Hugh. She swallowed and then managed to say, "I cannot marry the marquess if I am already promised to another man."

Hugh gulped down the last of his cup of tea and gawked at her. "What? Did you make some chap a foolish promise during a dance? I am sure if nothing has been formally arranged, there is still time to extricate yourself from such a dilemma. Who is it?" His face twisted into a snarl as he suddenly realized Charlotte's meaning. "Oh! You mean the vague suggestion I made when I helped you out of your dilemma. Well, it was never a formal arrangement. I never actually asked you to marry me and I haven't spoken to your father."

Misery drove Charlotte to her feet. She was the one who felt the need to pace now. She moved towards the window that overlooked the street, not wanting to face Hugh as she mentioned the secret that lay between them. Her voice was so soft, it hardly carried across the room. "What about the... other matter? If you are not going to protect me, then I could be ruined."

Hugh huffed. He had to think quickly. "I will still guard your secret, even when you are married to the marquess. It would not do for him to know your true character. Let yourself be guided by me and we will both prosper. I have a feeling that your father would approve of him more readily than he would accept me as your husband. He is, after all, one of the highest lords in the land, and one of the wealthiest. So, wed the marquess, but remain friends with me and I will continue to keep your secret."

Charlotte turned from the window, a frown on her face and despair in her voice. "I had always hoped that my marriage would be based on love and trust. If all you are saying is true, I will be married to a husband who does not love me, while I must keep secrets from him. It seems a dismal way to go through life."

Hugh shrugged. He stood up and crossed the room, coming to stand next to her at the window. He leaned close to her, gripping her arm tightly although his voice was still languid. "Happily ever after and love are only found in fairy tales read by silly little girls in schoolrooms. Society marriages are arranged along business lines and nobody gives a fig about your feelings. The marquess will most likely keep his mistresses even after he marries you." He leaned closer to Charlotte and ran his fingers suggestively up her arm. "And many married women have a cicisbeo or two to keep them happy."

His fingers trailed up her arm and across her shoulders, dropping over the exposed skin of her décolletage. Charlotte shuddered. Hugh's touch did not affect her the way Lord Theo's did. The shivers she felt when Lord Theo touched her ignited fires of desire in her. Hugh's touch left her as cold as the ashes of a long-dead fire. She wanted to pull away, but his grip on her arm tightened and she did not know how to repulse his advances.

"We are presuming much," she managed to say, trying to free herself from Hugh's tight hold. "The marquess has not offered for my hand in marriage."

Hugh tightened his grip on her arm. "Then you must make him want to marry you. It is not as if you are unaccustomed to leading a man on." His voice became a sinister hiss. "If you do not succeed, knowledge of your secret might just become known, and then you will have no prospects at all."

Her head whirled. Hugh's words turned her world on end. She had once dreamed of being married to the marquess, but that fairy tale had none of the sordidness of the future she now faced.

She frowned as Hugh's fingers continued their path over her exposed skin, pressing so hard that he left little red indentations on her arms that she feared might turn into bruises. She could not think how to answer him. Hugh moved closer and she could feel the lewd swell of his cock press against her thigh. She suppressed a shudder. She was finding it difficult to remember that she had one thought that marrying Hugh might not be unpleasant. But she had experienced real pleasure at the hands of a man she loved, and Hugh's touch was now abhorrent to her. She felt no corresponding desire as Hugh took liberties with her.

With a little gulp, she declared, hoping to get Hugh to release her from his hold, "If marrying the marquess is my only option, then I will try to convince him to marry me."

∼

HUGH AND CHARLOTTE were standing uncomfortably close together when the door opened and Mrs. Drake entered, followed closely by the Marquess of Oakdene.

Hugh slowly let his hand run down Charlotte's arm before he released his hold on her, watching the marquess all the while. Charlotte stood frozen in shock at the sudden arrival of Lord Theo, only vaguely aware of Hugh's possessive hold on her arm.

Mrs. Drake was completely oblivious of the compromising position of her daughter and Hugh Parsiville. The tension in the room did not penetrate her complacent glee. She swept across the room, her arms extended, as she gushed, "My dear Charlotte, just think what wonderful news there is. This is everything that we have been working for, everything we had hoped for. The marquess has brought a letter from Summerhill that gives your father's permission and approval. Just think, the season has hardly begun, and we have only just arrived in London. What a success you have been!"

Charlotte did not move. She could not make sense of her mother's words that were swirled around her like a fog. She did not notice either Hugh's triumphant sneer or Lord Theo's irate glare.

With a snide chuckle, Hugh pushed her forward. She stumbled to a halt as he said, "Well, it appears that everything is sorting itself out very nicely, just as we hoped. I think that is my cue to leave. Lord Raeburne, Mrs. Drake, good day." He sauntered out, leaving Charlotte with her mother and a highly incensed marquess.

Lord Theo had not uttered a word. Charlotte glanced at him and then back at her mother. She did not move from her position at the window. She did, however, finally recall her manners. She dropped a curtsey and murmured, "Good day, Lord Raeburne."

Her greeting galvanized the marquess. He strode across the room. "Good day, Miss Drake." His voice was hard, cold. This was the man who intimidated her, who twisted her stomach into knots and made her forget how to speak. The affable man who had shown her such kindness, such tenderness, such attention had vanished. Charlotte hunched her shoulders and pulled back against the curtains, trying to hide in the folds, as she had done when she was a little girl hiding from her mother's scolding when she had neglected practicing the piano to play outside with the dogs.

The marquess was holding a letter in his hand, which he flicked towards her. "I have been in Worcestershire. While I was there, I asked your father's permission to seek your hand in marriage. This is his reply to you. He is very happy for the union to take place, if it is something that you desire," he spat out. "Your father would like the marriage to take place as soon as the banns have been read. He sees no reason for a long betrothal. We will be married before the end of the season."

Charlotte stared at the letter. She heard the words the marquess spoke, but they made as much sense as the whirl of wind that heralded a winter storm. Bit by bit, the words rearranged themselves in her mind and she realized that he was proposing to her. A little cry of distress escaped from her throat. She had spent hours dreaming of what it would he like to receive a proposal of marriage from the marquess, but this reality bore no resemblance to her childish dreams. There was no declaration of love, no promise of affection. The tears that had hovered at the back of her eyes since Hugh had begun talking now spilled over.

She fisted her hands in the folds of the curtain next to her and tried to keep her face hidden. The marquess took a few paces closer to her. He watched the tears drip down her face and his stance softened. A tinge of tenderness warmed his next words. "My little lamb, I did not expect you to be so distressed by the thought of marrying me." His finger reached up and caught a tear that was falling down her cheek. He sipped it off his finger and then traced the other tears that were following its path. "I am sure that if you would rather not marry me, then your father will understand. He wants you to be happy," his voice hardened again even though he tried to sound gracious, "and if you would prefer to be with High Parsiville, then you should tell your father that."

Charlotte was looking up into the dark eyes of the marquess as he spoke. The tenderness, the vulnerability in his eyes and voice was like spring sunshine pushing away the heavy clouds of winter. She shook her head. "It isn't that. I d-do like you, my lord. I w-would l-like to be m-married to you. It was j-just so unexpected, and n-not quite how I imagined a p-proposal would be."

Lord Theo swore softly and cupped her head in his hand. His fingers tangled in her hair, loosening the pins as his fingers dug into her scalp. He drew her face closer to his. "I am sorry, little one. I was startled to see you and Hugh Parsiville alone and standing so close to each other. That is not how a betrothed man wishes to find his fiancée."

Charlotte felt her cheeks redden as the blood rushed to her face. The marquess was looming over her, studying her face as if he was reading a book that he needed to understand. After a few moments, he nodded and stepped back. He handed her the letter her father had sent. Numbly, she took it.

"Well," her mother's voice intruded, "I will leave the two of you to discuss matters while I arrange dinner. You will be staying, won't you, Lord Raeburne?"

Theo glanced at his future mother-in-law. His mouth twitched, but he answered as politely as years of breeding had taught him to, "Thank you, Mrs. Drake. I would be delighted to join you for dinner."

Mrs. Drake swept from the room, leaving the marquess alone with his soon-to-be bride.

Theo looked at Charlotte, who was still half hidden in the curtains. "Should we sit down?" he asked.

Charlotte nodded and then, as Theo began to frown, quickly said, "Yes, Your Lordship." She left the shelter of the curtains and, without looking at her future husband, made her way to the settee. As she sat, she realized she should have chosen a chair. Lord Theo sat down next to her, close enough that his thigh pressed against hers. She trembled at the pressure of his hard muscles and curled her fingers into her palms to try to control the thrill of being close to him, but she could not prevent the heat of desire from swirling through her body.

The marquess turned towards her so that he could watch her expressions as he spoke. "We do not seem to have made the best beginning to our marriage."

Charlotte glanced at him. Her face looked troubled. Instead of joy, sadness clouded the blue of her eyes.

Theo placed his hand on the back of her neck, a gesture that spoke of possession, of protection. "What is it, my little lamb? What is wrong?"

Charlotte choked back a sob. The emotions of the last two hours threatened to overwhelm her. All that Hugh had said echoed through her mind. "My lord, I know it is not my place to ask, and you have most likely discussed this with my father, but I can't help wondering…" She hesitated and looked away from the marquess.

"Look at me, little one. What can you not help wondering?"

His implacable tones compelled Charlotte to turn to him. She was quiet for a few moments. The marquess studied her face while she struggled to find the words. Finally, she managed to say, "I have found, my lord, that the interest I have garnered since my arrival in London has centered on the inheritance I will receive from my father."

Theo continued to watch her. Silence filled the room. After a minute or so, he tucked a tendril of hair behind her ear. "You did not ask a question, but I think I understand what you want to ask. I am wealthy in my own right. I am not in need of an heiress to prop up my fortunes, as Sir Trenwith and others of his ilk are. Of course, acquiring Summerhill is not something to be sniffed at, but I was considering buying it long before I thought of marrying you."

Charlotte let out a startled gasp but said nothing. She simply watched the marquess carefully, drawn by the sincerity in his expression. She also detected a glimmer of something that could be affection in the dark depths of his eyes. But Hugh's words and her own thoughts cautioned her not to read too much into what she saw.

Theo traced the outline of her face. "I like you, little lamb. I believe that you and I will suit each other very well, that your enthusiasm for life, your delightful opinions, reflect my own philosophies. I think you will be a good wife for me, and I will be a good husband to you."

Charlotte felt herself capitulating to his kindness, and it was a few moments before she realized that, charming and sweet as his words were, Lord Theo had still said nothing of love. All her hope of happiness rested on the tenuous thread of affection she thought she had seen in his eyes. She nodded slowly.

Theo's shoulders straightened and his face took on a grim expression. Charlotte pulled back as the tenderness in his eyes turned to hard annoyance.

"Charlotte," he began, his voice as rough as the thunder that sometimes crashed over the hills surrounding Summerhill, "clear, open communication is something that is necessary if our relationship is to succeed. A few times today, you have resorted to nods instead of using words. It displeases me when you do not try to obey my wishes."

Charlotte's eyes were wide and the dark blue of a lake before a storm. "I'm sorry, Your Lordship," she managed to utter. She blinked twice and then asked, "Will you punish me again?"

A grim smile curled the corners of Theo's lips. "You did enjoy your spanking the other day, and usually, it is a very effective way to remind you to focus on ways to improve yourself, to be the best person you can be." He ignored Charlotte's little squirm as her buttocks clenched, remembering the pleasure from her last spanking. "However, considering the time and place, I believe a spanking might not be prudent. This time, you will write out lines for me. You will write, 'When Lord Theodore asks me a question, I will politely and respectfully give a clear and articulate verbal answer.' That sentence, repeated fifty times, should remind you to put aside your habit of hiding behind silence."

Charlotte stared at him, indignation and a flash of anger in her eyes. "You cannot make me do that! I am not a child under the supervision of governesses!"

Lord Theo looked at her steadily, his eyebrow raised and his mouth set in a stern line. Charlotte subsided into the cushions of the settee. His calmness, his unwavering certainty, quelled her flash of temper.

"I-I'm sorry, my lord. I do not mean to be rude or ill-tempered," she managed to apologize.

Theo took her hand and his thumb stroked over her palm, soothing her. "Apology accepted, my little one. I know that you are not a child or even a girl. You are very much a woman, but you do still retain some girlish habits that you need to break, with my help." He gazed pointedly at her body, taking in the curve of her breasts and the swell of her hips. He leaned forward and brushed a kiss on her forehead. "As your husband, it is my duty to develop the best parts of your character, to show you how the goodness of pleasure is often the result of a little pain."

Charlotte squirmed, enticed by his words but also anxious. "Will you expect me to follow a lot of instructions? I am not very good at remembering all the things I am expected to do."

Theo was more relaxed now. He chuckled before he

answered, "There are many instructions I will give you over time, but we will begin with only a few." He drew Charlotte onto his lap. She sat stiffly at first, never having been in such a position before, but he tugged her closer to his chest and began to move his hand in comforting circles over her arm and back. She breathed slowly and relaxed against the solid warmth of his body, enjoying the rumble that came from his chest as he spoke.

"An arrangement such as ours will take years to grow, to develop fully. It will only succeed if we share openly and honestly, and if we trust one another." Charlotte stiffened, and Theo frowned. After a few moments, his caresses lulled her and she relaxed again.

Her mind settled. She convinced herself that she could keep her secret safe. Surely, the marquess meant that they needed to speak openly about the topics of conversation that would arise between them, and the matter of her secret would not need to be discussed. He would not know about it, would never ask about it, and she would be safe. Even as she came to this conclusion, she felt uneasy, as if she was lying to herself and to him.

The marquess, satisfied that Charlotte was agreeable to his views, explained, "Your pleasure will be enhanced if you submit yourself to me and let me guide you. I enjoy your candor and like the originality of your opinions. I certainly have no desire to see you become a timid mouse who mindlessly repeats what other people think. However, we will both be happier if you let me take control of certain aspects of our life together, if you defer to me. Sometimes, physical rituals are good reminders of the dynamics of our relationship, so I will often ask you to kneel next to me, the way that you have seen Amelia kneel next to the duke. Also, when you enter a room, no matter who is there, you are to come directly to me and stand slightly behind my right shoulder. You will not speak to anyone until I give you permission to do so."

Charlotte sat up and bit her lip, consternation creasing her forehead. "Won't people consider me impolite if I do that?"

Theo placed his finger under her chin and tilted her face so that she was looking at him. He studied her for a few moments before saying, "Do you trust me, little lamb?"

Charlotte nibbled her lip as she considered her reply. Did she trust the marquess, the man who was to be her husband? She had observed him over the years and knew that he had remarkable control, immense intelligence and real compassion. He would not hurt her. She nodded. "Yes, my lord, I trust you."

A radiant smile lit up Theo's face. "I am pleased you thought carefully before giving your answer. You are a remarkably intelligent woman, and I am glad that you have decided to trust me. I promise I will never allow anyone to think of you as unmannerly or accuse you of impropriety."

"Thank you, my lord," Charlotte said, relief evident on her face.

Theo kissed her forehead. "It would be good to practice some of what we have spoken about." He shifted her off his lap as he spoke so that she was standing between his legs. "I want to see how sweet you look when you kneel at my feet."

He placed his hands on her hips and she trembled as the heat of his touch surged through her, but she made no move to kneel.

"It is not a difficult request, my little lamb. Try it and you will see just how rewarding it is." Theo tugged at her hips and Charlotte found her knees bending. Quickly, she sank down and allowed the marquess to ease her into position. She knelt back on her heels, her back straight and her hands resting on her thighs. Uncomfortable as the position was, it felt right to be here in front of him. She smiled shyly at him.

"Very pretty, my angel," the marquess praised. "However, there are a few improvements needed. It is better if you do not clutch at your dress, so turn your hands palm up and rest them on your thighs." He smiled as Charlotte followed his instruction.

"Then, although your back is beautifully straight, I would like your head a little more tilted down. Yes, just like that. Beautiful. Now, the last change is that I would like you to move your thighs a little wider apart."

Charlotte jerked her head up at this, color flooding her face. The marquess simply stared at her, his eyes steady and his face implacable. After a few moments, she maneuvered into the position he had requested.

"Good girl. You are very beautiful, especially so when you yield yourself to me. Of course, you will look even more gorgeous when you are naked."

Charlotte managed to look both shy and eager, and Theo shifted forward, trying to ease the throbbing of his painfully engorged dick. He wanted nothing more than to fill that succulent mouth with his cock, to feel the sweet heat of her mouth surround him, to thrust into her throat and feel her tightness grip him, but he was in her mother's house and he needed to restrain himself.

He sat back and admired the gorgeous woman kneeling in front of him. Such a mix of submission and feistiness, of intelligence and naivety, of compassion and defiance, would ensure that his life would never be boring. Soon, he would take his nymph back to the countryside, to the woods and fields and rivers that were her natural habitation and then her chestnut curls would flow freely around her shoulders, her naked body would warm beneath his touch, and they would revel like ancient deities, exploring their passion and reaching heights of pleasure he had only ever imagined.

For now, he stretched forward and ran his fingers down her throat, savoring the shiver that rippled through her body. He tugged her bodice down, exposing more of her breasts, and kneaded the soft, firm mounds. She squirmed.

"Stay still while I explore what is mine." His voice was quiet but carried the unmistakable sound of authority.

Her deep breaths heaved her breasts upwards. He wanted to rip her bodice off completely, but it was almost time for dinner. Reluctantly, he dropped a kiss on each beautiful swell and then pulled her dress back into place. Then he kissed her on her mouth. His kiss was hard, thorough, possessive. With his mouth, he conveyed his control of his little lamb.

When he drew back from the kiss, he held out his hand and helped his betrothed to her feet. Charlotte looked down, her face revealing arousal and caution, but most of all, the sweet surrender of a woman who had yielded herself to a powerful man. "Thank you, my lord," she said softly.

Theo smiled as he led her to the dining room.

CHAPTER 12

$\mathcal{A}$ dignified butler, quite befitting the household of a marquess, led Charlotte through the brightly lit foyer of Raeburne House and up the sweeping staircase to the formal drawing room. She looked around, interested in all she could see. This was soon to be her home in London. She was going to be married to the marquess.

Charlotte took a deep breath, admiring all that she could see. The house was elegant and attractively decorated. Although there was a stateliness befitting the rank of the marquess, it was also gracious and welcoming. Beautiful paintings hung on the walls, and fine drapes covered the windows. The floors of the foyer were marble, but these gave way in the passageways to gleaming wood, which was covered with rugs and carpets in warm, rich colors. Chandeliers glittered from the light of the candles that burned brightly in them. This was a house that was decorated with taste as well as an eye to comfort.

Dawson, the butler, stopped before cherry wood doors, and a footman, neatly dressed in the deep green colors of Raeburne House, opened the door of the drawing room. Charlotte entered. The low chatter of Lord Theo's dinner guests filled the room.

Although she recognized many of them from the events she had attended since her arrival in London, she scanned the room, looking for the marquess, mindful of his instructions to her.

Lord Theo, resplendent in a dark grey dinner jacket and embroidered dark blue silk waistcoat, was talking to the Earl of Sherbonne near the fireplace. She quickly made her way across the room and drew near to the marquess, her betrothed. With an effort to remember what he had said to her, she stood just to his right, her head slightly bowed, her hands at her sides. She did not know if he had seen her. He continued discussing the latest news from the Spanish peninsula and how Napoleon would likely respond to the presence of the English army.

Charlotte began to feel awkward. She wanted to fidget. She wanted to look up at the marquess and tug his sleeve to let him know she was there. She was not used to being so still.

Baron Loxley joined his friends and the conversation turned to horses. One of Lord Theo's favorite mares was about to drop a foal, and the baron was interested in buying the baby horse. This was a subject that greatly interested Charlotte. She loved horses and she had seen the magnificent mare that the marquess pampered and treated with great affection. She was also fairly sure she knew which stallion had been used to breed with the mare. Her fingers twitched and she bit her lip. The only reason she did not join the conversation was her deep desire to please her betrothed and the memory of the creative ways he had punished her for not obeying him. Her fingers still ached from writing out lines.

Eventually, when she thought Lord Theo might never acknowledge that she was there, he turned to her. A smile flooded his face and his voice was warm with approval. "Good evening, my little lamb." He leaned forward and pressed a kiss to her forehead. "You have been very patient, and you will be rewarded." The low timbre of his voice rumbled through her, and she trembled at the promise in his words.

"Good evening, my lord," she managed to murmur.

The marquess kept his hand on her arm and drew her into the circle of his friends. "What do you think?" he asked her. "Should I sell Persephone's foal to Adam?"

Charlotte glanced up at her betrothed. His eyes were serious. He really was interested to know her opinion. She drew a deep breath. "That depends, my lord. I believe that if it is a colt, it might be better to keep him, and then later on, you might be able to breed with him, especially if he is from Saturn."

Loxley laughed. "Well, I can only try."

Charlotte glanced around, suddenly realizing she had been rambling about matters her mother deemed completely unsuitable for a drawing room or for a young lady to discuss at all. A blush covered her face and she caught her lip between her teeth.

The marquess nodded at her answer, although a slight frown creased his brow. "That is exactly what I have been saying to Loxley. I am not really considering selling that foal at all, colt or filly." His finger stroked her palm. "But Adam is making me neglect my duties as host. Little one, I was expecting your mother this evening, yet she does not seem to have accompanied you?"

Charlotte squirmed and turned an even deeper shade of red. "My lord, I should have made her apologies immediately. She has a headache and is indisposed. She thought it would be acceptable for me to come on my own, considering that we are betrothed and Lady Amelia would be here."

The marquess nodded, his features softened by a smile. "Ah, of course. I trust it is nothing serious?"

Charlotte shook her head. "No, only Mama has been extremely busy with all the arrangements for the wedding. It has been quite a whirlwind. I had not realized what a big event it would be."

Lord Theo studied the face of his young wife-to-be. She did not have the excited appearance of a young lady preparing for the most important day of her life. Her face was drawn and her eyes were shadowed with anxiety. Too much stress or a lack of sleep had left faint dark circles under her eyes. He tried to quell the irritation that surged through him. Was Charlotte still regretting giving up Parsiville to marry him? Had he misread her entirely, mistaking her compliance for affection?

He examined the way she was standing, so demurely next to him. Everything in her nature was designed to want to please those she respected. She might have run wild on her father's estate as a child, but deep down, she needed the approval of those she esteemed and admired. Was she marrying him to please her father while she still held a torch for Parsiville?

Theo took a deep breath. He could not, would not, believe that she preferred someone as insipid as Parsiville. She was lively, so enthusiastic about life, that she would never find true satisfaction with a weak man. She needed someone strong, to guide her, comfort her, to help her become all that she could be.

He still held her hand in his. He squeezed her fingers gently. "I am sorry that becoming a marchioness is such a very important social event." His voice had a slight mocking lilt to it but was mostly filled with understanding and concern. "What arrangements has your mother been making?"

Charlotte looked down to where his fingers entwined with hers. "Apparently, I need a whole new wardrobe even though I had new dresses when I arrived in London. There have been hours and hours of dress fittings every day and visits to warehouses to select materials and trips to haberdasheries to buy gloves and stockings. Mother is constantly fussing about menus and flowers and decorations and candles and table linens and silverware and plates, until she has a headache and I..." she petered off.

Theo cocked an eyebrow. "What about you? You are at your wits' end and wish you had never heard of weddings?"

Charlotte's eyes were wide as she looked at him. She nodded.

"I think it would be so much easier just to slip off quietly and marry in the stillness of the morning in the woods around Summerhill."

Theo's eyes were soft. "That sounds delightful. Unfortunately, I do not think your mother or society would deem that as a proper wedding and so the big social event must continue."

Charlotte laughed softly. "Yes, it must."

"And one of the aspects of what society expects is this dinner party, so we need to be polite and good hosts and mingle with the guests." Just then, Dawson announced that dinner was served and the marquess led the way to the dining room, Charlotte on his arm.

As the guests assembled around the long cherry wood table in the dining room, Charlotte noticed a tall, handsome lady, dressed in opulent green satin and wearing a striking emerald necklace, enter. There was a proprietary air about her as she took the seat that indicated she was the hostess. Charlotte glanced at Theo.

Theo's face had hardened. He turned to Charlotte, but his eyes were still fixed on the woman at the end of the table. "That is my sister, Lady Winifred. I am sorry she was not in the drawing room earlier and so did not meet you. I will introduce you later."

Charlotte nodded, but as she began the cream of mushroom soup, she was aware that Winifred was glaring at her. She could not understand why Lord Theo's sister should be so antagonistic when they had never met.

She was not given long to ponder the matter. As she enjoyed the exquisite meal, she was distracted from the glares of Theo's sister by the pleasant chatter of the guests around her. Soon Charlotte had relaxed enough to join the conversation, easily and intelligently presenting her view on things that interested her and quietly listening when the topic veered to something she did not know about. The conversation flowed rapidly from books and poetry to opera and philosophical thoughts of love and pleasure, to politics and the war in the Peninsula. Nobody suggested that young ladies should have no opinions and she found herself joining the discussions with a fervor that would have appalled her mother.

As she was enjoying a slice of deliciously cooked chicken in tarragon sauce and listening to Viscount Donnington and Baron Loxley discuss the paintings of William Turner that were causing a sensation in London, she felt the hand of the marquess on her thigh. She stiffened and looked at him, beginning to shake her head.

He raised his eyebrow and squeezed her leg. He leaned closer to her so that his mouth was next to her ear. "My little lamb, I want to play with you while I enjoy my dinner. You need to be as discreet as you possibly can be."

Charlotte nodded, her eyes fixed on her plate. "Yes, my lord," she murmured softly.

Theo continued his instructions. "Carry on eating and conversing politely, if you can." As he spoke, his hand was moving along her thigh in slow, firm caresses. Her skin tingled at his touch, not only where his hand was moving, but every-where, ricocheting deep within her intimate places.

"Yes, my lord," she managed and slowly nibbled a piece of chicken.

Theo's hand was relentless. He made some comment about attempting to purchase one of Turner's paintings and sipped his wine as if nothing unusual was happening under the table. Char-lotte had finished her chicken. Her hands were now on her lap, clenching the fabric of her dress as she tried to control the way her body responded to Lord Theo's touch. She was sure that everyone could see how her nipples had bunched into hard points, how her breasts were tight and swollen and how she was breathing hard.

The marquess leaned towards her again. "My little lamb, I

want to touch your skin, not just feel you through the fabric of your skirt. I want you to pull your skirt up until it is around the top of your thighs."

Charlotte's eyes widened until they seemed to fill her face. For a moment, she simply stared at the marquess. He looked back at her, as all around them, the dinner guests conversed and footmen began to clear the table, preparing for the next course. Dawson filled wine glasses.

Lord Theo's eyes were fixed on Charlotte, compelling, unrelenting. She looked down, making sure that the tablecloth covered her discreetly. Slowly, she began to tug at the smooth silk of her dress. She wriggled to set it free from where she sat on it. Bit by bit, her legs, encased in silk stockings that were tied just above her knees, were exposed under the table. Lord Theo's hand helped ease the material up. Finally, it was bunched at the top of her legs. Above her stockings, her thighs were bare. She squirmed.

Lord Theo's hand now began to rub lightly along the smoothness of her naked skin. His fingers were hard, firm, and calloused from the work he did on his estates but competent, skilled and eager to get what they wanted.

Charlotte could hardly concentrate on anything except Lord Theo's hand on her thigh as the strokes became firmer, more insistent, more intense. She held on to the material of her skirt and kept her eyes on the face of the marquess. The other guests faded away, until they were nothing more than a distant murmur, a blur on the edge of her vision.

Lord Theo molded his hand around her warm flesh and began to knead her thigh under his strong, capable fingers. He still seemed to be following the conversation at the table, which had now turned to music. Baron Loxley asked if she played the harpsichord.

She was so lost in the sensations the marquess was wringing from her that she hardly heard the question. She managed a small shake of her head. Lord Theo smirked at her and spoke softly so that only she could hear him. "That is not the most polite way to answer, my love. Usually, it is better to use words. This is a matter we have discussed." As he spoke, his fingers slid into the crevice between her thighs and he pressed into the slippery silky flesh, soaked from the juices her body was producing. She was sure she must be leaving a mark on the chair.

Charlotte bit her cheek to stop herself from crying out as the sensations built up. The marquess was making it impossible for her to think clearly, and she could not find the words to protest. She subsided when she saw the glimmer of laughter in his eyes. He knew exactly how his touches were affecting her.

Adam Loxley grinned knowingly as he turned to answer a question Viscount Donnington had asked. Lord Theo kept his eyes on Charlotte's face. "Little lamb, I think you would enjoy some of this blancmange. You really should try some." He dished some onto her plate and used the movement to force her legs apart.

Under the table, she was now splayed open. Lord Theo's fingers slipped up the center of her private parts. She could feel how slippery she was, how easily he was able to glide his fingers along her folds. She was red with embarrassment. She was going to leave a mark on the chair from the wetness that was dribbling from her core.

The marquess did not seem to care about that. He rubbed his fingers along the folds of her womanhood, tugging the labia and exploring the crevices of her pussy, causing more and more juices to flow. His fingers slid easily along the center of her being. One digit found the pulsing nub at her very core. It rested there for a moment and then, very slowly, he pressed hard. She let out a low cry. He flicked the little core where her pleasure was centered. He flicked the nub leisurely, almost careless in his attentions. She pushed against his hand, trying to get him to move faster as her body sought the new thrill. He pressed her back against the chair, glancing at her, amusement and under-standing gleaming in his eyes. She tried to glare at him, but he just smiled.

The marquess ceased all movement, and after a few moments, the raging heat had subsided a little, then he began his languid attention to her nub yet again. This time, Charlotte clutched the edge of her chair and let him play with her. Just when she felt the burning desire build to a peak, he pulled back a little and stroked the inside of her thighs and the outside of her mound. He was paying close attention to her every response.

She was so sensitive now that every touch was like a sizzling coal on a fire, but she wanted his touch on her nub. And she wanted more. There was an emptiness in the very center of her that needed to be filled. She felt the muscles of her passage clenching around the hollowness. She wanted the marquess to sweep her up in his arms, carry her to the nearest bedroom and plunge his manhood into her. She wanted to open herself to him completely. Her heart had belonged to him for months already. She was ready to let him have her body.

But Lord Theo simply stroked her, almost casually. He ran his fingers along her center, now avoiding her nubbin. She was sticky and wet where he spread her juices along her mound and between her legs.

Again, he leaned towards her. "My little lamb, I want nothing more right now than to watch you come, but I think you will not be able to be quiet and still, so I am going to stop playing with you. We will continue this game later on, when we have more privacy and I can see how prettily your pussy is flowering for me. Now straighten your dress." He smirked, "For the rest of the evening, you will be aware of me whenever you move."

Charlotte whimpered as he removed his hand from between her legs. He kept his eyes on her as she let her dress fall back into place. He lifted his hand to his mouth and slowly licked his fingers. Charlotte's breath was ragged and her face was flushed.

She could not believe that the marquess was tasting her juices right here in front of all his dinner guests. She bit her lip, uncertain of what she would see when she looked up, but the guests near her were continuing their chatter as if nothing unusual had happened to her.

With great effort, she sipped her wine, nibbled on the last dishes that were served and chatted with the guests, but all of that was made more difficult by Lord Theo's hand, which was on her thigh until Lady Winifred indicated that it was time for the ladies to withdraw.

CHAPTER 13

*C*harlotte sat quietly on a settee in the drawing room, sipping a cup of tea. It was a pleasant room. Comfortable chairs were covered in soft cream brocade. Beautiful paintings of the countryside graced the walls. Colorful arrangements of flowers reminded her of Summerhill. She imagined herself in this room, comfortable and happily married to Lord Theo.

Some of the ladies had asked the footmen to open the grand piano that filled one corner, and three of the ladies were animatedly discussing which pieces of music they should play.

"Are we to expect you to impress us with your talent on the pianoforte, or do your accomplishments lie more with the harp?"

Charlotte looked up as the harsh tones of Theo's sister cut through her thoughts. Lady Winifred was a striking woman, one who would easily be called handsome. It was clear to see that she was related to the marquess, but where his face often showed his enjoyment with life, his sister looked peevish and bitter. She was tall and dignified, but there was something hard about her mouth and eyes that made Charlotte feel uneasy. She stumbled for words. "I-I am not very accomplished. I believe it would be better for everyone if the other ladies played."

Winifred looked her up and down as if she were a specimen in a museum. "I have been watching you all evening and I find it difficult to understand what would possess my brother to select you as a wife. It was inevitable that he had to marry someday, but I thought he had enough sense to choose a society woman, one with connections, from a titled family, one with at least the basic accomplishments, as befits the Raeburne name."

Charlotte blushed at the cutting words. She had her own qualms about why the marquess wanted to marry her, but hearing his sister so openly criticize her was both painful and humiliating.

Winifred sat down next to her, the emerald necklace sparkling in the light of the candles. "Ever since Theo was old enough to be considered as a prospective husband, he has been hounded by young ladies, all wanting to be the Marchioness of Oakdene. He is considered a catch, but he is not all he appears to be. If you expect a happy marriage, you will be disappointed. I do not know what you hope to find in a marriage to my brother, but I can assure you that you will not find generosity or love or kindness. He is selfish, and his main priority has always been the prosperity of his estates. He always gets what he wants."

Charlotte shifted uneasily in her seat, not sure how to respond. She could not help remembering that Lord Theo had never mentioned love to her. All his attentions and caresses were not sufficient to calm her qualms and uncertainties. Summerhill was a greater attraction than she was. Charlotte gaped at Lady Winifred, her brow wrinkled in a frown, but Winifred continued. "My brother can be very charming when it pleases him, but he is a different person at home. I have heard that you are an heiress. To put it bluntly, my brother is very fond of money." She touched the emerald necklace as she spoke, and when Charlotte looked at it, Winifred smirked. "This is one of the Raeburne jewels. It has been in the family for many generations and belongs to a true Raeburne."

On that cryptic note, her future sister-in-law rose and left the room. Charlotte, confused and troubled, watched as Lady Winifred walked away. She had not known that Lord Theo had a sister. No one had mentioned her, not even the marquess himself. What other things had he not mentioned to her? Charlotte shuddered as Winifred's words echoed in her mind. Theo's sister was a bitter, angry woman who resented her brother. Charlotte was bewildered. Did her hero really have feet of clay?

Just as Winifred left, the gentlemen entered the drawing room. Charlotte would need to consider Winifred's words later. She watched Lord Theo walk across the room with Lord Sherbonne. The friends laughed as they shared a joke. Was the marquess a consummate actor, a gentleman who was one thing in public and someone quite different at home? Who would know him better than his sister?

As SOON AS Lord Theo entered the room, his eyes were drawn to Charlotte, like filings to a magnet. It had only been half an hour since he had seen her, but he wanted her. God, he needed her as he had never needed a woman before. All other women paled into insignificance before her. She was all he thought of, all he desired. He could not wait to make her his in every way. He wanted to claim her, every part of her appealing body, her fascinating soul. He wanted to see her naked, exposed to him, surrendering all her strength and beauty to him as he brought her to pleasure.

He frowned when he saw his betrothed sitting on her own. In a few strides, he crossed the room and sat down next to her on the settee. She was staring into her teacup as if she were trying to read her future in the tealeaves. He laid his hand on her arm. She jumped, clearly startled out of her reverie. Her eyes were glazed with unshed tears, her mouth pulled taut in an attempt to hold back a sob.

"My little lamb, what has happened? Are you upset because of what I did to you during dinner? Are you all right?"

She turned away from the marquess, trying to hide the distress in her eyes. "Oh, I had forgotten that." She gave him a watery smile. "I am well, thank you, my lord. I think I am just a little tired. All the preparations for the wedding are wearing me down, too." Her voice was prim and distant. "Perhaps, my lord, if it is not too much of an imposition, my carriage could be called."

Theo shook his head. "You have forgotten what I did to you during dinner? I will need to work much harder to keep your interest." There was laughter in his voice, but when she gave a little cry, he changed his tone, showing the tenderness he felt for her. "I understand that the wedding is overwhelming you, but I think something more specific has upset you." He cupped her chin and spoke with an unmistakable air of authority. "Look at me."

Charlotte could not help herself. She turned to face him. Her lips were trembling. Theo wanted to pull her into his arms and kiss those sweet lips. But he first needed to know what or who had upset her. "Now tell me, little lamb, what is the matter? I cannot help you or protect you if you do not tell me the truth."

"I'm just a little confused," she admitted.

"Yes. About what?" he prompted.

Charlotte looked into Lord Theo's eyes. Surely, Winifred could not have been right. The marquess could not be only pretending to care for her. She could not believe that the affection and tenderness in his eyes was an act, a ploy to gain her inheritance.

"I-I have heard, my lord, that you have mistresses and I know it is no concern of mine, but I was wondering if they are women I know, if they are here tonight and whether, when I leave, they, or she, w-will be... entertaining you."

For a moment, Lord Theo sat still, simply staring at his young bride. Then he actually chuckled.

Charlotte huffed, a delicious pout forming on her mouth. "Please don't laugh at me."

Theo stood up and reached out his hand. "My little lamb, there are some things we need to clarify. I think we should find some place a little more private. Come with me."

Charlotte was blushing as she placed her hand in his and allowed the marquess to lead her from the drawing room. As they passed groups of guests, chatting and drinking coffee, she hesitated. A young lady should not be alone with a gentleman, even her betrothed, but no one in the room looked concerned about the way the marquess was leading her away. And she did want to be alone with him. She hastened her steps to keep up with him.

A fire burned cheerfully in the library hearth, casting a warm glow onto the shelves and shelves of books. Charlotte longed to browse. She was sure she would find many treasures that she could lose herself in. She could see herself lounging in one of the comfortable leather chairs that were arranged all through the room, inviting readers to spend hours there. But the purpose of this trip to the library was very different.

The marquess settled himself into one of the large armchairs and when she looked around for a place to sit, he said, "Little lamb, I want you to kneel here in front of me, while we talk."

Charlotte nodded, and with a soft, "Yes, my lord," she dropped into the position he had taught her. The approval in his eyes calmed some of her riotous emotions. "Now, my little lamb, what have you heard about these mistresses of mine who are causing you such anxiety?"

Charlotte bit her lip. Her voice was unsteady. "I have only heard, my lord, that you keep some... one, I think, as most gentlemen do."

The marquess shook his head. "I am not going to ask who

mentioned that piece of gossip to you. I do, however, want you to listen to me carefully. It is true that I used to have two mistresses, but I broke off our arrangements some months ago. I let them go, in the usual way that such matters are arranged, before Christmas."

Charlotte looked up at him, confusion clear in her eyes. "I don't understand."

Theo quirked an eyebrow. "There is not much to understand. Towards the end of last year, I found that I no longer wanted what mistresses could give. I want a wife, and so I no longer have any mistresses. I have not had sexual intercourse since Christmas."

Charlotte shook her head. "Th-that sounds improbable."

Theo chuckled. "It probably does, but it is true. Now, you have no need to worry that I will entertain mistresses or anyone else once we are married. I believe in the sanctity of the marriage vows."

Charlotte was still nibbling her bottom lip. Theo's explanation had not eased her worries. There was clearly something else that had upset her.

She looked down at the carpet and then, coming to a decision, turned her eyes to him. Her voice was almost a whisper. "Ever since I arrived in London, it has been pointed out to me that my only value is linked to my inheritance. I have had many gentlemen vie for my attention, but each one has only been interested in the size of my dowry or the annual income from Summerhill." She paused, but the marquess said nothing, simply stroking her hair while he waited for her to continue. After a few moments, she sighed. Her voice was even softer now, and Theo had to lean close to her to hear what she said. "There are so many accomplished and elegant ladies you could marry. I am not sure why you have chosen someone as unsuitable as me."

Theo sat up straight as Charlotte spoke. His eyes glinted and his jaw was hard. "Charlotte, I do not like the way you constantly disparage yourself. Just because you do not have the same accomplishments as some of the other debutantes, does not make you less worthy to be married to me. You are not to belittle and undermine something that belongs to me. It seems that your spanking at the duke's house was not sufficient to teach you to value yourself. Another spanking might help you to remember."

When he drew back, he studied her for a few moments and then came to a decision. "Little lamb, I believe that more is needed for you to overcome this belief you have that you are not worthy of my attention. Stand up."

Charlotte looked at the marquess, a question in her eyes, but she obeyed him, giving his cock a slight reprieve. She stood before him, her hands at her sides and her head slightly bowed.

"I want you to realize how beautiful you are, how much you affect me. I want you to remove your clothes and show me your gorgeous body."

Charlotte stared at the marquess, her eyes wide and blue, dark with passion and trepidation. "My lord, right here, now? What about your guests?"

"My guests can look after themselves for a while. You are more important. I need you to learn to trust me and obey me." He smiled grimly. "Finding ways to delay following my instructions might not be good for your bottom."

Charlotte trembled with desire and enough fear to keep her on edge. Her hands slid around to feel where Lord Theo had spanked her. Then, slowly, she moved them to her buttons and began unfastening them, one by one. Her breathing was heavy and quick and her cheeks were flushed, but she continued until her dress was loose enough to slide off her shoulders. She wriggled out of it and the fabric pooled in a heap of pale blue at her feet. She stood, arrayed in her petticoat and undergarments with her hands clenched at her sides, but looked directly at Lord Theo.

"Beautiful," he breathed. "Seeing you stand there, so bravely, so enchantingly, is one of the most exquisite sights I have ever seen. But I want to see more. Take off the petticoat and the corset."

Charlotte was finding it difficult to control her breathing. She had not expected her evening to include undressing before the marquess. In spite of all she had seen and heard over the last few weeks, she still had the idea that husbands and wives kept themselves politely covered in the marriage bed and that ladies were not expected to enjoy physical pleasure. But there was a deeper, more elemental part of her that wanted what the marquess was offering her. She wanted the pleasure and passion he promised.

She undid the ties that kept her petticoat in place and let it fall to join her dress at her feet. She struggled with the fastenings of the corset but managed to loosen those as well. She dropped it and stood before her future husband clad in nothing but her stockings and shoes.

She tried very hard to keep her hands at her sides and not cover her nakedness. A little shiver rippled through her body. She could not tell if it was from the coolness of the night air or the strangeness of standing exposed before the marquess.

He leaned back against the cushions of the chair and studied her. His eyes roved over her, from her hair, falling loose and wild over her shoulders, to her breasts, round and pale with rosy, pink tips, puckered and pointing towards him. His gaze traveled down, taking in the curve of her stomach and the shapeliness of her thighs and calves. He lingered on the dusky triangle between her legs.

Charlotte wanted to squirm but managed to keep still. After what felt like hours but was probably only two or three minutes, Theo stood up and moved towards her. "Lovely," he declared. "You are the loveliest woman I have ever set eyes on." He walked around her slowly, looking at her from every angle. Once he was back in front of her, he held her eyes with his steady gaze.

"You, my little lamb, are the bravest, most intrepid, most delightful woman I know." He began to touch her. His fingers marked a trail along the contours of her face, outlining her cheeks, her chin, and then moving down the slender column of her throat. She shivered at the lightness of his touch and leaned forward.

"No, my gorgeous girl, we move at my pace." His voice was as sultry as a warm summer afternoon. His hands slid over her shoulders, shaping them, testing the smoothness of her skin, the subtleness of the muscles in her arms.

Then he cupped her breasts. She sucked in a breath as his hands molded the shape of them. He let the mounds fill his hands and squeezed lightly, watching her reactions. She shuddered but pressed towards him. He squeezed again, more firmly this time. A sound like a whimper emerged from her mouth. He continued to play with her breasts, brushing the sensitive skin underneath the curves, leaving a little trail of light pinches on the undersides and slowly circling the pretty orbs until his fingers moved closer and closer to the pink buds that were jutting forward in hard points. He ran his thumbs over the areolae and then flicked them back and forth across her nipples.

Charlotte let out a little cry and reached forward, grabbing his arms. Theo could see she was finding it difficult to keep her balance. The musky scent of her arousal filled the air between them. Gratified at her response, he bent down and took one of her breasts into his mouth. She jerked up onto her toes and then settled back.

Theo sucked gently on her breast and dragged more of her into his mouth. His sucking became more intense, more desperate. He licked and grazed her nipple with his teeth. He pressed the nipple against the roof of his mouth, enjoying the taste of her. Bit by bit, he released her, his tongue continuing to lap until he pulled his mouth away from her.

He moved back slightly so he could admire the swollen, red

breast now slick with his saliva. Charlotte was still clinging to him. His hands were cradling her back, drawing her close to him. He studied her other breast and decided it needed the same treatment he had given the first one. With a grin, he drew it into his mouth.

Charlotte was overwhelmed with unusual sensations. Her body arched as Lord Theo sucked her breasts. All thoughts of being embarrassed had vanished. Her body pulsed with anticipation and pleasure. Vaguely, she was aware that she was moaning and crying out. The word *please* echoed in the room as the marquess continued to explore her body. She wasn't sure what she was asking for, but she wanted these feelings to continue forever.

Her legs had been spread over one of Lord Theo's thighs and she was rubbing herself along the smooth silk of his breeches and hard muscle of his leg. There was a peak of pleasure that she was reaching for, but it remained tantalizingly out of reach.

Lord Theo released her breast and looked at her. Amusement and heat filled his eyes. "My little lamb, I owe you a climax as I stopped short of letting you come at the table." He ruffled her hair. "Considering the lovely noises you are making now, it is just as well I did not let you finish at dinner. We will have to work on ways to have you climax quietly in public, but when we are alone together, I enjoy the sounds you make."

Charlotte gazed at him, her eyes glazed and her breath coming in short puffs. She only vaguely followed what the marquess was saying. Suddenly, she felt one of his arms under her knees and the other around her shoulders as he lifted her. She tried to protest, but he carried her to the couch and sat down with her in his lap.

She wriggled as she tried to find a comfortable position and then stopped as she realized that she was moving over the hard shaft of his manhood. She stayed still but could feel it pushing against her bottom.

"Relax, my sweet little lamb. You will become better acquainted with my cock very soon. Tonight, I want to focus on your pleasure." The marquess ran his hands up her thighs as he spoke. She trembled beneath his touch. He tapped the top of her legs. "Open for me, little one."

Charlotte tensed her muscles, but when the marquess pinched the top of her thigh, she squealed and relaxed. Her legs splayed open and her wet, pink pussy was revealed to him. He pushed her thighs farther apart and then simply sat looking at her most private parts, studying her. After what seemed like an hour to Charlotte, he declared, "Very pretty."

Then he ran his fingers through the slickness of her core, slowly exploring the intricacies of her secret places. He traced a path between the petals towards her core and then back along the other side, to her nub, slowly, patiently, as if there was nothing else he needed to do. Charlotte squirmed, but he held her still as his fingers continued their relentless path.

Just when she thought she would scream from the build-up of sensations in her body, Lord Theo increased the pressure, rubbing more firmly, more quickly. She gasped and her back arched. Her breasts were tight and swollen. Theo concentrated on her nub, flicking his finger along the sides and rubbing circles over the top. Charlotte was panting. Her hands were clenched in tight fists and her eyes were closed. Her body pulsed as it reached towards a peak she had never known before. With a cry of pleasure, she surrendered to the climax.

Theo watched her face tighten and then relax. She was flushed pink. Her nipples were tightly pointed, such sharp nubs he swore he would cut himself if he took one into his mouth right now. A sheen of perspiration caused her body to glow in the soft candlelight of the library. Her hair was tousled and damp tendrils curled around her face. He had never seen anything more beautiful.

As she came down from the climax, her body still shuddering

from the intensity of her pleasure, the marquess sought her mouth and kissed her with exquisite tenderness. He was falling in love with the lovely young heiress who was soon to be his bride.

Slowly, caressingly, he ran his hands over her body, learning the shape and feel of her. She moaned lightly as he touched her skin, sensitive from the climax he had just brought her to. She lay limp in his arms, satiated with pleasure. She opened her eyes and looked at him with a satisfied smile. "I've never felt anything like that before."

Theo grinned at her. "That's just a small taste of all that you are yet to discover."

Charlotte snuggled against him, settling into a more comfortable position. His cock pulsed insistently beneath her buttocks, and suddenly she scowled. She reached up a hand and touched his face. "But you did not experience the pleasure that I did," she ventured, wriggling against his still rock hard cock.

Theo smiled. How sweet and giving she was, how concerned for his well-being. "I assure you, my little lamb, that I derive much pleasure from bringing you joy. And I believe it would delight me now to show you even more."

Charlotte twisted so that she could see his face more clearly. She frowned slightly. "I am not sure I could experience any more pleasure right now," she protested feebly.

Theo chuckled. "Oh, I believe you are capable of far more if you would let me continue."

Charlotte's eyes were wide; the dark of her irises seemed to have consumed most of the blue. She swallowed and then nodded. "Yes, please."

Theo needed no further encouragement. He bent towards her and began placing kisses along her throat and down towards her breasts. He lingered there, licking the soft skin with slow circles of his tongue. He enjoyed the whimpers of delight that escaped her lips.

Then, very slowly, he eased his way down her abdomen, swiping his tongue over her silky skin. As he continued his exploration, savoring the sweetness of her body, he manipulated her position so that her head and torso were resting on the couch and her hips were canted towards him. He slid his hand between her legs and cupped her blazing pussy. Gratified to feel the wetness there, he knew she was enjoying his ministrations. He lifted her left leg and placed it along the back of the couch. This left her pussy exposed to him. He tilted her up so that she was within easy reach of his eager mouth.

Charlotte lay still and quiet. He could feel the sudden tension in her muscles. Quietly, as if gentling a lamb, he murmured, "It's all right, little one. Just relax. I want to look at the pretty treasures you are keeping here for me." He rested his one hand on her stomach and the other on her thigh. His calm strength settled her and he took a few minutes simply to look at her pussy. It was plump and swollen with passion and musky juices were flowing from her core. Dark brown curls were slick with her arousal.

He hoisted her pussy closer to his face and took a deep breath of her sweet fragrance. Then he began to lap at the juices that she was making for him. His tongue ran in a long swipe up the fold between her lips and then back. This startled a mewling sound from her. Enjoying both the taste and sound of her, he continued to lick her folds, pausing occasionally to nibble a particularly luscious spot.

Charlotte was writhing and moaning beneath his hands and tongue. He repositioned her and then took a long, slow lap up the center of her pretty pink petals. He stopped just short of her clit, which was now swollen and peeking out from its hood. He repeated this steady circling of her folds a few times, each time ending with a firm swipe up the center.

The scent of her arousal was making him lightheaded, and his cock was so tight and full, he thought it might explode.

Finally, he focused on her little sensitive nub. He flicked the tip of his tongue around its base and then over the top.

Charlotte shouted out and gripped the cushions of the couch tightly. She tried to close her legs but his hands kept her open to his exploration.

He circled her clit with his tongue and then sucked it into his mouth. His teeth grazed the sides and then he bit lightly. Her hands moved from the couch to push against his torso, but he ignored her feeble attempts to move him away. She was sobbing out the words *please* and *more* in a heady rhythm. Her hands curled around his arms and dug in.

Her body was tense and poised to come. He released her clit and licked up the juices that were spilling copiously from her now. She subsided slightly, loosening her hold on his arms. His tongue swept up her center again and he licked her clit, flicking his tongue over the sensitive tip with hard, quick movements. He felt Charlotte tense beneath him again. This time, he did not slow down. He took the nub in his mouth again and bit down. A scream resounded through the library as Charlotte reached her peak and plunged over into her second climax. He kept licking and nibbling, not letting her cut short the powerful orgasm that pulsed through her body.

Only when the shuddering ceased, did he let go. Then he pulled her into his arms and cradled her against his chest.

Marriage to her was going to be a delight.

CHAPTER 14

*H*ugh Parsiville tossed down the cards he had been playing and pushed back his chair. Lord Danforth raised an eyebrow. "Are you out?"

Parsiville grunted. Danforth swept the pile of bills and coins into a neat pile as he said, "You owe two thousand to the bank."

Parsiville stood up, grabbing the piece of paper on which Danforth had scrawled the IOUs that would be added to the pile of vowels in his study. His luck had to turn one of these days. It was impossible to continue this losing streak for much longer. "I'll pay it, as soon as the next quarter's income is available from my estate."

A general murmur of disgust greeted this announcement from the gentlemen gathered around the faro table in the cardroom of the Danforth's house. Parsiville owed more and more debts of honor and was finding fewer and fewer gentlemen willing to play cards with him.

With a scowl, Parsiville stalked from the cardroom and entered the ballroom. A quick glance showed him where Charlotte was dancing with the marquess. He stood watching them, his mind plotting various scenarios. His initial plan had been to marry Charlotte Drake and use her fortune to get himself out of debt, but when the marquess had shown an interest in her, he had considered how he could manipulate the situation to his benefit. He just needed to play his cards right. He snorted softly at his own wit. Charlotte was naïve, gullible and his knowledge of her secret made her vulnerable to his machinations. In another week, she would be married to the marquess and Theo Raeburne's extensive riches would be available to him.

He was so focused on the marquess and Charlotte, he didn't notice that someone had stopped right next to him until a lady's voice interrupted his thoughts, "Are you one of the forsaken suitors of the heiress?"

Hugh turned to look at the lady who had spoken. She was taller than most, with a supercilious air. Her dark hair was fashionably arranged and her dark green dress had clearly been made by the best dressmakers. But what caught his eye was the heavy necklace studded with emeralds that embellished her neck.

He smiled. "I do not know that we have had the pleasure of an introduction. Hugh Parsiville at your service," he said as he bowed with as much charm as he could muster.

The lady sketched a quick curtsy. "Lady Winifred Raeburne. I suppose it is rather forward of me to approach you without an introduction, but I could not help noticing how you watch my brother's fiancée, and I heard that when she arrived in London, she was seen often in your company."

Hugh glanced at the dancers just as Charlotte looked up at Theo with eyes blazing with love. He sucked in a mouthful of air. His plan would only work if there was dissension between the two of them. He needed to keep her loyal to him. He turned back to Lady Winifred who was watching him keenly. "Charlotte and I have been... *friends* for a long time. We are distantly related, and I am pleased that she has managed to attract the interest of someone so distinguished as the marquess."

Winifred gave a light laugh. "That is a very diplomatic answer. If I did not know my brother better, I would imagine that he had lost his wits, making a fool of himself over such a little country dab who has no style or fashion. She will bring nothing to the eminence of the Raeburne family except her inheritance."

Hugh turned to face Lady Winifred more fully. He studied her for a few moments. Perhaps he could find a way to use her vitriol to ensure that Charlotte's fortunes were not wasted on the marquess. His need was, after all, much greater. "Poor little Charlotte. She is certainly out of place in the *Beau Monde*. And yet she has her uses. I imagine that the whole Raeburne family will benefit from her riches."

Winifred had the grace to blush, but fury flashed in her eyes. "My brother is very good at ensuring that his own fortune is intact and untouched, and yet he does not consider the needs of his family members." Her hand moved up to touch the necklace as she spoke.

Hugh eyed her, with his eyebrow raised. Nothing in Lady Winifred's outfit suggested neglect or approaching penury. However, he nodded and shifted the focus of the conversation. "That is a very distinctive necklace. It looks old."

Winifred puffed up. "It is one of the Raeburne family jewels, an heirloom, passed down through the centuries from Henry VIII's time. It has been worn by countless generations of Raeburne ladies, and I believe it suits me well." She almost spat out the next words, "I would rather see it sold than given to an upstart like Charlotte Drake."

Hugh smiled. "It really does look nice on you. And if, as you say, it belongs to the Raeburne family, then you, as a Raeburne, have every right to have it, to wear it or sell it as you please."

Winifred looked at Hugh for a few moments, her eyes thoughtful. It suddenly occurred to her that she had let her feelings be known to someone who was a stranger, and yet because of his association with Charlotte, he might just prove useful in her campaign against her brother.

The music drew to an end with a flourish and the dancers broke up the sets. Hugh bowed to Lady Winifred. "It has been a pleasure to make your acquaintance, my lady. I look forward to furthering our alliance."

LORD THEO LED Charlotte from the dance floor, a wide smile on his face. Every day, he was falling more in love with his lovely fiancée. Her eagerness and ebullience delighted him. She was responsive to him in every way, and in just less than a week, she would be his wife.

He brought her to where his friends had gathered. Sherbonne greeted him with a hearty slap on the back and a bow for Charlotte. "Miss Drake, you are looking remarkably well this evening. I believe that the prospect of marriage, even to Theo, delights you."

Charlotte smiled. "I am looking forward to being married to Theo."

Adam chuckled. "I suppose it was inevitable that we would all begin to settle down at some time. Somehow, I thought Donny would be the first of us, but Theo jumped ahead of him."

Donnington shrugged. "I am not without hope. I don't believe it will be long before I win the heart of my true love."

His friends turned to him, clamoring for an explanation. Donnington laughed and pointed to Loxley. "Adam can bear me out. I was viewing the exhibition of Greek statues, to get some inspiration, and Miss Blakeney arrived. We had a delightful conversation and she has promised to dance with me tonight."

The gentlemen, with the ease of long friendship, fell into a comfortable conversation and Charlotte stepped back. She knew that Theo needed his friends, and she was satisfied that he cared for her, and she did not need his constant attention. She gave a little start as a hand grabbed her arm. She looked up to see Hugh Parsiville, an echo of a smile making his face look strangely sinister. She took a breath. This was her confidant and friend, not someone wanting to cause trouble for her. "Hugh, you did startle me. It is good to see you," she managed to gather her thoughts and greet her friend.

Hugh pulled her farther away from the marquess and his friends. "Good evening, Charlotte. Would you honor me with the next dance?" He didn't wait for her answer, but pushed her into the set that was forming in front of them.

Charlotte glanced at Theo, who was still talking to his friends. He would not object to her being polite to an old acquaintance. She took a deep breath. "I have not seen much of you in the last few weeks, Hugh. Are you well?"

"Well enough, I suppose." He scraped a bow as the music began.

Charlotte eyed him thoughtfully. "I did not know that you had developed a liking for dancing." she ventured.

Hugh just smirked. "I wanted to speak to you and you have been so occupied with wedding arrangements and cozying up to your new friends that you haven't had time for me." He managed to sound somewhat aggrieved. "I suppose I am not as important to you anymore."

Charlotte took a deep breath and looked abashed. She focused on the first part of Hugh's comment, not quite sure how to apologize for her neglect of her loyal friend. "The wedding is a much bigger affair than I imagined it would be. Mother is making such a fuss that I hardly have time to breathe."

"I received my invitation, and so, it appears, has almost everyone in London. Everyone is talking about how you won such an eligible husband. You are quite the subject of gossip these days." His voice didn't seem to change, and yet Charlotte shivered at his next words. "People are always so eager to discover something scandalous. It would be quite a shame if the gossip about you turned to salacious matters."

Charlotte bit her lip, disturbed by the reminder of the secret she was keeping from the marquess and also by the implied threat in Hugh's words. "Hush, Hugh. We should not talk of such things where anyone might hear." She glanced nervously at the other dancers moving through the steps of the cotillion.

Hugh laughed. "No one is listening. You manage to present a rather believable façade of sweet innocence."

Charlotte swallowed. "What did you want to talk to me about?"

Hugh smiled. "I just wanted to remind you that when you need a friend, and you *will* need one, I am the one who knows you and your... history best. You relied on me in the past when you needed help, and you and I have a special... arrangement. I just wanted to make sure that you will not forget your good friends, that I have not been replaced by your new companions. There might come a day when your assistance might just be necessary."

Charlotte stumbled, suddenly finding it very difficult to remember the steps of the dance. Hastily, she tried to appease Hugh. "You know that I am grateful for your support. Of course, we will continue to be friends once I am married."

Hugh nodded. "That is all I ask."

VISCOUNT DONNINGTON SAUNTERED off to find Miss Blakeney for the dance she had promised him. Theo turned around and frowned. Charlotte had disappeared while he had been talking to his friends. She was not with her mother, who was describing to Lady Armstrong in excruciating detail the lace that had been purchased for Charlotte's wedding clothes. He looked towards the refreshment room, but there was no sign of Charlotte's pale blue dress and deep chestnut curls.

His eyes flickered over the dancers and stopped as he saw her circle the leading couple, ready to move down the set with... Every muscle in Theo's body tensed. She was dancing with Hugh Parsiville and clearly engaged in an intense and intimate conversation.

Daggers of jealousy shot through him, so sharp, he almost staggered under their attack. Theo knew it was not polite or possible to prevent Charlotte from dancing with other gentlemen. Indeed, she had danced with each of his friends earlier. But he had not expected her to seek out Parsiville's company.

"Say, old chap, isn't that Parsiville dancing with Charlotte? How did that happen?" Sherbonne's voice carried only a hint of teasing.

Theo swallowed and glared at his friend. "They are acquaintances from childhood. I am sure there is nothing untoward in her accepting him as a partner for one short dance."

Sherbonne's eyes narrowed with concern. "She is looking very flushed, more than the exertion of dancing would cause. Is she angry or enjoying her time with her old friend? I'm not sure that I would want my betrothed to be so familiar with Hugh Parsiville."

Only good manners prevented Theo from punching the earl. Sherbonne saw the rage simmering in Theo's eyes and offered a quick apology. "Sorry, old chap. It is an unsettling scenario. Charlotte was most likely lured into accepting the dance."

With clenched jaws and fisted hands, the marquess stared fixedly at his betrothed and her childhood friend as they completed the dance. He did not reply to Sherbonne but emitted a hiss of displeasure as he saw Hugh lead Charlotte to the other side of the ballroom, rather than returning her to the protection of her mother or him.

He turned to his friend with a plea for help. "Why is he taking her to the terrace?"

Sherbonne's voice now held a tinge of real concern. "We both know that gentlemen use the terrace to engage in a little intimate exchange with young ladies who are not overly concerned with propriety. We need to get over there and put a stop to any plans he has."

Theo was already moving through the crowded ballroom. "I am not about to let Charlotte disappear into the shadows with Hugh Parsiville. If she needs some fresh air, then I will be the one to escort her outside."

CHARLOTTE TRIED to tug her hand out of Hugh's grasp. "I need to return to my mother," she declared.

Hugh laughed. "All in good time. I thought it would be interesting to see just how sincere your promises of friendship are. The terrace will be very cool. And private."

Charlotte looked around the ballroom, frantic for assistance. She did not want to be found in a compromising position with Hugh. With tears burning the back of her eyes, she remembered how angry the marquess had been when he had come upon her alone with Hugh on the day of her proposal. She did not want to endure such cold rage from her betrothed again. And she really did not want to spend more time with Hugh. He frightened her, as he never had before. She pulled harder and finally tugged hard enough to force him to let go.

Blushing furiously, she staggered away from him. She stumbled against someone, and a gentle voice greeted her, "Pardon me, Miss Drake, but can I be of assistance?"

Charlotte spun around and faced Miss Blakeney and Viscount Donnington. The smile that had filled the viscount's face while he had danced with Miss Blakeney faded when he saw how distressed Charlotte was. His quick eyes noticed Hugh Parsiville glowering a few steps away and he quickly came to the rescue. "Miss Drake, Miss Blakeney, allow me to escort you to the refreshment room. A glass of lemonade or champagne will be just the thing."

Clarissa Blakeney smiled. "Thank you, Lord Donnington. That is very kind of you."

Charlotte said nothing but, with one last desperate glance at Hugh, took Lord Anthony's offered arm and sighed.

As the viscount led the ladies away from a scowling Hugh, Miss Blakeney observed, "It can be awkward for a young lady to be seen going onto the terrace with a gentleman, even one she knows well. It is always better to be overly cautious to ensure that one's reputation remains unblemished."

Charlotte scowled as she stumbled along with the viscount and the perfect Miss Blakeney, who would never find herself in a compromising position with anyone, whose reputation was pure and not besmirched by secrets and unsavory friends. She would never have to fight off unwelcome advances from a very persistent gentleman whose very presence was a threat to her peace of mind.

"It isn't as if I wanted to be with Hugh," Charlotte murmured rebelliously under her breath, so softly that not even Lord Anthony could hear her.

And then her humiliation was compounded by the sudden appearance of her betrothed. As they turned into the refreshment room, Lord Theo took her hand and nodded curtly to the viscount. "Thank you, Donny, but I will see to my fiancée now."

Donnington merely smiled and stepped away with Miss Blakeney, but Charlotte shuddered. Lord Theo's voice seethed with suppressed anger and irritation. He took a glass of lemonade from a passing footman and handed it to Charlotte but said nothing. And Charlotte had no words to excuse herself. She had landed in this predicament because she had accepted

Hugh's invitation to dance. She deserved any punishment Lord Theo administered, but his disappointment was more than she could bear.

She sipped her lemonade slowly, not daring to look at her husband-to-be. Finally, when her glass was empty, he removed it from her hand and she looked up at him. "I'm sorry," the words were little more than a whisper but she could see Lord Theo's face soften.

"I'm not sure which of your transgressions you are apologizing for, but I do believe that it would be good for you to be reminded that you belong to me and that I do not like it when you slip off with another man."

CHAPTER 15

"Lord Danforth will not mind if we use his library. It won't be the first time someone at one of his balls has found it necessary to use it to punish a young lady who has displeased her Master." Lord Theo spoke blandly as he led Charlotte from the ballroom.

Charlotte tried to protest, but only because of the memory of Clarissa Blakeney's words. When Hugh had tried to maneuver her out of the ballroom, she had been very reluctant, but she liked spending time with Theo and had willingly followed him. With a sigh, she wondered if she was going to become intimately acquainted with all the libraries in London. And then her body flushed with the remembrance of the last time she had been in a library with Lord Theo. Every cell in her body tingled in both dread and anticipation.

She was a pace or two behind the marquess and took the opportunity to freely admire and appreciate his broad back, his confident gait, his muscular thighs. She was gazing at the way his hair, thick and dark, curled against his collar when he stopped abruptly. She bumped into him.

Lord Theo turned at the library door and grasped her arm to keep her from falling, a quirk of his eyebrow the only indication that he knew what had distracted her. With a blush, Charlotte entered the large library, sparing only a moment to take in the dark paneling and shelves and shelves of books. The marquess was already making his way to a deep leather couch, not unlike the one in his library at Raeburne House.

He sat down, looking as comfortable as if taking a young lady out of a ballroom for a spanking was nothing unusual. Charlotte squirmed and was about to sit next to her betrothed, when the marquess cleared his throat and, with a tilt of head, indicated the carpet in front of him.

Charlotte bit back a retort. She had forgotten his injunction that this kind of conversation would always occur with her kneeling in front of him. Gracefully, she slid to her knees, bowed her head slightly and placed her hands palm up on her thighs, which were splayed open. Even though she was fully dressed, she felt her face warm at the suggestiveness of the posture.

The marquess studied her, his face impassive, and then a slight upturn of his mouth showed his approval and admiration of her. He leaned forward and placed his hand on her head. "Good girl," he said with such warmth that all of Charlotte's qualms fled. His approval was like warm summer rain to a parched flower.

Lord Theo leaned back a little, placing his hands on his thighs. "Well, my little lamb, do you understand why we are here? Why I intend to punish you?"

Charlotte began to nod and then remembered that the marquess had stipulated that she was to use words. "Y-yes, my lord. I think so."

His eyebrows shot up. "You think so? Perhaps I should make it clear so that in the future, there will be no misunderstandings."

Charlotte raised wide blue eyes to him, brimming with trepidation, but trust and desire were also evident in their bright depths. "If you please, my lord."

"I do please." Lord Theo smiled and perused his betrothed with approving eyes before raising his hand and holding up three fingers. "There were several offences. Firstly, you disappeared from my sight without a word. I did not know where you were. Anything might have happened to you." Charlotte opened her mouth to explain that he had been occupied with his friends and a ball was not a dangerous place, but a sharp look from the marquess silenced her.

"Secondly, I am not happy that you chose to dance with a gentleman such as Hugh Parsiville." Charlotte frowned at her betrothed. She had been uncomfortable with some of Hugh's words and actions, but she could not understand why Lord Theo particularly objected to her old friend. Then, before she uttered a word, a vision of her betrothed's face when he had found Hugh leaning over her in her mother's drawing room rose in her mind's eye. She subsided. Her history with Hugh was complicated, too involved to explain to Lord Theo, and yet she found his jealousy strangely endearing.

Theo lowered his third finger. His voice dropped and took on a grim timbre. "Lastly, it is not appropriate or proper for my fiancée to be seen disappearing onto the terrace with another man. I expect my wife to behave with decorum and decency. You belong to me and me alone."

Charlotte flushed a deep red at these words. They stung. Her head dropped and she bit her lip between her teeth. She had not wanted to go anywhere with Hugh, but any protest would sound like an excuse. There was no latitude for her to play with. Her reputation was a fragile thing, so easy to shatter into sharp shards that could tear apart her tenuous happiness. She could not bear thinking of the derision and disappointment that would fill Theo's eyes if he discovered that she was tarnished. She sat in silence for a few moments, not daring to look at her husband-to-be.

His voice finally broke the silence. "Now you know why I need to punish you." His tone gave no indication of his feelings. She took a deep breath and nodded.

"I suggest you answer clearly if you do not wish to add to your punishment," his words snapped out this time.

"I'm sorry, my lord," she rushed. "Yes, my lord, I understand and accept."

"If you keep forgetting to speak, I will show you another use for that lovely mouth of yours." His voice was tinged with amusement and Charlotte glanced up at him, bewilderment clouding her eyes, but she said nothing. Theo sighed and a smile teased the edges of his mouth. "Stand up and remove your clothes."

Slowly, Charlotte rose to her feet. She had undressed in front of the marquess before. He had already seen every inch of her but, somehow, after what he had said about decent behavior, she was reluctant to undress. She felt more vulnerable, more embarrassed, more wanton with his words ringing in her ears.

She glanced at him. He was leaning back on the couch, his chin resting on his folded fists, his eyes focused on her. He raised his eyebrow and Charlotte squirmed. Slowly, she raised her hands to the buttons that fastened her bodice and began to loosen them.

She pushed the sleeves off her shoulders and the soft, blue silk slithered to a heap at her feet. She tugged at the ties that fastened her petticoat, and soon that joined her dress. She reached behind her to loosen her corset. She frowned as she struggled with the tight bows her maid had tied to create a shapely form under her ball gown. After a struggle, the first one came loose, but she could not untie the next.

She looked up at the marquess, who had leaned forward and was watching her closely. His eyes were warm and glazed with desire. She hesitated then took a step forward. "Please, sir," she asked, "could you help me?" Her voice was low and husky.

Theo smiled. "It would be my pleasure, little lamb. Turn around." Charlotte expected him to deal with the ties of her corset so was startled to feel his hand move slowly over her bare bottom. She rose up on her toes as his hand moved lower and slid between her legs. She squealed—and then felt disappointed when he withdrew his hand and quickly unfastened her corset. He tugged the garment off her body and dropped it to the floor, placed his hands on her waist and pulled her towards him.

Charlotte hardly had time to realize what was happening before she found herself arranged over Lord Theo's lap. Her legs were dangling over his thighs and her hands were reaching towards the carpet. Her bottom was positioned within easy reach of his hands. She wriggled, but his left hand splayed out on the small of her back, steadying her.

"Well, my little lamb, I am going to spank you until I believe that you understand the seriousness of your misdemeanors, so there is no need to count this time."

Charlotte took a deep breath. She felt Lord Theo's hand smooth over her buttocks and she squirmed.

"Keep still!" he instructed. Then he lifted his hand and it came down in a hard strike in the very middle of her left buttock. She cried out as the pain seared through her. Before she could absorb the sensations, he struck again, this time on the right side. His hands were large and hard. He covered a large section of each of her mounds each time he struck her.

Charlotte was tense, and every time the marquess brought his hand down, it stung. But after a while, she began to relax and the bite of pain began to diffuse into the warmth of pleasure that seeped into her body. Her body softened against the hard muscles of Lord Theo's legs and she began to drift on a sea of pleasure.

From what seemed like a long way away, she heard Lord

Theo say, "What a pretty shade of pink your arse is turning. I do believe I should keep it this color. Regular spankings will remind you that you are mine."

He brought his hand down in one final slap and then left his hand on her buttocks. His fingers stroked the path down to her soaking pussy and rubbed her folds. "Mmm," he remarked. "I'm not sure how much of a punishment it is if you enjoy it this much."

Charlotte lay in a daze, letting Theo touch her as he wanted, offering no protest. She was strangely comfortable on his lap, naked and exposed as she was. But she stiffened when his fingers drew up towards her back hole. Slowly, he fingered the puckered flesh that protected her dirtiest parts. She tried to sit up, tried to cover herself with her hands. Sounds of protest fell from her mouth.

Theo smacked her hands away. "Keep these in front of you and do not stop me from touching you wherever I want to. Every part of you belongs to me and is available for my pleasure." With these words, his finger jabbed into the back opening. Charlotte gave a startled cry as her muscles resisted the unexpected intrusion. The intrusion felt hard and knobby and the stretch was painful. But as Theo began twisting his finger slowly, she settled into breathing in an easy rhythm. Nerves inside her that she had never even thought existed soared in response to his movements. The unusual sensations began to send shivers of pleasure through her body.

After a while, his other hand moved between her legs and found her core of nerves that was throbbing with anticipation. She shifted to push herself harder against his finger as he rubbed circles over her nub.

Charlotte was panting hard. One of Theo's fingers continued to thrust into her backside while another stimulated her clit. Her nipples were tight little buds and her skin felt as if it would burst. She raised her hips, trying to increase the pressure that would bring her to the peak of pleasure, to the cusp of release.

Theo increased the pace of his thrusts, his finger sliding more rapidly into her arsehole and flicking her nubbin harder and harder.

Her whole body tensed and she let out a cry as she exploded around his fingers.

CHAPTER 16

*C*harlotte gazed around the ballroom of Raeburne House. It had been transformed into a banqueting hall for her wedding breakfast. Guests roamed amongst exquisitely decorated tables, covered in white damask cloths and laden with delectable dishes on large silver platters. Delicate pink roses and ferns were arranged in graceful vases. A beautiful cake stood on a side table, waiting to be cut.

She took a deep breath. She was married. It felt like a dream, but as she caught sight of her husband, the Marquess of Oakdene, she smiled. All she had experienced with him in the weeks before the wedding boded well for her future.

She turned as her mother bustled up to her. "Well, my dear, I always said that your dowry and the fact that you will inherit Summerhill would land you a good marriage. And here you are, Lady Raeburne. I could not be happier. I am only sorry that your father was not able to travel to London to enjoy the triumph of our success."

Charlotte winced at her mother's words. The weeks leading up to her wedding had taught her to hope that Lord Theo appreciated her for more than her inheritance. Her anxiety was appeased as she looked across the crowded room and saw that her husband was watching her. A glimmer of a smile lit his face. Charlotte smiled at him and her tense shoulders relaxed. Her mother was distracted by Lady Danforth, and Charlotte took a glass of champagne offered by a passing footman.

She watched the bubbles rising in the glass and smiled. The effervescence reflected her mood.

"You do look happy," Lady Amelia exclaimed as she came up to Charlotte, her elegant green gown barely able to disguise the swell of the baby she was carrying.

"I am indeed," agreed Charlotte. "I did not think that every-thing would work out so well, that I would be married to the marquess."

"Of course, things worked out well. I knew from the night of the duke's birthday ball that Theo was entranced by you, that he responded to you in a way he had never done with any other woman. I am delighted that we can be friends, and I am so glad that I was able to be here today."

"I am happy that you are here." Charlotte smiled. "You have been a good friend and I look forward to spending more time with you. I am going to need all the help I can get as I settle into this very strange new life." Amelia had spent an afternoon regaling Charlotte with the story of how she had become the wife of the duke and how difficult she had found it to adjust to life in London. Now the duchess was one of the leaders of society and Charlotte was pleased that she would have such a friend beside her as she learned how to be a marchioness.

But Amelia frowned. "Oh, my dear Charlotte, I am afraid that this is my last public appearance before I am confined." She rested her hand gently on her rounded stomach and a soft smile replaced the frown. "The duke is insisting that I leave London tomorrow and remain at Broadwell until after this little one arrives."

Charlotte smiled bravely, but her eyes remained somber. "Of

course, you must go. The duke is right. You are so active in London that you will not rest here, especially with all that needs to be done to prepare the house for girls in Cheapside." She glanced at Lord Theo, who was talking to his friends, the Earl of Sherbonne and Viscount Donnington. "I will, after all, have my husband to guide me."

Amelia laughed, but before she could respond, the ladies were interrupted by the duke. "Lady Charlotte, as I have already conveyed my congratulations to both you and Theo and been polite to all those who would be offended if I ignored them, I am going to take my wife home. She is looking a little peaked and she needs to rest before our journey tomorrow."

Charlotte bade the duke and duchess farewell and then stood quietly in an alcove, surveying the wedding guests. She still felt somewhat awkward in social settings, not quite at ease discussing the fashions and pastimes that occupied the ladies of high society.

She was startled from her reverie by Hugh Parsiville. She had not seen much of him since the day of her betrothal and that one disastrous dance at the Danforth's ball.

His voice now was low and smooth. Charlotte shuddered, wondering how she had ever considered that she could have liked him enough to have thought that marrying him would solve her problems. His presence reminded her of the secret he shared, the secret she did not want to think of on her wedding day.

"Well, my dear, everything is working out splendidly. But now it is time for us to have a little talk, somewhere a little less crowded than this room." He gripped Charlotte's arm as he spoke, his fingers digging into her arm.

Charlotte took a deep breath. "Hugh," she pleaded, "this is not the time or place. Surely, we can find a better time to… to talk."

Hugh chortled, but there was no humor in his eyes. "There is no better time than right now. We need to consider just how things are going to work between us from now on. Of course, if you like, we can have that discussion right here in front of all these gracious guests. I am sure they would be very interested to hear about your past."

Charlotte clenched her fists. She would have to talk to Hugh, take him to a more private room, if she did not want to cause a scandal. Reluctantly, she turned to the door nearest them and led Hugh out into the quieter hallways of Raeburne House, her new home. She was disconcerted to see Lady Winifred just outside the ballroom, a smirk on her face as she observed Charlotte and Hugh. However, her sister-in-law said nothing and Charlotte walked past her quickly, Hugh still gripping her arm.

A small private sitting room was situated just across the corridor and Charlotte quickly led Hugh inside. Hugh closed the door with a click that sounded like the lock on a prison cell to Charlotte.

She remained standing, and so Hugh, who had some manners, could not sit.

He came and stood right in front of her. His voice had never sounded so menacing. "Now that you are married, your dowry has been released. You are also married to one of the wealthiest men in England." He studied her for a few moments and Charlotte shivered at the cold, calculating look in the eyes of the man she had thought was her friend. "You are looking quite elegant today, every inch the wife of a marquess. I wonder what Lord Raeburne would think if he discovered that his new wife is no better than a common hussy who likes to roll in the hay with the sons of farmers."

Charlotte could feel the sting of tears behind her eyes but fought to keep them from falling. She would not let Hugh Parsiville see how his words affected her. She said nothing, only stared at him as he continued.

"My... situation puts me in more need of the money you now have access to than either you or the marquess need. You will let me have whatever I ask for, whenever I ask for it." He stroked her arm with a lascivious glint in his eye as he spoke. "I also know that someone with a base nature such as yours will be ready to serve my *other* needs." He licked his lips. "By fulfilling my needs for money and sex, you can guarantee that your secret is never revealed to your aristocratic friends and family."

Charlotte tried to pull her arm away from Hugh, but he tightened his grasp on her. "I-I thought y-you were well off," she managed at last, trying to ignore the more carnal aspects of Hugh's proposal.

Hugh scoffed. "The expenses a gentleman incurs at the clubs, in playing cards and entertaining in the city, are many. My estate is mortgaged to the hilt and costs more to run than it produces in disposable income every year. I need access to ready cash, which you will provide."

Charlotte stalled, although her heart was pounding and her hands felt damp with the anxiety that clenched her stomach. "I do not have access to much, only the allowance, the pin money, that was agreed on in the settlement."

Hugh's eyes flashed with an unpleasant leer. "Then you will have to please your husband well enough to get him to increase that allowance. In the meantime, those diamond pins you are wearing to keep your hair in that very stylish arrangement are worth quite a bit. I could sell even one for at least fifty pounds. Give me one now, and then I will call on you soon for the next installment, or I will present a letter to your husband describing your reprehensible conduct. I also have a contact in a newspaper office who would be quite delighted with the morsel of gossip I could offer him about a newly married marchioness."

Charlotte swallowed, but she could not dislodge the lump that constricted her throat. Hugh had released her arm and she slowly, reluctantly raised her hands to her hair, feeling for the pins. A sudden memory of Lord Theo sliding the pins from her hair in the library, just a week ago, assailed her, and she could not hold back the tear that slid down her cheek. She had been so very mistaken in Hugh's character. He had never wanted to help her, only use her. She had been such a fool.

She managed to loosen a pin without disturbing too much of the elaborate style her mother's maid had spent so much time creating that morning. Slowly, she passed it to Hugh. "There, I hope you find it useful." She tried to sound forceful, sarcastic, but the dryness in her mouth made the words come out as a whisper.

Hugh smiled. "I will indeed. And now, as with all good arrangements, our partnership needs to be sealed with a kiss."

Before Charlotte could object, Hugh grabbed her and pulled her toward him. He lowered his face to hers and pressed his lips against her mouth, bruising her lips as he plundered her. He held her there for at least a minute, even though her hands pushed against his chest. Finally, he let go and pocketed the diamond pin. Without another word, he left. Charlotte covered her face with her hands, distraught, uncertain of what to do to extricate herself from the dilemma she now faced, certain only that her husband could never know.

LORD THEODORE RAEBURNE, Marquess of Oakdene, was enjoying his wedding. He raised a glass of champagne to his friends and swallowed the bubbling gold liquid that reflected his mood. Champagne was definitely the right drink to serve at weddings.

He looked across the room to where his young bride was talking to Lady Amelia. Her silk wedding dress, overlaid with chiffon, swirled around her as she swayed in time to the music played by the string quartet. Theo smiled, even though his cock ached just at the sight of her. Soon, just as soon as he could politely rid the house of the wedding guests, he would take his wife and make her his own in every sense of the word. A vision of her standing naked before him, succumbing to the pleasures of the flesh, flashed into his mind. Her pussy, that had been dripping with arousal when he had explored her body, would welcome his manhood. His cock swelled and hardened even more at the thought of pounding into her tight, welcoming body.

"The heat you are radiating is enough to keep a furnace blazing," observed Loxley as he took a bite of a *vol au vont*.

Theo just grinned. "Wait until your wedding day. I will remember all your sarcasm and play it back to you!" His teasing tone softened as he added, "Sexual pleasure is very different when love is involved."

Sherbonne sniggered. "There's more to do with lust than love with what you're feeling right now. Love exists only in the stories made up by romance novelists who want gullible girls to believe that romance is real and that the right man will love them forever."

Theo and Donnington shook their heads as Sherbonne spewed his cynicism. Donnington slapped him on his back as he laughed. "One of these days, Sherry, you are going to fall in love and we will all laugh at how hard you fall. We might not even pick up the pieces. It will give me great pleasure to leave you scrabbling in the dust when that happens."

Sherbonne had the grace to look ashamed. He turned to the marquess. "I apologize, Theo. I don't mean to put a damper on your wedding day, but I can't help but feel cynical about love. Too many ladies declare everlasting love while they are calculating how best to spend your fortune. However, Charlotte is a delightful woman and I'm glad you found someone who makes you happy, even though you broke our pact of not marrying before we turn thirty."

Theo laughed. "Charlotte is all I could hope for. I cannot

imagine being happier. You should try love. I think it would suit you."

"That is not going to happen. I will remain blissfully unmarried for the next two years and then select a wife carefully, one who will fit my position in society, not fulfill the whim of emotion."

Donnington and Theo laughed with the superiority born of understanding the power of love. Theo glanced across the room to where Charlotte had been standing a moment before. She was no longer there. He looked around the room. Some of the guests had left and the room was not as crowded as it had been earlier. It was easy to see everyone who was there. Charlotte was not to be seen.

Theo felt as if some part of his heart had left. Where had she gone? He had not meant to neglect her, but she had seemed relaxed and confident when Amelia had been with her. He knew that the sophistication of society still intimidated her, and he wondered if she had sought a moment's reprieve from the formalities of the day.

He needed to find her, reassure her that the guests would soon leave and then it would be just the two of them. With a quick excuse to his friends, he strode across the ballroom and into the quieter corridor. A murmur of voices filtered through the door of the little sitting room that was seldom used. He thought he discerned Charlotte's voice, but she was talking to a man. Alone, behind a closed door. He frowned.

Quietly, Theo opened the door. Charlotte was standing very close to Hugh Parsiville, too close for politeness. The marquess was riveted to the spot. He watched silently as his bride loosened a diamond pin from her hair and handed it to Hugh.

"There, I hope you find it useful." Her words were soft, almost husky, but Theo heard every syllable. His heart turned to a fist of ice in his chest. His Charlotte, his wife, was alone behind closed doors with the man she had been quite attached to when she had first arrived in London. Was there more to their friendship than he had realized?

Hugh smiled. "I will indeed. And now, as with all good arrangements, our partnership needs to be sealed with a kiss."

Theo was paralyzed, unable to move, scarcely able to breath as he watched them together. Hugh kissed his wife, his little lamb, with the intimacy of familiarity and Charlotte did not protest. Instead, she accepted his embrace, yielded to it, rested her hands on his chest.

Theo turned away quietly, leaving them undisturbed. Rage rose within him, but he held it back, tempered it down. He was aware of others in the corridor, guests bidding him congratulations and farewell. His sister, Winifred, was standing near the door of the ballroom, a smug look on her face.

Without really knowing what he was doing or saying, the marquess played the consummate host to the end of his wedding. He conversed blandly, he accepted congratulations, hoping he presented an impassive face to his guests. But anger and bitterness roiled within him constantly. Charlotte reappeared in the ballroom. She smiled and spoke to Lady Watford as if she had not just moments before been in an intimate embrace with a man not her husband at her wedding. Disgust joined the anger in Lord Theo's gut. He had been fooled, duped by a pretty face and sweet manners.

Once the guests had all departed, Theo ensconced himself in his study. He tugged off his cravat and poured himself a brandy. He glanced at his desk where a pile of papers awaited his attention. A bitter laugh erupted from between his lips. At least he had Summerhill as compensation for a fickle, disloyal wife. He had been cuckolded before he had even taken his wife to their wedding bed. Sherbonne was right. Love was just a fable, a fairytale, and he had been a gullible fool to let his heart lead him into its trap.

~

A FEW HOURS LATER, the marquess emerged from his study. The house was quiet, the servants having cleared away the detritus of the wedding. He could hear no one in the lower rooms of the house. He strode upstairs to his rooms. His anger was contained, simmering beneath his façade of politeness. He knew how to present himself as implacable, contained, controlled in society, but in private, he could vent his anger. He entered his chambers and was disconcerted to see Charlotte sitting on a chair near the window.

She looked up when she heard the snick of the door closing but said nothing. Lord Theo stood where he was, just inside his bedroom.

"What are you doing here?" He managed not to snarl, but his voice was cold, distant. He noticed the bewildered flash in Charlotte's eyes but reminded himself that she was a good little actress.

"I was waiting for you," she said, her voice not quite steady.

"Did your maid not show you your own bedroom? It is across the hallway from mine." His tone was ruthless, his stance rigid.

Charlotte rose from her seat. Her voice trembled. "She did, my lord, but I-I thought that…" she was unable to finish her sentence but walked quickly towards the door, not looking at him again.

Theo continued to glare at her. "Well, you thought wrong. If and when I need your presence at night, I will let you know." He opened the door and gestured her out. Without another word, but with her head held high and her shoulders back, Charlotte walked out.

CHAPTER 17

"*A*re you going to Bond Street today?"

Charlotte looked up from the handkerchief she was attempting to embroider. Her sister-in-law, Winifred, was standing in the doorway of the ladies' sitting room, attired in a dress and coat suitable for shopping.

Charlotte shook her head. "Thank you, Winifred, but I wasn't planning to go out at all. There isn't anything I need. My mother ensured that I had everything necessary before the wedding."

Winifred scowled and strode into the room. "It might be worth your while to buy as much as you can now, before you realize that your resources will be limited before long."

Charlotte looked at her sister-in-law, a frown clouding her eyes. "I am not sure I understand you."

Winifred scoffed. "You have been married to my brother for three weeks now, and even I can see that he is not as enamored with you as he pretended to be before the wedding."

Charlotte winced and could feel her face grow warm with the blush of her embarrassment. She peered at the embroidery, which was a tangled mess, much like her life. She had no answer for Winifred's remarks. She could not deny that the marquess had been a distant and detached husband. He was seldom at home and she accompanied him to dinners and balls, only to be left alone as soon as they arrived. He no longer touched her or called her his little lamb. When he did look at her, his eyes were cold and hard. And he had not once spent the night in her bed.

Winifred tugged impatiently at the linen handkerchief Charlotte was working on. "Oh, do stop pretending to be a good little wife. Your embroidery is as atrocious as your playing on the harp. You should at least do something useful. I want to go to Bond Street. I need to consult my milliner about a bonnet and a visit to the haberdashery might not be amiss. I think it would be a good idea if you accompanied me."

Charlotte stared at her sister-in-law, her mouth open in surprise. "Why? I did not think you were particularly fond of my company."

Winifred managed to look a little awkward. "I thought, considering that we need to live in the same house, perhaps we should become allies."

Charlotte sighed and put her sewing down. Winifred had not been friendly to her, and her conversation was focused on bonnets and dresses and ribbons, all things that Charlotte did not find interesting. But perhaps she should become better acquainted with her sister-in-law. After all, spending time with Winifred was surely better than the long days she spent alone.

TWO WEEKS LATER, Charlotte smiled at the housekeeper as she set out the tea on the glossy wooden table in the drawing room. "Thank you, Mrs. Redmond. It looks delicious, as usual."

The housekeeper straightened a plate of scones and withdrew, leaving Charlotte alone. The young bride had grown accustomed to taking meals on her own. Even Winifred, her self-proclaimed ally, usually made sure she was invited to other houses as often as she could be. Charlotte surveyed the table. As well as the scones, there was a rich fruit cake, a gateau with cream and berries, sandwiches and little pastries. She sighed. She had little appetite since her wedding and did not eat much of any of the meals prepared by the French chef the marquess employed. Although this meal was as impeccably prepared as usual, there was no one to partake of it. She hoped the servants would enjoy it when it was sent back to the kitchen.

She poured a cup of tea and began to sip it slowly. In the silence of the room, her thoughts played over the encounter from earlier that day. Hugh Parsiville had paid her a visit. Since her wedding day, she had seen him a few times, including briefly at Lady Cartwright's ball and when she had accompanied Lord Raeburne to a dinner given by the Earl of Merton. Hugh had taken her aside at both these events and reminded her of the arrangement they had made.

Charlotte had not expected that Hugh would call on her at home. The half an hour he had been at Raeburne House had been extremely uncomfortable for her. She had only managed to persuade him to leave by giving him two hundred and fifty pounds and the promise of more money as soon as she could arrange it. That had been all the money she had, but she did not need it for anything. Getting rid of Hugh was worth every penny she could gather for him.

Charlotte shuddered as she recalled how Hugh had grabbed her and kissed her. He had hurt her. Even now, she could feel the bruises on her arm. There was nothing pleasurable in the feel of his lips on hers. It sickened her, but she could not cry out and cause a disturbance. If the servants knew what had happened, there would be a scandal. She could never let the marquess know that she and Hugh had an arrangement. She would not give her husband further reasons to despise her.

Her life was entombed in secrets that were casting darker and darker shadows over her each day. The gloom of London settled into her soul. She had almost forgotten what the grass felt like beneath her bare feet, or how the fall of water in the streams called to her soul. She could no longer picture the green of the trees she loved so much or envisage the carpets of blue-bells or daffodils that danced freely under their protective boughs.

Her tea grew cold as her thoughts plagued her.

The thud of a door opening brought her back to the present. She looked up with a start as her husband strode into the room. The marquess never took tea with her, was never at home in the afternoons. A quick glimpse of his face showed her that he was not here to engage in a polite conversation over a cup of berg-amot tea and a scone.

Charlotte shuddered. She had been intimidated by the marquess when she had met him at Summerhill, and everything in his demeanor now reminded her of her girlish apprehension of his powerful presence. He was a dominant man, a man of consequence and authority. He did not need to rant and rave when something angered him. His anger was quiet, still, but more fierce, more intense because of that. He was a force to be reckoned with.

Charlotte knew he was angry but could not think of a reason for the rage that simmered beneath his detached but polite façade. She could not think of anything she might have done to anger him, to disappoint him, but her guilt ate away at her confi-dence. Her secrets were enough to disturb the promise of happi-ness she had hoped to find in her marriage, but she did not believe that Hugh would have revealed her secret to the marquess. No hint of scandal surrounding her had appeared in any newspapers.

Every muscle in Lord Theo's body was tense. He held himself rigidly under control, aware that letting go would unleash a tempest. Charlotte had never before seen eyes that could be as hard as granite yet as sharp as a surgeon's scalpel. They pene-

AN HEIRESS FOR THE MARQUESS

trated to the very heart of her. She felt ripped apart, as if every one of her carefully guarded secrets was bared to his view.

She bit her lip and clutched the tea cup so tightly that her knuckles turned white and the cup almost broke. Lord Theo came to a standstill next to her chair. She looked down at the table. She could not bring herself to keep her eyes on his formidable face.

He tossed a handful of bills onto the table and began to speak without preamble. His voice was as cold as ice, guarded, lacking any emotion. "I suppose I should have expected this. You are deceitful on every level. You led me to believe that you had no interest in fashion, in acquiring a dozen bonnets or two dozen pairs of shoes. I thought you understood from the marriage settlement that you are to have a set allowance, a very reasonable one, in fact more generous than you deserve, and are expected to keep to your budget. However, I now find that in your avarice, you have run up debts in my name all over town because you cannot live with only eight bonnets."

Charlotte turned her face to him, her eyes bright with unshed tears. How could she explain to him that she had not bought anything for herself? She had gone shopping more than once with Winifred, and her sister-in-law had cajoled and pleaded, until Charlotte had used her name, her husband's name, for Winifred's purchases.

The marquess clenched his jaw. His eyes seemed to grow even harder. "I am not going to be moved by foolish tears. Your father might have pandered to your every whim, but I will not do so. I have had to live with the selfish extravagance of one woman; I will not endure the same from another. My secretary has also informed me that you applied for an advance on your next quarter's allowance. It appears that you are a spendthrift, careless and selfish. Of course, I have vetoed the advance so you will not have anything to spend until September. Perhaps by then, you will have learned a little economy. Furthermore, to

KATHY LEIGH

curb your recklessness, from now on, you are to present an account to me, or my secretary, every week, of every penny that you spend."

Tears were pouring down Charlotte's face, but she did not move to wipe them away. The marquess might think she was responding to his scolding, but she was overwhelmed. No matter what she did, she was trapped. She was married to a man who thought she was frivolous and tiresome. Her childhood friend had betrayed her, using her for her money and treating her like a harlot, taking kisses from her whenever he wanted to. She was cut off from her family, who were far away in Worcestershire, and she was fairly certain her mother would have no sympathy for her predicament. Her father was very ill, so her letters to him mentioned only the lightest trivialities. The only person who had offered her friendship in London, Lady Amelia, was now confined in the country, awaiting the birth of her child. Charlotte's secrets wound around her, stifling her, suffocating her.

The marquess did not move. She could hear his breathing as he stood over her. In spite of everything, her body softened, opening itself for him at the closeness of his large body, his firm muscles, his solid presence. Her breasts swelled and her nipples peaked into tiny, aching points. Her pussy grew slick and soft. Her clitoris pulsed, wanting his touch. The marquess could arouse sensations in her just by entering a room. Every part of her wanted to turn to him, to beg him to love her as a man should love his wife. But she sat still. No matter how much she loved him, he did not consider her as anything but an heiress who had increased his wealth and brought him the property he wanted. She had been fooled into thinking he might care for her, just a little. She should have known better, she had known better. No man could consider her desirable.

"Well, brother," Winifred's sardonic tones cut through the room, "I do congratulate you on presenting such an excellent portrayal of a good husband." She sauntered across the room and sat down at the table. She selected a scone and took a small bite. As she surveyed the rest of the items on the table, she commented, "I did warn you that the marquess is a very different man at home. He cut off my allowance and is now doing the same with yours because he is cruel and miserly, concerned only with his own selfish interests. He does not like other people to have the pleasure of spending money on the things they like, but he has no qualms about buying yet another horse for himself, when he already has three hunters."

Theo turned to glare at his sister, barely able to keep his irritation in check. He did not owe either of these ladies an explanation for the horse he had bought. He had selected the mare a few weeks back, before his marriage, as a gift for Charlotte. Now the mare stood in his stables, being cared for by his grooms. He brushed away his irritation. "Winifred, your spending habits are not under discussion, nor are mine. This is a private conversation between my wife and me. What are you doing here?"

Winifred raised an eyebrow and cocked her head at the table. "It is teatime, a meal conducted in most civilized homes at this hour. I am enjoying my tea. Besides, Dawson mentioned that you had asked to see me."

Theo made an impatient noise with his tongue. "I do need to talk to you, but I did not expect you to interfere in a conversation I was having with Charlotte."

Winifred had finished her scone and reached for a sandwich. Ignoring her brother, she turned to Charlotte. "I heard quite a bit of what he said to you, Charlotte. I do find it interesting that a woman can bring a large fortune into a marriage—what was your dowry? Something close to a hundred thousand pounds, I believe, as well as the property that will come to you when your father dies, or has that already been given over to my brother? I am not sure of the details of your inheritance. But the interesting point is that you brought all that to the marriage and my brother now generously allows you to have a pittance to spend each quarter, not even enough to cover your expenses. All that property is now his. I think it should be yours and you should do with it as you please. If you want to buy a thousand bonnets, then that should be your choice."

Charlotte stared at Winifred. She knew that the marriage laws gave her husband the control of her property, but it had not bothered her. Before her marriage, she had dreamed of sharing the responsibility for her beloved Summerhill with the marquess. He had implemented some very interesting improvements for the tenants at Oakdene, and she had been eager to help him do the same at Summerhill. But her dreams of being his partner in his enterprises had crumbled together with her dreams of a happy marriage.

She began to get up. "I do not want a thousand bonnets," was her only response to Winifred. She glanced at the marquess. "My lord, as you wish to speak to your sister, please excuse me."

Theo shook his head and laid his hand on her arm. She flinched as he touched one of the bruises Hugh had left. Lord Theo frowned, but he removed his hand. His voice was no longer quite as icy as it had been. It might not have thawed to the warmth of spring, but it was softer now. "No, I need you to stay. There are one or two other matters that concern you."

Charlotte sank back to her seat. She did not know how much longer she could be near the marquess. She had spent hours trying to think of how she had disappointed him, of what she had done to turn him into this remote, polite man who bore no resemblance to the passionate lover she had known before their marriage. He had taught her so well that she just being in the same room in him made her long for his touch, for the pleasure that he had shown her.

Lord Theo turned to his sister. "Winifred, your extravagance and recklessness with money has been an issue for a long time, but there are other matters that have recently come to my attention that are a grave cause for concern. You have been in London for six years and are no longer considered a debutante. In spite of your dowry and connections, you have not attracted any interest from prospective husbands, mostly because you are considered disdainful and dismissive. Something must be done before you are so damaged that no one will want to be near you. I have decided that you need a firmer hand, a different environment, where you can develop a more amenable approach to life. A break from society will give you time to contemplate how best to save your reputation and prepare for a better future."

Winifred scowled, but before she could retort, Theo continued. "You might remember Papa used to speak of an aunt of his, Edwina, who lives in Edinburgh. I have written to her and she is willing to have you live with her for a while. You will be leaving on Monday."

Winifred dropped the sandwich she was holding. She jumped from her seat, her face ashen. "What? You cannot send me into exile! I refuse to go. Do you have any idea how isolated Scotland is?" she shrieked.

Theo watched her, unmoved. "You are twenty-three years old. It is time you learned to control yourself and act in a more ladylike manner. Being born into the ranks of the aristocracy does not endow you with the qualities of a lady. Those need to be learned. Great Aunt Edwina assures me that she will help you to do so."

Winifred grabbed a cup and threw it across the room. It crashed against the wall and broke into pieces. "I hate you! You'll be sorry for the way you treat me!" she declared and stormed out of the room.

THEO WATCHED his sister and then turned back to his wife. Charlotte's face was still streaked with tears, although she was no longer crying. He ached with the desire to take her in his arms and comfort her, to kiss her all over her face, to lap up her tears, to tell her that everything would be all right. She was so small, so fragile, and she looked so vulnerable. His little lost lamb needed to be rescued.

He shook his head. He could not, would not, fall for her manipulations again. He had been fooled by her innocent act. She had made him a laughing stock in society and among his friends. He hardened his heart. He wondered if she and Hugh Parsiville mocked him when they were together. Did they congratulate themselves on their well-executed plan? Did she look at him, Lord Theo Raeburne, and despise him for his gullibility?

He reminded himself that she was crying now only because she had not been careful enough and had been caught in her little game. Her tears were not an indication of remorse. There was nothing tender or kind in her. She had married him so that she could support her profligate lover. Theo should have listened to his instincts that night at Sebastian's ball. He should have left her to Hugh Parsiville and not sought to win her for himself.

He looked down at her now where she sat quietly at the tea table. A half-empty cup of tea was in front of her, but nothing else. He studied her face for a moment. She had lost weight in the weeks since their marriage. She was also pale, no longer kissed by the sun as she was when she ran freely in the grounds at Summerhill. Theo stiffened his shoulders. He would not pity her. He would no longer allow his heart to rule him.

"Now that the matter with Winifred is sorted out, there are two further issues I need to mention to you." His voice was clipped.

Charlotte raised her eyes to him but said nothing.

"I have received a letter from Sebastian. Amelia has given birth to a son. I will be leaving for Gloucestershire on Saturday to see my godson, and I do not know when I will return. My estates need my attention and most of my friends will leave London during the heat of summer, so there is nothing to bring me back here soon."

"Oh! I am so happy for Amelia." Charlotte smiled briefly, and then her face returned to its sadder expression. She fumbled as she looked at her hands in her lap. She did not have much practice in asking her husband for favors. "My lord, may I come with you? I would so like to see Amelia and her baby." She swallowed and then added, "London is not very pleasant in the summer and I would love to go into the country."

Theo hardened his heart. He was not going to let that little quiver in Charlotte's voice, that sadness in her eyes, manipulate him. His voice was smooth, detached. "There is no need for you to go to Broadwell. You can see the child when he is old enough to be taken out in public. At present, the duke is allowing only family to see the duchess and his son."

Charlotte flinched at Lord Theo's words. She might be married to the marquess, the cousin of the duke, but that did not make her family. She bit her lip and tried to make her voice steady. "Yes, my lord. What was the other matter you wished to discuss?"

Charlotte had not thought that her husband's voice could become harder, but it did now. "Dawson mentioned that Parsiville called on you this morning. I would prefer it if you did not entertain your friend here in my house."

Charlotte could not help notice the inflection on certain words the marquess used. This was his house. Hugh was her friend. She could see Hugh, but not here. Tears stung her eyes. She wanted to turn to Theo and bury her face in his chest, to feel his arms around her as she sobbed out the whole story. But she sat still as the marquess stalked from the room.

CHAPTER 18

*C*harlotte was in her sitting room, a copy of Fanny Burney's novel, *Evelina,* open on her lap, although she had not been reading much. She sighed as she glanced at the page in front of her. Life was not like a story. Evelina, the fictitious heroine of the story, had experienced so many misadventures, but she had found love, been rescued by love. Charlotte was married but was alone and there was no prospect of love for her. She was miserable. She hated London. The years stretched before her, a barren wilderness empty of love and joy.

She shook her head as she closed the book and put it down. Hugh Parsiville had been right; the marquess wanted only her inheritance. She was not the kind of woman men wanted, desired or loved. She was completely alone. Even Hugh had disappeared from London, and she was abandoned by the last person who had tolerated her. The days stretched ahead of her, empty and lonely.

She rose from her seat and wandered to the window that looked out over the hazy heat of the London afternoon. It had been almost seven weeks since the marquess had left for the country. The warmth of the London spring had turned to the suffocating heat and humidity of the summer. The city was unbearably hot, stuffy and unpleasant, but she had to endure it. There had been no letter or note from her husband and she did not know if he would return to the city before the end of the year and he had probably not given a thought to her discomfort, to how she was pining for the coolness of the countryside.

Her mind wandered back to that morning of his departure. Although she was not very good at sewing, she could crochet quite well and had managed to produce a decent baby bonnet for the duchess's newborn son.

CHARLOTTE HEARD the preparations for Lord Theo's departure. She picked up the little parcel containing the bonnet and a letter she had written to Lady Amelia and slipped down to the foyer. Footmen were carrying trunks and boxes out to the carriage, while Dawson kept an eye on the proceedings. She stood on the landing of the staircase, clutching her parcel, uncertain what to do. Eventually, the marquess strode out of his study, tugging on his leather gloves.

Charlotte quickly made her way down the stairs. She bit her lip as she approached her husband. She had not seen him since he had left her in the drawing room that dreadful afternoon, but she wanted Lady Amelia to receive her gift.

She stood in front of her husband, who frowned at her. She curtsied and kept her face as impassive as she could. "Good morning, my lord. I wanted to ask if you would take this little parcel to Lady Amelia for me?" She held it out, trembling, dreading his rejection.

The marquess nodded and took the parcel. His eyes showed no emotion and his voice was cold, curt. "Yes."

He said no more. Charlotte curtsied again. "Thank you. I trust you will have a pleasant journey." She turned away to return upstairs to her room where she could indulge in a fit of sobbing but stopped when the front door of the house opened and a woman entered. Charlotte stared. She recognized Lady Mary Hatfield, who had been widowed a few years back, but was still quite young and very attractive. She had the air of a woman who knew how to please men. And she was well-acquainted with Lord Theo. Charlotte had heard whispers that Lady Mary had been a mistress to the marquess, probably still was. Charlotte choked back a cry.

Lady Mary walked up to the marquess and dropped her hand on his arm in a very familiar manner. "Oh, Theo, it is so good of you to take me with you. You are always so helpful and so good to me!"

Lord Theo had led Lady Mary out to the waiting carriage without even a backward glance at his young wife standing on the stairs.

CHARLOTTE HAD SPENT many hours wondering just how helpful and good Lord Theo was to Lady Mary. As much as she tried to dismiss the thoughts, they played around the edges of her mind every waking moment.

Every time she thought she had no more tears to cry, new ones formed in her eyes. Her shoulders heaved now as she turned from the window. She wiped her hand across her eyes, brushing away the teardrops.

A knock at her sitting room door surprised her. She never received visitors, and the servants usually left her alone except for mealtimes. The knock was repeated, a polite but insistent call for her attention. "Come in," she said.

The door opened. "His Grace, the Duke of Broadwell, my lady," Dawson, the butler, announced, then bowed and left.

Charlotte stared for a moment. Her mind was confused. It took her a few deep breaths before she could gather her thoughts well enough to remember her manners. She curtsied. "Your Grace, how are you? I am afraid that the marquess is not at home."

Sebastian chuckled. "Good day, Lady Charlotte. I am aware that Theo is not here. It is you I have come to see."

Charlotte was flustered. She glanced down at the plain dress she was wearing, one that she had often worn when she rambled in the woods and fields around Summerhill and that her mother had tried to get rid of. She touched her hair, which was pulled back in a simple knot. "I do apologize, Your Grace. I was not expecting visitors. Please sit down. Can I offer you some refreshments?"

Lord Sebastian sat on the settee, leaning back as if he felt more at home here than she did. He crossed one leg over the other and smiled at Charlotte. "A cup of tea would be very welcome, thank you."

Charlotte fumbled for the bell pull and, when a footman arrived, hastily organized for refreshments to be brought up. Then she turned back to the duke. "I thought you were in the country."

Sebastian nodded. "I had some business I needed to attend to in town and decided I would come to see how you are doing while I am in London."

Charlotte blushed. "I do apologize. I did not mean to be rude. It is only I do not receive many visitors and I am a little out of practice. I am sure that you have better things to do than visit me. However, I am glad that I can wish you well on the birth of your son and ask how Lady Amelia is doing?"

Sebastian's aristocratic features softened as a smile lit up his face. "My little son is very well and Amelia is strong, too. I have brought a letter from her for you." He reached into his pocket and drew out an envelope which he offered to Charlotte as he spoke.

"Thank you, Your Grace, but you could have sent a footman with the letter. You did not need to waste your time bringing it to me yourself."

Sebastian scowled. "I do not consider seeing you a waste of my time. I do not do things that I do not want to do."

Charlotte looked at him, bewilderment in her eyes. "I do not understand. I am not a very important person."

The sound that emerged from the duke could almost be described as a growl. "I do not like to hear you talk about yourself so disparagingly. If I think it is worthwhile spending time with you, then you are important. However, for now, I suggest you read the letter my wife wrote."

Charlotte was about to protest that reading while she should be entertaining her guest was not polite, but the duke was even more forceful than Theo. His orders were not to be gainsaid. She glanced at him, as he sipped his tea, and opened the letter.

My Dear Charlotte,

Thank you for the delightful little bonnet you made for my son. He looks even more perfect when he wears it. He is to be called Sebastian, after his father, and Theodore, after his godfather. His third name is to be Gilbert, after my father. I am not yet sure which of those names will be used as his daily name. I simply call him my little angel.

I was very disappointed that you did not come with Theo to visit me. Letters are not as personal as visiting. I am sorry I have not been in London to help you settle in to your new life. My duke tells me that I should focus on my son and not let other matters concern me for now, but I cannot help but worry about you. I was so certain that you and Theo would be very happy together. I trust that I was not wrong about you. You do love him, don't you? I am sure I did not mistake the way you look at him. However, he would not talk about you when he was here. Any time your name was mentioned, he changed the subject.

The duke would not let me come to London to see you and so I have sent him to see what he can do. Love is such a delicate thing and yet, paradoxically, how robust it is. It conquers all, all the mistakes of the past, all the flaws of Theo's character (and yours, if there are any), all the misunderstandings that might have arisen between the two of you. Do try to remember that men can sometimes be foolish in the matters of the heart and we women need to keep on loving them until they understand the power of that love. Whatever foolish things Theo has done, forgive him and love him until all is right again.

I cannot wait to introduce you to my son.

Yours affectionately,

Amelia Montgomery

CHARLOTTE DID NOT REALIZE that tears were running down her face as she read this letter. She felt the smooth linen paper begin to crumple in her hand. She had forgotten that the duke was sitting next to her on the settee and was startled when a warm, strong arm slipped around her shoulders and a handkerchief was pressed into her hands.

"There, little one. A good cry is sometimes a way of letting out all the bad feelings, all the poison that has been eating away at your peace. Cry as much as you need to."

Even as the duke's soothing voice washed over her and she nestled into the safety of his arms, Charlotte shook her head. "I have cried and cried and cried. It doesn't make anything better, and now Lady Amelia's letter has made me cry again because she is so kind, and yet some of what she says reminds me of all my sorrow," she sobbed.

The duke chuckled wryly. "Amelia has a knack for ferreting out her friends' troubles, but as she is not here and I am, perhaps you should tell me what is troubling you."

Charlotte could not stop the flood of tears that was pouring down her face, but she managed to speak coherently enough for the duke to make sense of what she said. "If Lady Amelia knew the truth of my situation, I think she would not want to be my friend. Her letter is so kind and yet she is wrong. I deserve to have been left alone like this, to be abandoned by my husband. I am not a very good person and I have done things that cannot be forgiven."

Sebastian stroked her head while she spoke, not interrupting, simply letting her pour out her woes. For the first time in many months, Charlotte began to feel a little sense of peace. They sat like that in silence for a long while, while she sobbed into the duke's solid chest. Finally, Charlotte's sobs eased to sniffles.

Sebastian still did not let her go. This was a young woman in need of comfort and his cousin had been stubborn, refusing to find a way to solve the problems in his marriage. Sebastian was not beyond prying into the difficulties he had noticed. He was determined to find a way to help Theo and Charlotte realize that love was powerful and that their marriage could become something very beautiful, something that could bring pleasure to them and others.

After a long while, he spoke quietly, "Little one, I read Amelia's letter. I want to ask you the question she asked. Do you love Theo?"

Charlotte managed to pull back a little, enough so that she could answer the duke. "Yes, I do. But he does not love me, and if he knew the truth about me, he would despise me even more. Lady Amelia is wrong. My love for him does not matter. Love is not powerful enough to eradicate what I have done, to cover my sins. I cannot force the marquess to love me, and just because I love him does not mean that I deserve his love."

Before Sebastian could begin to untangle her reply, another voice cut through the room, sharp and cold as tempered steel. "My wife is correct. She does not deserve to be loved. And you, cousin, seem to think that as your wife is indisposed, you are free to do as you please with other men's wives."

Charlotte pulled back from the duke with a gasp, but Sebastian simply tugged her closer again. He was relaxed and his voice was nonchalant. "Good day, Theo. I trust you had a pleasant journey. Would you like a cup of tea? Dawson brought this tray up when I arrived, but I am sure a fresh pot could be made. Oh, Donnington, you here too? How are you?"

Viscount Donnington strolled into the room and sank into a

chair. "Duke, Lady Charlotte, good day. Tea is just what is needed after a dusty journey into the city on a hot afternoon." He settled into a comfortable armchair and addressed the marquess. "Theo, do sit down. Perhaps you need to listen to the duke. You know he loves Amelia and would do nothing to harm her."

The marquess glowered at his friend and then took a chair near the settee. Charlotte was still nestled in Sebastian's arms but her face was turned to her husband. She was nibbling her lip in that very distracting manner of hers. Her eyes showed a mixture of emotions, ranging from uncertainty to trepidation. But lurking deep behind the obvious feelings, there was a glimmer of desire.

"My lord, I did not know that you were expected home." Her voice was almost a whisper.

Theo arched his eyebrow. His voice dripped with derision. "Clearly. Perhaps you would have been a little more discreet, had you known when I was due to return to my house."

Sebastian shook his head as he felt Charlotte stiffen. "Do calm down, Theo. I arrived just over an hour ago, to bring your wife a letter from Amelia. I found Charlotte in a state of distress and in need of comfort, which I gave her. She might not have known you were on your way to London, but I did. There is nothing untoward in our interactions, except in your imagination."

The marquess snorted indignantly. He was once again on his feet and stalked across the room, to stand in front of the settee where his cousin still had his arm around Charlotte's shoulder. Theo's voice was cold and hard. "Do you know the real reason why my wife is so upset? Do you know what kind of woman I attached myself to? If the scandal should be revealed, it could bring ruin to my family name. All I have worked so hard to achieve would be lost. If I could have the last few months back again, I would not have tied myself to her."

Charlotte uttered a little cry and covered her face with her hands. She did not know how the marquess had discovered her secret, but he must have heard somehow. Had Hugh reneged on his promise because she had not been able to give him more money?

The duke held her close, but the comfort of his arms could not ease the pain that tore through her heart.

Sebastian looked at his young cousin, his eyes hard, his voice like flint. "What is it that you are accusing your wife of? You say she is not the kind of woman you would want to associate with. Why?"

Theo scoffed. "She knows what she has done. Look at her. There is guilt in every line of her body. I have had to return to London to settle the matter and to ensure that innocent servants are not accused of the theft she has committed."

Charlotte was stung by these words, but something did not make sense. "Theft! I am no thief," she protested, sitting up straight and staring at her husband.

Theo paced across the room, clearly agitated. Disgust flooded his voice. "What would you call it when you take a family heirloom and attempt to sell it off to a jeweler for a fraction of its worth, simply because you ran through your allowance as heedlessly as the most spoilt of society brats and are in need of ready money to give your paramour?" Once again, he came to a standstill in front of the settee. His voice was so cold, it could ice up the room, but his eyes conveyed a vulnerability that suggested he had been deeply hurt by all that had happened. "I know all about the money you give to support your lover, which would be enough to cause a scandal if it became known to society, but taking valuable heirlooms and implicating honest servants is something I thought even you would not stoop to."

Confusion and embarrassment swept over Charlotte's face. She pulled free from the duke's hold and stood to face her irate husband. She had never been more fearful of him, but her own rage fired her indignation and gave her the courage to answer. "It is true, my lord, that I have given money to Hugh Parsiville. I gave him what I could from my legally apportioned allowance. He received nothing beyond what was rightfully mine to dispose of. I did so, not because he is my lover, but because he knows a secret about me and threatened to make it public if I do not pay him." Her voice faltered toward the end of her defense, and she ignored the gasps of all three men as she concluded more quietly, "I have never touched any of your heirlooms. I would not even *think* of taking something that does not belong to me."

Donnington breathed out a long, low whistle. "I did tell you, Theo, not to be too hasty, although, perhaps your goading has been beneficial. I doubt Charlotte would have mentioned half of that mess if you had not pushed her."

The duke had crossed his arms and now quirked his eyebrow. "I thought you had learned to control yourself, boy. However, I must agree with Donny. There is much you and your wife need to discuss."

Theo was simply staring at his wife. Charlotte had frozen after her rant, as if the realization of what she had said had immobilized her. Now she clutched her skirts and began to turn towards the door. Theo reached out and stopped her. "No, you need to stay and talk about what you have just revealed."

Charlotte bit her lip, a sheen of tears in her eyes, but she found herself responding to her husband's instruction. She shook her head, but her shoulders sagged wearily. "Why, my lord? You have accused me of being frivolous, extravagant, deceitful and dishonest. You do not care for me and I accept that you married me so that Summerhill could be yours. I ask for nothing from you. I am sorry that your friends have heard that I am a disgraced woman, but I am living as quietly and unobtrusively as I can. I see no one; I go nowhere. As long as I can keep Hugh quiet by giving him what he wants, my scandal will not hurt you. I know nothing about the missing heirloom and I am sorry that any servant has been harmed by its disappearance, but I do not believe that there is anything more that you need from me now."

Theo glanced at his cousin. Sebastian was leaning forward, his face somber. The duke nodded at Theo, indicating that the marquess needed to handle this if his marriage had any chance of surviving this chaos.

Theo stepped forward. He placed his hand on Charlotte's arm. His voice was quieter than it had been but still held the thread of command that compelled obedience. "Charlotte, I apologize. It seems that I have been mistaken. There has been much wrong between us since our wedding, and I have done nothing to set it right. Hugh Parsiville is a rogue, a scoundrel. I was jealous that you favored him, right from the moment that you arrived in London. He was always at your side. Even the day I proposed to you, he was with you, speaking to you with a familiarity that suggested intimacy." Theo took a deep breath. "On our wedding day, you disappeared. I looked for you and found you with Parsiville. I saw you give him one of the diamond pins from your hair, and then you kissed him. I was convinced that you had married me to have access to my wealth so that you could support your impoverished lover."

Charlotte uttered another cry and then dropped her face into her hands. Through her fingers, she managed to say, "I did not know you were looking for me or that you saw what happened. I did not want to kiss Hugh. I do not like his kisses. He hurts me when he touches me. But he says you would not care be-because of your mistresses." She stared at the carpet, scared to look into the eyes of her husband, uncertain of what she would see there.

Theo cupped her chin and tilted her face upwards, until her eyes were caught by his. He was frowning, but there was soft-ness now in his expression that conveyed concern and tender-ness. "I told you that I do not have any mistresses, that I have not had any since shortly after I began to know you properly. What mistresses are you referring to?"

Charlotte could not turn her face away because the marquess still held her chin in his firm fingers, but she bit her lip. "Lady Mary went with you to Broadwell."

Even Sebastian laughed at that. "Mary Hatfield is not, and never has been, Theo's mistress. Even *he* has better taste than that. She did not come to Broadwell, either. I believe Theo took her only as far as Bath because her mother is ill and she has no carriage of her own. Theo has always been a soft touch for a woman with a sad story."

Theo took up the conversation again. "Loxley was with us for the whole journey and I was never alone with Mary. I was very glad to see her go. She speaks of nothing but the latest gossip." The marquess paused and let his thumb rub Charlotte's mouth. "I am, however, extremely annoyed to hear that Parsiville has been blackmailing you. This cannot continue. It is preposterous for him to have such a hold on you that you give in to his demands. You are no longer to give him money or kisses."

He took a step backwards and looked at his cousin, although his hand still held Charlotte's chin. "If we are to bring his game to end, we need to know what information he is using to black-mail Charlotte." As he spoke, he led Charlotte to a chair and sat down. Charlotte stood before him, her head bowed, her hands twisting in front of her. Her husband nodded briefly and gestured with his right hand. Charlotte stared blankly for a moment and then sank to her knees in front of him. She clenched her hands and then slowly relaxed them, turning them palm upwards on her thighs, as he had taught her to do. An unexpected peace settled over her. Her head was slightly bowed but he could see her eyes, bright with the tears that still glistened in their depths.

Charlotte took a deep breath, trying to find the words to tell

Theo about the muddle of her life. "I am not sure that I understand what you want me to say," she prevaricated.

Theo looked at her steadily, his eyes intense and filled with
determination. "There are a number of issues that need explana-
tions. We will return to the missing necklace later. However, you
have been spendthrift with your allowance, running up debts
with dressmakers and haberdashers, although you told me that
you cared nothing for fashion. You have entertained Parsiville,
and by your own admission, given him money. You have indicated that he knows some secret about you that he is using to
coerce you into compromising behavior, and you did not
mention any of this to me. Does this summarize the issues?"

Charlotte nodded. Her eyes were wide as anxiety drew lines
of tension at the sides of her mouth. She noticed Theo raise his
eyebrow and she quickly stumbled out an answer. "Yes, my lord."
She took a deep breath. How could she explain these points?
Perhaps it would be best to begin with the secret she had hidden
from the marquess for so long. She felt her face turn red as she
gathered the courage to admit what had darkened her days and
led to her current predicament.

"Lord Raeburne, I know that when you married me, you did
so only because you were interested in Summerhill." She ignored
the impatient click of Theo's tongue and continued. "I am not
the kind of woman gentlemen in your position seek to marry. I
prefer the country to the city, riding out in the fields and woods
to perfecting my technique on the pianoforte, and I enjoy talking
to the farmers' wives about their daily concerns. All of these
idiosyncrasies, of which you were aware, you overlooked,
because of the inheritance I brought into the marriage."

Again, Theo clicked impatiently, but Charlotte proceeded,
more at ease now that the words were falling freely from her
mouth. "However, if you had known the full extent of my
wickedness, you might have hesitated to procure Summerhill
through marriage to me." She glanced up at the marquess. He

was sitting still now, leaning forward, his eyes fixed on her. She could not discern the emotions or thoughts in their depths.

"Hugh Parsiville is the only one who knows, apart from... those who were involved, and initially, he implied that he would marry me to protect me from my wickedness." Theo snorted at that but said nothing. Charlotte bit her lip and then continued. "However, when it was evident that you were interested in marrying me, Hugh said he would continue to keep my secret and ensure that there would be no repercussions related to my past."

Charlotte paused. Theo's eyes did not waver. They focused steadily on her as he summed up how Parsiville had manipulated the situation. "So, Parsiville had you pay him to keep your secret from me." It was a statement, but Charlotte nodded. Theo continued, "And he suggested that I would despise you if I discovered the truth." Again, Charlotte nodded. Theo reached out and ran his finger down her cheek. "Did it never cross your mind that perhaps telling me might be your best protection against his machinations?"

Charlotte blinked back the tears that once again threatened to spill down her cheeks. She shook her head. "No, my lord. We married so quickly and then after the wedding, it was... difficult to approach you."

Theo smiled, but there was more regret than humor in his eyes. "I was rather angry to discover you in an embrace with Parsiville just after you had promised to love and honor me. What did Parsiville know that was so dastardly it would have caused me to despise you?"

The room was silent. In the distance, Charlotte could hear the servants moving through the house, preparing rooms for the gentlemen who had arrived unexpectedly, but here, in her sitting room, there was a silence so profound that she could almost hear the beating of her heart.

The words of Walter Scott flitted through her brain as the

silence dragged on. 'Oh, what a tangled web we weave when first we practice to deceive.' She had been caught for so long in the web of deception that she had woven its thick cords around herself and those close to her. She had heard it said that truth set one free. Perhaps finally bringing her secret into the open would set her free from the prison in which she was trapped.

She glanced at the duke, who was looking at her with sympathy, and the viscount, whose eyes showed concern. She looked up at her husband. His face had softened a little and his eyes held a glimmer of affection. She dropped her gaze to her lap. She did not want to see that tenderness turn to disgust.

"I was very foolish. No, it was more than foolish. I did something scandalously wicked." She choked slightly on the last word but swallowed. These gentlemen would not let her go until she revealed the full extent of her indiscretion. But once they knew of her wickedness, they would quickly dismiss her, no longer willing to be associated with her. She would lose the tentative friendship she had begun to form with Lady Amelia. Briefly, she wondered how soon the marquess could and would send her away in disgrace.

With a deep sigh, she gathered her courage. Keeping secrets had festered in her soul. Telling the truth would ease the infection in her heart, but it would create new problems she would have to face. Finally, she spoke in a low voice, surprised at how steadily she was able to form the words. "There was a young man, the son of a farmer, with whom I became... friends." She knew her face was bright red, but she let the words tumble out. "I often rode out to his farm. His father was elderly and often bedridden and Tom usually worked the fields on his own. One day when I arrived, he was in the stable. His mare was giving birth. I helped with the foaling. Afterwards, we were cleaning up and, well, he had removed his shirt and I was not wearing a coat or bonnet. We began to kiss and touch."

Charlotte glanced up at her husband. Theo was leaning

forward, his face expressionless. His voice conveyed nothing as he asked, "Did you love him?"

Charlotte was not sure how to respond. She knew that honesty now was the best option, but somehow the truth made her actions seem even more tawdry. "I like Tom. He is a decent, hardworking man. I do not think, however, that love is part of our friendship." Her eyes closed tightly and then she opened them, pain clear as she looked up. "I have not seen him since that day."

"What happened?" the duke turned the conversation back to the basic facts.

Charlotte took a deep breath. "I am not sure how long we had been… kissing, when Hugh arrived. He hauled me to my feet and escorted me back home. He promised never to say anything to my mother or father, or to anyone else. I believe he went to speak to Tom, but I do not know what arrangements were made."

Theo shook his head. "That is your secret? For that, Parsiville has been bribing you for money and taking liberties with you?"

Charlotte looked up, startled at the lightness of her husband's voice. "I was so very wicked," she tried to explain. Her voice was monotonous as she kept her emotions under control. "If a young lady is caught with a half-naked man, passionately kissing… it is enough to destroy her reputation entirely. If her buttons were loosened, her bodice open and her dress pulled up near the top of her thighs, and if they were… lying down together on the grass, there can be no hope for her to be considered decent." With a quick glance at the three gentlemen, she mumbled, "I know that girls who engage in such behavior are wicked, but it is even more reprehensible if a young lady of breeding is prone to such wickedness. Those of us who have been given better opportunities in life should know better than to let their baser natures overcome their prudence." She swallowed and brought her explanation to a halting conclusion. "You implied as much at

Lord Danforth's ball when you said that my reputation would be ruined if I had gone onto the terrace with Hugh. If a lady finds herself in a compromising situation, then she is degraded, wanton, sullied. No gentleman would consider her decent or respectable. No gentleman would want her for a wife." She ended with a sob.

Charlotte could not understand why all three men laughed. She bit her lip and looked at her hands that were now clasped in her lap.

Theo stroked her hair as he spoke. "I am glad that you were prevented from going any further with Tom, not because I consider your actions perverse, but because I do not like to think of another man touching you or taking what belongs to me."

Charlotte frowned and choked back her sobs. This was not the response she had expected.

The duke was now standing behind her. "Little one, you have spent some time with us. You must know that our ideas differ from society on many matters. You were the instigator in rescuing Mary from the hands of louts. We would not despise you for being friends, even intimately, with a farmer. We believe that men of all classes have merit, just as men of all classes can be despicable. We also understand that denying passion and pleasure can do more harm than good. Your passion is a wonderful indication of the brilliance of your personality."

Charlotte tilted her head and looked up at the duke. His voice was firm, his eyes were kind and his presence exuded stability. She nodded slowly.

Theo reached out and helped her to her feet. "We will discuss all of that further. However, right now, it is time for dinner. That tea was not sufficient to satisfy the hunger created by the emotions of today, or by all the traveling we have done. We will continue this discussion while we dine."

CHAPTER 19

"What I would like to know," the marquess said as he cut a piece of one of the lamb cutlets his French chef had prepared for dinner, "is how Parsiville has continued finding money since Charlotte has not had any available funds since May."

Charlotte squirmed, but the gentlemen focused on their food and ignored her response.

The duke agreed, "From all that I have heard, in spite of his almost bankrupt state, he has had ready money to indulge in his usual luxuries. However, he has not been seen in London for a few weeks now and no one seems to know where he has gone."

Theo looked at Charlotte, who was pushing her cutlet around on her plate. "What is it, little one? Are you not hungry? Dupre has created a marvelous meal, considering he had no warning of our arrival, but if you would prefer something else, I am sure he will make it for you."

Charlotte pierced the lamb with her fork and took a little bite. "This is delicious and quite a treat. I have been used to a bowl of soup on a tray in the evenings."

Theo frowned. "Has Dupre not been well, that he has not cooked for you?"

Charlotte hurriedly shook her head. "He is well, only, it seemed overly extravagant for him to create an elaborate meal when I was the only one here to eat it. I thought it prudent and economical to simply have a portion of whatever was being made for the servants."

Theo touched her cheek gently. "What would have happened if visitors arrived?"

"I have seen no one other than the servants and been nowhere since you left for Broadwell."

"And yet Dawson tells me that Parsiville was here a day or so after I left." Theo's voice was expressionless, but Charlotte cringed at the suggested accusation.

Shaking her head, she glanced up at the butler who was standing near the sideboard, presiding over the wine. "That cannot be. I know I did not see him," she denied emphatically.

Donnington reached for his wine glass. "More mysteries. This is a far more interesting trip than I anticipated. Laurie and Adam will be disappointed that they went to Yorkshire."

Theo glared at his friend for a moment and then turned to his butler. "Dawson, when did Mr. Parsiville last visit Lady Charlotte?"

Dawson stepped forward to refill the wine glasses. "My lord, Mr. Parsiville visited her ladyship a few days before you left for Broadwell; however, a few days *after* you left, he was here again. It was the day before Lady Winifred left for Edinburgh. They had tea together in the library."

"I did not know that they were acquainted," Charlotte blurted out.

"I believe that they became acquainted sometime during your betrothal, my lady." Dawson cleared his throat and faced the marquess again. "I have also heard that Mr. Parsiville has been seen in Edinburgh in the last week or so."

Theo glared at his butler for a moment before saying, "It appears that there has been miscommunication on all sides. I will be leaving for Scotland in the morning. The answers to the last parts of the puzzle will be found there, I believe."

DINNER CONTINUED PLEASANTLY and Charlotte's appetite recovered enough for her to enjoy the meal. Now, she had left the gentlemen to their brandy and was standing near the window of the drawing room, looking out into the London night.

The darkness of the night wrapped around her soul. The despair of the last few months clung to her. The marquess might believe that he would find answers to his problems in Scotland, but she was still unsure about her own future. She did not want to be left alone again in the stifling heat and loneliness of London, while her husband set off across the country once more.

The door opened and Lord Theo entered.

"Where are the duke and Lord Donnington?" she asked.

"They are still enjoying their brandy and cigars. They will be here shortly. I came to see how you are."

Charlotte straightened her shoulders as she pulled her armor back around her heart. "I am well, thank you. However, I did want to ask if it might be possible for me to visit my father in Worcestershire. His last few letters have indicated that he is losing strength and I have not seen him since I came to London."

Theo walked across the room. "I visited Oakdene briefly last week and spent a little time with your father. He is comfortable, but the heat of summer is draining his health. He is eager to see you."

Charlotte took a deep breath as a wave of disappointment swept over her. It should not have surprised her that her husband was so quick to acquiesce to her request to return to her father's house. After all, he had spent almost no time with her since their wedding. In spite of his earlier apologies, there was no reason for him to change his ways now. Keeping her voice as steady as she could, she ventured, "I wonder, my lord, if it is not inconvenient, could you take me as far as Worcestershire on your way to Scotland? I do not have my own carriage and I am not sure how to arrange such a trip."

Theo observed his wife closely, silent for a few moments. Charlotte shifted uneasily under his penetrating gaze. "I do not mean to be any trouble, my lord. It is only that I thought it might be possible for me to travel with you for a little way, and then, perhaps I could remain at Summerhill, and all would be... settled."

Theo clenched his jaw. "Settled? You want to return to your childhood home?"

Charlotte nodded uncertainly. His question seemed to suggest something more than she could understand. "London has never held much appeal for me, and I miss the countryside. I am sure it will be a relief to the servants not to have me here, and it will not concern you whether I am here or in Worcestershire."

A rumble slid from Theo's throat. "At dinner, I said that *we* will be going to Scotland. I thought we could go to Oakdene when we return, and you will be able to see your father daily when we are there."

Charlotte shuffled uneasily and looked at her husband from under downcast eyelids. "I-I did not think you m-meant that I was to go with you."

Theo stroked her cheek with his knuckle. She shivered and he tilted her face so that she had to look at him. "I do want you with me. There are many things that we need to discuss, and a long journey will give us time to sort through some issues."

Charlotte blinked and tried to bite her lip. "What about Lord Donnington and the duke?"

"What about them?" Lord Theo repeated. "The duke has business here and then he will return to Amelia and his son at Broadwell. Donny can find his own way home." As he finished speaking, his lips moved closer to hers and brushed across her mouth with gentle insistence. She opened to his touch, feeling her whole body softening to him, yielding to him.

"Well, it appears that my work here is done." The duke's voice held a hint of amusement as he strode into the drawing room, interrupting the kiss.

Theo pulled back slightly and chuckled. He kept his arms around Charlotte, holding her close to him, and looked at his cousin over the top of her head. "My wife and I will manage this part of our lives, I think. However, I did want to ask your advice about handling my sister and the other issues. You dealt with your sister-in-law efficiently when she threatened your marriage."

Charlotte raised puzzled eyes to Theo's face, but he was looking at the duke. The duke simply raised his eyebrow. "I believe there is very little to compare in the two situations. However, it might be valuable to discuss your options before you descend on your sister in a rage and estrange her completely. Sometimes gentleness achieves so much more."

Theo huffed but pushed Charlotte away with a soft kiss to the top of her head. "My little lamb, perhaps it would be best if you arranged your packing while I finalize matters with Sebastian. I will see you later." He cupped her bottom as she turned and left, the squeeze suggestive of further attentions he would give it later.

CHAPTER 20

*T*he barouche box rumbled comfortably along the country road, pulled by a well-trained and lively team of four grey horses. The marquess kept his own horses at the first few changing posts and his coachman and grooms were competent and drove well, ensuring that the passengers were jostled as little as possible. The coach itself was extremely comfortable, with luxurious cushions and wide seats. The windows were big enough to let in ample light and allow those inside to see the countryside they passed, but velvet curtains were provided for privacy.

Charlotte leaned back and placed the book she had been attempting to read on the seat next to her. Because the day was so warm, she had removed her traveling coat and only her light muslin dress covered her slender body. She was agitated from sitting still for so long. They had left Raeburne House just after an early breakfast and it was now almost one o' clock. Only once, had they stopped to change horses. At the bustling inn, Theo had led her to a private sitting room and ordered a cup of tea for her, which had done much to refresh her.

Now she was becoming restless. It was difficult to read as

even the slight up and down movement of the carriage made the words on the page jump, leaving her a little nauseous. Because the book did not keep her attention, she found her thoughts drifting to all that had happened the day before.

She looked at the opposite bench, where Lord Theodore, the Marquess of Oakdene, her husband was seated. She tried to make her glance unobtrusive. She need not have bothered. Her husband did not suffer from the malady she did; he had no problem reading in the carriage. Since they had left London, he had been absorbed by numerous documents and papers and articles that were in a leather satchel beside him on the seat. Although he had said that they had much to discuss, he had hardly spoken a word to her in the hours they had been together, and she was too timid to interrupt him.

Suddenly, Lord Theo shuffled together the pages he had been perusing and stuffed them back into his satchel. He looked across at Charlotte with a smile. "I am sorry, little lamb. There is always so much correspondence that I need to consider, but now I have neglected you long enough."

Charlotte tried to think of a polite response but no words formed in her mind. She felt the warmth of her cheeks as they turned rosy. She dropped her eyes under his steady gaze.

"Look at me." Theo's voice was calm but implacable. Charlotte raised her head. Lord Theo nodded, a quirk at the corner of his mouth the only indication that he was pleased with her quick response, but also warning that her lack of a verbal response would bear consequences.

"You look very charming when you are so uncertain, my little one," Theo remarked. "Last night was too fraught, too emotional, for me to come to you as a husband should come to his wife. All the crying you did, all the emotions I experienced, would have caused our union to be too intense for your first time. You were so exhausted that sleep was the best solution."

Charlotte nodded slowly, her eyes not leaving Lord Theo's

face. It was difficult for her to discuss matters of the flesh with him, in spite of the encounters they had enjoyed before their wedding.

Lord Theo raised an eyebrow. "Charlotte, I believe we have discussed a number of times that words are the best way to communicate."

Charlotte blushed. "Yes, my lord. I'm sorry, my lord." She bit her lip and looked down at her fingers that grasped her dress. "It's just, sometimes, I'm not sure how to say what I want to say when I am with you."

Theo chuckled at this. "My sweet little lamb, you can say whatever you want to. I am not such an ogre that I will censure your opinions and thoughts. Indeed, I want to hear what you are thinking. And I will let you know what I am thinking, too, especially when we are alone together."

Charlotte looked up at this, her eyes even wider than usual. "You will?"

He nodded. "Yes. Right now, I am thinking that we are alone together in this carriage, we have a while before we stop, and my wife is sitting too far away from me." He reached out his hand and Charlotte placed hers in his, briefly noticing how delicate hers looked in his large, strong one.

Theo pulled her across the space until she tumbled into his lap. "There are so many things that I want to share with you, my little love," he murmured against her hair. He began loosening the pins until the mass of curls tumbled loose around her shoulders and down her back.

The silky mass caused his cock to thump in anticipation. All morning, as he had been working through documents and considering how the heirloom necklace had so strangely appeared at a jeweler's he had never used, his cock had been aching and hard, aware of the proximity of his lovely young wife. Now he was determined to indulge the pleasure that had been so long denied.

Charlotte shifted on his lap and his cock throbbed as her bottom pressed against it. She turned to him with a gleam in her eyes. His lips found hers and they kissed for many minutes, sweetly, passionately, intensely, communicating all that had not been said in those days and weeks of misunderstanding.

Eventually, Theo drew back. They were both breathless. "My sweet little one, I have been quite insistent on communication, but I have been guilty of not speaking to you when I did not understand what was happening. I was too quick to judge what I saw rather than discuss issues with you. Will you forgive me for that?"

Charlotte nodded, running her fingers down his cheek. "Yes, my lord. I do forgive you. We do not know each other very well, and things I did were very suspicious."

Theo chuckled. "They were indeed. However, you also need to promise not to keep secrets. You need to trust me with whatever happens or has happened in your life. I love you and will do all I can to help you and protect you, whatever situation you find yourself in."

Charlotte gasped. "Y-you love me? Really? I did not think that was possible."

Theo pressed a kiss to her forehead. "Why do you think I married you if not because I love you?"

Charlotte blushed. "My inheritance gave you Summerhill, which increases your lands substantially."

Theo clicked his tongue impatiently. "Summerhill is a very fine estate, but as I mentioned before, I could have and would have bought it from your father with my own resources. I did not need to marry you to acquire it." His hand moved in slow circles over her back as he spoke, and Charlotte stiffened when she realized he was loosening her buttons.

She raised her eyes to his, still overwhelmed by his declaration of love. "I'm not sure I understand. Last night, I revealed my secret to you, and if nothing else, it shows how unsuitable I am for polite society."

Theo nuzzled the soft place where her neck joined her shoulder. His reply was muffled against her skin. "My sweet love, the things I want to do to you are not very polite. What first drew me to you was exactly how different you are from all the starched and stuffed society ladies who clamored for my attention. I admired your willingness to get muddy to help a lamb in distress." Leaving one last kiss on her throat, he pulled back and looked at her with serious eyes. "I kept my distance after our wedding because I was confused and hurt, thinking you and Hugh had deceived me."

With a little cry of distress, Charlotte turned and buried her face in his chest. "Oh, I am so sorry. Hugh was so plausible in all he said, and I was so certain that you would despise me, and there was no one I could talk to."

"From now on, you will talk to me, no matter how serious or trivial things are." Theo had unfastened her dress and petticoat by now and was tugging the material down until her breasts bounced free. "That's better. Now we can concentrate on what is important." Theo slid his hand into her loose hair and gripped hard as he lowered his mouth to her breasts. With deliberate, slow strokes, he began to lick.

Charlotte shivered but arched her back, offering herself to her husband. Theo sucked the nipple into his mouth, laving her with his tongue. She moaned under his ministrations. Sparks of fire rippled all the way to her core. Warmth collected in her groin.

Theo's clever fingers caressed her naked skin, heightening her responses to him. He plucked at the nipple of her other breast while he continued to suckle the first, pulling hard between his fingers. They were hard points when he released them. Charlotte moaned her protest at the loss of his touch. Her eyes were glazed as she gazed up at him.

Theo grinned. "I think it's time for something a little different." He reached behind him and found one of the soft velvet cushions that added comfort to the benches of the traveling coach. Still keeping his arm around her, he tossed the cushion onto the floor at his feet. Then, using her hair to guide her, he slid her onto the cushion.

Charlotte knelt between his feet, her dress half-off, with her breasts, swollen, wet and pink from his attentions, exposed lewdly. Her hair spread around her like a cloud of dark silk. Her face was level with his groin.

His cock pulsated against the seam of his breeches. Her eyes focused there and the point of her tongue slipped out of her mouth to lick her lips. Theo was not sure that he could last much longer. He could feel his balls tighten and his cock grow heavy and hot. He clenched his fists and silently counted backwards from ten.

"Open my breeches," he instructed, his voice rough and raw.

Charlotte hesitated a moment, and then her hands reached for his buttons. Her delicate fingers brushed against his stiff erection as she fumbled with the fastenings, made tighter because of his swollen dick. He moaned each time she bumped his cock, each time her fingers touched the bare skin beneath his buttons, each time she exposed more of him.

Finally, the last button was open and she pulled back the soft wool of his breeches. His cock sprang free, already hard and red. She pulled back for a moment and then resumed her position. Fascination filled her eyes as she gazed at his member.

"Touch it," Theo said. "You've already felt it, that night at the opera. Now you can see it and feel it without the encumbrance of clothes."

Charlotte knelt forward and, using the tip of her index finger, traced the throbbing vein that pulsed insistently along the length of his cock. Then, gaining confidence, she used more fingers and touched the smooth, hot skin. She wrinkled her nose. "It's softer than I thought. I mean, it's hot and hard, and yet the skin is so soft. It's a strange combination."

Theo smiled. "Do you remember how you gripped it at the theater? Take hold of it in your hand now. Yes, like that. Rub your hand up and down, harder. Squeeze as you do, twisting slightly near the top. It isn't going to break."

A little frown formed between Charlotte's eyes as she concentrated on her task. "It's growing longer and harder!" she exclaimed after a few minutes of intense work.

Theo gritted his teeth, trying to control his response to Charlotte's touches and her innocent wonder. He wanted this experience to last. He reached down and rested his hand on hers, stopping her. She looked up with startled eyes. "Did I do something wrong?"

"Not in the least, but I want you to do something else." He guided his cock to her lips as he spoke and rubbed the tip against her mouth. She opened slightly and her tongue came out to lick him tentatively. "That's right. Taste me, the way I've tasted you."

Charlotte's tongue slid around the top of his cock slowly and then more insistently, testing the texture. She spent some time probing his slit and then poked the loose skin that surrounded it. She began lapping as if she were enjoying an ice at a summer picnic. Her tongue swept down the length and then up again. He shuddered as she moved over the sensitive underneath parts.

Her hand gripped the base and she looked up at him, her eyes conveying glee as she discovered her power to give him pleasure. He leaned forward and grasped her hair. Using it as leverage to control her movements, he pushed his cock past her delightful lips into the welcoming warmth of her mouth.

Charlotte tried to pull back at the invasion that stretched her jaw, but Theo held her steady, and she began to suck. Her mouth closed around his shaft, enclosing him in her heat. The warmth and wetness of her mouth brought his cock to a hardness he hadn't thought possible. He pushed in until she began to gag, and then he pulled out slowly. He repeated the movement, over and over, getting faster and faster as he felt his climax approach. His balls tightened.

He pulled free of her mouth with an audible pop. Charlotte looked up at him, her cheeks red with her exertion, her eyes showing the disappointment at the loss of her treat.

Theo managed to smile. He looked down at his cock that was between them, dripping with her saliva, rigid and swollen. He took her hand in his and rubbed his dick fiercely, quickly. He aimed at her exposed breasts as the first spurts of his seed surged up in a hot stream. Ropes of white, sticky semen landed on her round tits, her pink nipples, her upraised face.

"I love you, my sweet, sweet wife," he gasped as the last of his sperm landed on her chin and dripped down onto her breast.

CHAPTER 21

*L*ord Theo entered the drawing room of his great aunt Edwina's house in Edinburgh. All frivolity and pleasure had been set aside, although a warm glow still lingered in his body and heart, reminding him that matters between Charlotte and him had vastly improved.

"Lady Edwina and Lady Winifred have not yet come downstairs but will join you here in quarter of an hour," a stately butler informed them.

The marquess sank into a chair near the fire and pondered, yet again, how to approach the matter of his sister. He watched Charlotte, who was wandering around the large room, admiring the well-chosen paintings that hung on the walls and the knick-knacks on side tables. She looked so innocent, so ingenuous, as she paused to examine a portrait by van Dyck. Theo shook his head, wondering how he could ever have thought her guilty of theft or even of extravagance. Even now, she was dressed in a simple gown of pale blue poplin and wore only her wedding ring as embellishment.

Charlotte glanced at him, her lower lip caught between her teeth. Her eyes were wide with nervousness. "If this person is related to you, or your great aunt Edwina, then I am glad I did not meet him before I knew you. He is somewhat formidable."

Theo chuckled, and reaching out his hand, he pulled her onto his lap. She felt so tiny, so fragile, as she snuggled against him for a moment, but then she sat up and pulled away, "No, Theo, not here. Let me go. It would be unseemly to be found in such a position the first time I meet your great aunt."

Theo chuckled and drew her face closer to his so he could kiss her thoroughly. When she was breathless from his attentions, he drew back and murmured against her lips, "We have a little time before Aunt Edwina and Winifred come down, and kissing you distracts me from thinking about the conversations that need to occur." He placed a kiss on her lips and then added, "Besides, I have a lot of catching up to do."

Charlotte raised her mouth to his, and Theo indulged in a second, longer, more passionate kiss. Kissing her, claiming her so completely with his mouth, exploring every part of hers, thrusting his tongue into her welcoming warmth, was satisfying. Theo could dedicate hours to nothing more than kissing his wife, just for the pleasure it gave. He was so immersed in the kiss that he was not aware the door had opened, had not noticed that anyone had entered the room, until a voice penetrated through the haze of his passion.

"Well, nephew, it is good of you to come all this way to introduce your bride to me, but I might have preferred a more formal introduction."

Theo released Charlotte with a laugh, and Charlotte scrambled off his lap, blushes suffusing her face as she turned to meet Lady Edwina. She dared not raise her eyes as she curtsied and murmured, "Good morning, my lady."

Theo's aunt studied her for a moment and then looked at her nephew. "She's a fetching little thing. I can see why you find her so irresistible."

Theo grinned, his face showing his love for Charlotte, but he said, "Much as it is a pleasure to see you, Aunt Edwina, I have not traveled all this way to exchange pleasantries about my wife." His face became much more somber as he looked toward the door. "I do not see my sister?"

Lady Edwina settled onto the settee opposite Theo and Charlotte. "Winifred will be down shortly. Perhaps it is best that I have a moment to discuss a matter or two while she is not here." She poured a cup of tea from the tray a housemaid brought in, and when she had taken a sip, began, "Winifred is a very attractive lady, and two or three suitors have shown an interest in her. However," Edwina rushed on, seeing that Theo wanted to interrupt her, "I believe that much of her appeal relates to the size of her dowry. She has an odd way of treating her suitors with disdain. I have noticed that she is much more amiable when one gentleman, Lord Darrow, is near. I have sent a note asking him to join us for lunch."

Charlotte shuffled uneasily at the reference to suitors who were interested in a lady because she was an heiress, but Theo took her hand in his and squeezed it lightly. She relaxed, beginning to accept that her husband loved her, and her fortune was simply an added bonus.

Keeping his wife's hand in his, the marquess focused on the problem of his sister. "I would be interested to meet Lord Darrow and see if Winifred can be persuaded to accept him if he makes an offer. It is time that she settled down. However, I am most interested in a suitor who might have pursued her from London. Has Hugh Parsiville been among her admirers here?"

A frown flashed across Lady Edwina's face, but she was not the one who answered.

"Hugh did follow me from London. He is, I believe, still in Edinburgh, but I do not count him among my suitors."

All three occupants of the room turned to look at Winifred as she paused in the doorway. Theo rose from his seat and faced his sister. "Winifred, it is good to see you."

Her eyes flickered from the marquess to Charlotte, and then she strode across the room and sat stiffly in a chair facing Theo. "So, you have taken time out of your busy life to come and visit me in this godforsaken place. That is very considerate of you." Her eyes slid towards Charlotte once again but seemed not to focus on her. "Or did you bring your wife to join me in exile?"

Charlotte squirmed, but Theo's reassuring squeeze of her hand comforted her.

The marquess leaned forward and studied his sister. "I had hoped that spending time with Aunt Edwina would help you to see things a little differently." He shook his head slowly. "However, I do believe I owe you an apology."

Winifred lifted her chin and smirked at this, but before she could gloat, Theo explained, "I have done you a disservice. When Mama died, I indulged your every whim and employed governesses who taught you to think of nothing but fashion and appearance and that because you are the daughter of a marquess, you are somehow superior to others. It is my fault that you are extravagant and self-centered."

Winifred turned a bright shade of red as Theo spoke. "It is your fault that I am living in this wretched place!" she spat out.

Aunt Edwina stifled a cough behind her hand, but Theo spoke calmly. "I would like to ask you about some things that occurred just before you left London."

Winifred glanced pointedly at her great aunt and Charlotte. "Is this interrogation intended to humiliate me entirely?"

Theo was implacable. "Considering that some of it concerns Charlotte, and Aunt Edwina is here as your guardian, it is fitting that they remain. Whether you will be humiliated depends on whether you have done anything disgraceful."

Winifred gave an elegant snort but said nothing.

Theo's voice became almost conversational. "The first matter is one that is easy to deal with. I limited your expenditure at various fashion houses and haberdashers in London, not so?"

Winifred's lips tightened into a straight line. "You did, because you are too miserly to pay for the clothes I need."

Theo ignored the accusation. "Yet, you coerced Charlotte into running up her accounts to pay for the fripperies you wanted, leading me to believe that she was extravagant as you are and causing dissension between her and me."

Winifred glowered at Charlotte. "You needed to know what kind of husband you married. But I suppose you bleated out to Theo that all of those shoes and bonnets were for me, and now my brother despises me even more than he did!" She turned back to Theo, vitriol burning in her eyes. "I told you I would make you pay for sending me here."

Theo stood and walked to the fireplace. He turned and faced his sister. "I am sorry you believe I despise you. That is not so. I remember the delightful girl who was my companion in the schoolroom. I curbed your extravagance in an attempt to help you overcome your spendthrift proclivities, to reach the kind-hearted girl I played with in the nursery. Unfortunately, I believe that my attempts were too late. I have reason to suspect that those tendencies led to something far more serious than running up debts in my wife's name."

Winifred's shoulders stiffened, but she said nothing. Theo let the silence hang in the room for a few moments. Finally, he sat down again and broke the silence, almost conversationally, "I received a very interesting letter from a Mr. Goldblum, a dealer in fine jewelry, although not the jeweler I usually use. He wanted to meet me, and when I met him, he brought me an antique emerald necklace that he offered to sell me. Imagine my astonishment, when I was shown one of the central pieces of the Raeburne collection, that I had thought was safely stored in a box in my study with the rest of the family jewels, where it belongs."

The room was silent as the three women listened intently to the marquess. Theo kept his eyes on his sister, although Charlotte's hand was in his. He took a breath and continued. "Mr. Goldblum had not been in his shop when a young gentleman brought in the necklace. His younger son, seeing a chance to acquire a piece of great worth, bought it without question and for much less than its worth. When Mr. Goldblum saw it, he recognized it and contacted me." Theo looked at Winifred. His voice was deceptively mild, but his eyes conveyed a hardness that indicated he was not to be trifled with. "Do you know how the necklace came to be in the hands of Mr. Goldblum and Sons?"

Winifred bristled. "You have wasted your time coming all this way to question me. You should simply have asked your wife. I believe she is in the habit of giving pieces of jewelry to her lovers. She would not know the difference between a bauble and a priceless heirloom."

Charlotte let out a little cry and sank back against the cushions of the sofa, trying to cover her face, but Theo turned to her with a gentle look and ran a finger down her face. "It's all right, my little lamb. I know you did not give the necklace to Hugh."

Neither of them noticed the vulnerability that softened Winifred's expression as she watched the care her brother took of his wife. But she straightened her back and clenched her jaw, re-erecting her defenses before Theo turned back to her.

His voice was once again grim. "If you are going to persist in prevaricating, then I will tell you what I know. Mr. Goldblum and his son were quite precise in the details they gave. The son received a visit from a gentleman who, to save time, I will state has been identified as Hugh Parsiville. He said that he wanted to sell an old family necklace as he needed ready money. He was given five thousand pounds for it, which is, of course, far less than it is worth. Parsiville traveled to Scotland with the money and met with you. I have come to reclaim the money and clear the name and reputation of the second footman, Angus, who was blamed for the loss of the necklace."

Winifred rose to her feet at the end of this and faced her brother. "What of it? Am I not a Raeburne? Do I not have the right to the Raeburne jewels?"

"Being a Raeburne is more than simply a name. It entails a sense of honor and understanding of what that name means, not simply the privileges it entitles you to. It comes with responsibilities and duties," Theo intoned slowly.

Winifred clenched her fists and glared at her brother but added nothing to her defense.

Theo studied her for a moment and then continued, more gently. "Your allowance and dowry are very generous. You inherited some excellent pieces of jewelry that belonged to Mama, but the necklace that you took was not yours to sell. Indeed, even selling pieces that were left to you by Mama without consulting me would have been inappropriate. But that emerald necklace needs to remain in the Raeburne collection that has been handed down from one generation to the next of Raeburnes for centuries. It is mine, not yours. Mr. Goldblum is too much of a businessman simply to return it, even though he realizes it was sold to his son without my permission. I am forced to buy back an item that belongs to me. The money you received for it needs to be returned, to cover the repurchasing of something that should never have been sold. Of course, it would be best if this could all be settled without any recourse to the law. Parsiville was selling a stolen necklace, after all."

Winifred had gone pale as the implication of her brother's words struck her. She sank back into her seat. "No," she whispered. "You wouldn't." Regaining some of her strength, she admitted, "I don't have the money."

The marquess raised his eyebrow and looked at her. Winifred sat up a little straighter but dropped her head. Her cheeks were flushed. "I arranged with Hugh Parsiville to sell the necklace, which I kept after the last time I wore it. He was to bring the money to me here and he was to keep a percentage of the money as a fee." She gave a bitter laugh. "I underestimated his devious-ness. He wants to marry me and will give me the money only if I agree to be his wife." With a flash of indignation, she declared, "I do not intend to marry him."

Theo gave a little snort. "Parsiville is a gold-digger of note." He turned to his aunt. "I believe he is staying in Edinburgh? Do you know where I can find him?"

While Lady Edwina was writing down an address, the butler announced the arrival of a visitor. Charlotte saw Winifred's shoulders sink as Lord Darrow, a stern looking gentleman, entered the room with a curt bow to the marquess and his wife.

After greetings had been exchanged, the newcomer drew Theo aside and spoke to him. "I am pleased to meet you. It saves me having to send a letter to London. I intend to marry Winifred. She is in need of a husband to look after her, and I intend to be that man. We can draw up marriage settlements while you are here."

Theo raised his eyebrow. "I see that you are not someone who procrastinates. Your abrupt approach would be considered rather offensive in London."

Not even a glimmer of a smile softened Lord Darrow's face. "I see no need to waste time on beating about the bush. I say what I mean, I get what I want. I see no reason to delay."

Theo's face hardened. "Are you certain you want to marry her? Do you know all that you need to know about my sister?"

Both gentlemen turned to look at Winifred. Theo was surprised to see how Winifred's face softened as she looked at Lord Darrow. A gentle smile hovered in the corners of Lord Darrow's mouth as well. Theo gave a mental shrug.

Lord Darrow drew his attention back to the matter at hand. "I have spent some time with Winifred and have become quite fond of her, in spite of her prickly manner. Winnie has told me something of what happened. I am not blinded by her beauty or her wealth, yet I am finding myself falling in love with her. She is willing to give me her hand in marriage. Her tough façade hides a very sensitive character and I believe I can help her to fulfill her potential and become the woman she is meant to be. I live a very quiet life and she is beginning to realize that there are consequences for her unruly behavior."

The marquess studied Lord Darrow's face, noting the emphasis he placed on the word consequences, and then he nodded. "Discipline and control, tempered with trust and love, go a long way to making a marriage happy," he agreed.

For the first time since his arrival, Lord Darrow smiled.

EPILOGUE

*C*harlotte sat quietly next to her husband as the carriage rumbled through the busy evening streets of London. She had spent a pleasant two months at Oakdene with her husband and enjoyed seeing her father regain some of his strength as he handed over the running of Summerhill to his new son-in-law. Now, they had returned to London. She was much more comfortable with her husband, and the city was no longer a place of horror. With Lord Theo at her side, she could face anything.

Well, almost anything. They were on their way to Briar House for dinner. She nibbled her lip nervously, uncertain what to expect. She pulled at the skirts of the white muslin dress the marquess had asked her to wear but kept her eyes on the view outside the window. She did not know what to say to Lord Theo, who was lounging back in his seat, a small smile playing on his face.

As the carriage turned a corner, she ventured a question. "Will you not tell me anything more? I asked Lady Amelia and she said that Briar House is quite an unusual place. Who owns it?"

Theo took her hand in his. "I promise that you will enjoy the dinner this evening, but it will indeed be unusual. The house was, until about thirty years ago, the property of Viscount Thorne, and he bequeathed it to the Lords of Voluptas. It is presided over by a retainer who ensures that the house is always ready for those who want to use it and that special events such as tonight's dinner are properly organized." He gave Charlotte a slow smile that sent shivers down her spine. "This is a place where we can openly indulge our desires without fear of being judged by those who do not understand our views of pleasure, and I regret not having brought you here right at the beginning of our marriage. Some of the misunderstandings we both harbored would have dissipated."

As he finished speaking, the carriage drew up outside a large white house. Charlotte peered out the window and felt a little disappointed. "It looks like any ordinary house," she commented.

Theo chuckled. "What did you expect? From the outside, that's what it is. Inside, things are somewhat different."

Theo led his wife up the wide steps to the large entrance doors. Charlotte stepped inside and looked around. The foyer was disappointingly similar to the entrances of every house she had ever known. Elegant furniture and tasteful paintings adorned the room. A butler and footmen came towards them to take their coats and gloves.

They followed the butler upstairs to a drawing room. Charlotte entered behind her husband and then stopped, her mouth agape. She had entered a different world. The room was furnished with large sofas and chaises lounges in various shades of blue from pale ice to deep midnight. A few comfortable armchairs were also scattered around. But it was the people who shocked Charlotte. Several of them she knew, but she had never seen them like this.

Many of the women, and some of the men, were in various stages of undress. Other gentlemen were fully clothed in black evening suits. Lady Sylvia, whose soiree she had attended the previous week, clad in only a pair of white stockings and shoes, was kneeling at the side of a sofa, her bare breasts in the hands of a gentleman Charlotte recognized from that same soiree.

The Earl of Sherbonne was reclining on a chaise with a lady kneeling on the floor between his legs, as she herself so often sat with her husband. Theo simply nodded as they walked past, looking for the Duke of Broadwell and Amelia, who were occupying an armchair farther back in the room. Charlotte was startled to notice as she followed her husband that a naked man was following another man on what looked like a dog leash. She turned to Theo with startled eyes, but he simply slid his hand around the nape of her neck and spoke softly. "At Briar House, we allow everyone to find their pleasure in whatever way they desire. You and I have been exploring our own pleasure and you have found much freedom in it, so it will not do to judge what others find pleasurable."

Charlotte nodded and managed a low, "Yes, my lord," just as they reached the duke and duchess.

Amelia looked at Charlotte with a delighted smile. The duke remained seated, partly because Amelia was on his lap, but he studied Charlotte closely. He nodded after a few moments. "Yes, you are definitely improved since the last time I saw you. It seems my cousin has learnt how to be a husband."

Charlotte blushed, but Theo only laughed. Charlotte asked Amelia about the baby and the duchess was describing how her son was able to sit on his own when dinner was announced. It was a strange procession that led into the dining room.

Charlotte's eyes were wide when she saw that the footmen were arrayed in very tight breeches and nothing else. Their torsos were bare. Furthermore, all along the table, chairs had been interspersed with large, comfortable cushions. She looked up at Theo. He smiled at her and led her to a place near the center of the table. He sat down but gestured for her to kneel on the cushion. She wanted to protest, but a quick glance around the room showed her that most of the other women, including the Duchess of Broadwell and Lady Watford, were kneeling beside their husbands.

Charlotte was between her husband and the duke, but shifted closer to Theo so that she could lean against him as the meal was served. It was a position she often took when they were alone together at home. She felt protected and safe when she knelt next to him. Now, in this unfamiliar place, the familiarity of his body, of his smell, comforted her. She smiled when he placed his hand on her head and whispered, "My good little lamb."

The strange meal began. The gentlemen conversed as they would at any other dinner, but Theo made sure to hand her pieces of food from the dishes that were served. Always, he chose for her the things he knew she liked best. Every time he offered her a forkful of food from his plate, he touched her cheek or hair. Every now and then, he gave her a sip of wine from his glass. When he did so, his fingertip trailed over her shoulder and down to the top of her breasts.

Charlotte was becoming more and more aroused as the meal progressed. Her body was on fire and she wanted more touches from her husband, but he was sparing in those he gave her. He paused in his discussion about some paintings with Viscount Donnington to give her a taste of veal in raisin sauce. His finger traced the outline of her chin. She shivered. He smiled. "Not yet," he promised, running his hand over the mounds of her breasts.

The duke drew Theo's attention away from Charlotte. "So, I believe Winifred is finally married."

The marquess nodded. "Yes. Lord Darrow is an unusual choice for her, but I believe he will help her to settle down. He is not a man given to excess, but he has taken a fancy to my sister, and for some reason, my sister has developed some affection for him. They were married last week and she will now live in Scotland. I have not seen her so happy or relaxed for many years."

"Were you able to recover the necklace?" Donnington asked.

"Now, that's an interesting story. Mr. Goldblum had given it back to me, for a sum, before we left for Scotland. He did not want to keep in his possession what he knew was actually a stolen item, as he did not want his business to suffer the possibility of a scandal. However, the real question is what happened to Parsiville." Lord Theo took a bite of veal and looked down the table to where Lord Danforth was seated. "Parsiville's debts have become increasingly large and he has no means to settle them. He owes debts of honor all over London and his estate is in ruins. He has been a parasite for too long and there is no one left to capitulate to his games." Theo looked down at Charlotte as she wriggled uncomfortably. He smoothed her hair but continued his story. "Parsiville is now languishing in the Marshalsea Prison until his debts are paid."

A murmur of approval ran around the table at this announcement.

Theo glanced at the butler and ensured that all the glasses were filled. He rose to his feet. "However, we are not here to mull over such morbid matters. We are here this evening to celebrate the good that is to be found in pleasure."

"Hear! Hear!"

Theo smiled down at Charlotte, who was looking up at him. Her white muslin dress was almost transparent and he could see the outline of her nipples pushing against the flimsy material. He had asked her not to wear a corset or petticoat. He wondered if she knew how delectable she looked.

He raised his glass. "I propose a toast to the delight of pleasure, to the satisfaction that is found in fulfilling our desires with those we know and love."

When he sat down again, he reached for Charlotte and scooped her onto his lap. She pressed her face against his chest, embarrassed and uncertain about what would happen next.

The footmen had removed the previous course and now a

splendid array of creams, jellies and blancmanges was being set out on the table. Theo took Charlotte's face firmly in his fingers and tilted it up. "There's no hiding. There is nothing to be embarrassed about. Your passion is a beautiful thing to be enjoyed openly. No one here will think any less of you for yielding to me and enjoying yourself." With a chuckle, he inclined his head towards the other guests. "They're all too busy enjoying themselves to bother about us, anyway."

Charlotte twisted her head and, with a quick glance along the table, realized that Theo was right. Most of the other guests were engaged in various intimate embraces and were not concerned with what Theo was doing to Charlotte. There was a freedom here that Charlotte had never known.

She raised her face to her husband's and slid her arms around his neck. He kissed her deeply and passionately. His hands roamed over her back as he did so, molding the softness of her shape and pressing her close to him. His tongue entered her mouth, taking possession of her.

His hands cupped her breasts and squeezed hard until she squealed as the sharp pain shot through her with an arrow of pleasure. Theo shoved his hand under her bodice and slid it around one plump globe. He fondled her naked skin, caressing the silkiness with firm strokes of his strong fingers.

Suddenly, without warning, he grasped the edges of the delicate material of her dress and ripped. The dress tore and her breasts bounced free. She looked up at him and slowly arched her back so that her breasts were on display. Lord Theo grinned. "I want to admire what belongs to me, and I believe that I will enjoy dessert much better this way."

Charlotte was still baffled.

Theo pulled her torn dress off her completely, leaving her naked. Charlotte tried to cover herself with her hands, but Theo caught them in his and put them behind her back. "Keep your hands there until I give you permission to move them. You will not need them and I have need of your beautiful body."

Charlotte tried to keep still, but it was difficult to keep her balance on Theo's lap, especially when he spread his thighs and splayed her legs open. He had turned her so that her back was resting against him. Now, he leaned forward and perused the desserts on the table. After a few minutes of deliberation, he selected a creamy sabayon. With a twirl, he dropped a dollop on Charlotte's one breast. She arched up as the cold cream met her cool skin. "Careful," warned Theo, "it wouldn't do to spill my dessert." She tried not to wince when a second dollop landed on her other breast. "Perfect!" announced her husband.

He ducked his head and began lapping up the creamy dessert in slow sweeps of his tongue across her breast. He began at the edge of the pile of cream and worked his way slowly in towards where it covered her nipple. He alternated breasts, treating them with equal attention as he worked his way to the center.

Charlotte moaned as heat built up in her body. Theo paused and she looked at him with desperate eyes. He grinned. "I haven't finished with you yet. But I think you might want to taste this delicious dessert."

He scooped up a portion by running the side of his finger through the sabayon on the underside of her tit and lifted it to her mouth. She stuck out her tongue and enjoyed the contrast of the roughness of his finger and the sweetness of the dessert. She drew it into her mouth and clamped down with her teeth. He winced and laughed lightly.

"Bad little lamb!" he scolded and tugged his finger away.

He squeezed her nipple hard and she winced in turn. Thoughtfully, Theo watched her as he circled her breasts with his fingers and mouth, lapping up the remaining cream. He took a last mouthful, holding it on his tongue, and sought her mouth. She opened for him and he shared the treat with her, the taste of one another adding to the flavor of the sabayon as he kissed her tenderly.

"I love you, my sweet wife," he murmured against her mouth.

"I love you, too," she replied dreamily.

WATCH for the next book in the Lord of Voluptas series, *A Paragon for the Viscount*, which tells the story of Lord Anthony Donnington and Clarissa Blakeney.

The End

KATHY LEIGH

Kathy Leigh has loved books and writing since she could first follow the stories in her bedtime tales. She began writing stories in old school notebooks when she was eight years old but only recently thought that others might want to read her stories, too.

A romantic at heart, she is inspired by thunderstorms, sunflowers, and the belief that every princess deserves to find her prince. Recently she moved to a small village in France where long walks in the meadows and woods are wonderful inspiration for her writing.

She loves curling up on her couch with a good book, a glass of wine and her cats for company. As a young girl she particularly enjoyed the novels by Georgette Heyer and Jane Austen, and sighed over Mr. Rochester in *Jane Eyre*. She now enjoys historical and contemporary romance with an edge. She also enjoys fantasy, especially if it has a touch of romance.

Visit her website here:
https://kathyleighauthor.wordpress.com

Don't miss these exciting titles by Kathy Leigh and Blushing Books!

Lords of Voluptas Series
A Wife for the Duke
An Heiress for the Marquess

To the Manor Born Series

Arabella's Journey
Dorothea's Quest
Lilian's Journey
To the Manor Born collection

BLUSHING BOOKS

Blushing Books is the oldest eBook publisher on the web. We've been running websites that publish steamy romance and erotica since 1999, and we have been selling eBooks since 2003. We have free and promotional offerings that change weekly, so please do visit us at http://www.blushingbooks.com/free.

BLUSHING BOOKS NEWSLETTER

Please join the Blushing Books newsletter
to receive updates & special promotional offers.
You can also join by using your mobile phone:
Just text BLUSHING to 22828.

Every month, one new sign up via text messaging will receive a
$25.00 Amazon gift card, so sign up today!